P9-CEX-694

We Have This Moment

Tales from Grace Chapel Inn®

We Have This Moment

DIANN HUNT

Guideposts.
New York, New York

We Have This Moment

ISBN-13: 978-0-8249-4731-6

Published by Guideposts
16 East 34th Street
New York, New York 10016
www.guidepostsbooks.com

Copyright © 2008 by Guideposts. All rights reserved.

This book, or parts thereof, may not be reproduced, stored in a retrieval system,
or transmitted in any form or by any means, electronic, mechanical, photocopying,
recording or otherwise, without the written permission of the publisher.

Distributed by Ideals Publications, a Guideposts company
535 Metroplex Drive, Suite 250
Nashville, Tennessee 37211

Guideposts, *Ideals*, and *Tales from Grace Chapel Inn* are registered trademarks of
Guideposts.

The characters and events in this book are fictional, and any resemblance to actual
persons or events is coincidental.

Library of Congress Cataloging-in-Publication Data

Hunt, Diann.
  We have this moment / Diann Hunt.
    p. cm. — (Tales from Grace Chapel Inn)
  ISBN 978-0-8249-4731-6
  1. Bed and breakfast accommodations—Fiction. 2. Sisters—Fiction. 3. Pennsylvania—
Fiction. I. Title.
  PS3608.U573W4 2008
  813'.6—dc22

                                2007041779

Cover and interior design by Marisa Jackson
Cover art by Deborah Chabrian
Typeset by Sue Murray

Printed and bound in the United States of America

10 9 8 7 6 5 4 3 2 1

A special thanks to Leo Grant and Regina Hersey for their editing expertise, and to my agent Karen Solem for her wise guidance. Finally, I dedicate this story to my sisters-in-law Julie Hunt, Patti Hunt and Beth Wallace. I love you all!

GRACE CHAPEL INN

A place where one can be
refreshed and encouraged,
a place of hope and healing,
a place where God is at home.

Chapter One

*A*lice Howard arrived for work at Potterston Hospital after her short drive from the peaceful atmosphere of Grace Chapel Inn, the charming bed and breakfast that she and her sisters owned in Acorn Hill.

The hospital presented a very different environment from that of the inn. Alice stepped into a world of stainless steel counters, wobbly-wheeled carts, bleeping machines, pungent antiseptics and paperwork—endless paperwork. By ten o'clock, however, the usual hustle and bustle brought on with new patients, and doctors on their rounds, had settled to a comfortable hum. Quiet reigned on Alice's floor.

Well, except for Wilma Rinker, the patient in Room 305. Alice decided to check on her. She padded across the scrubbed floor beyond the colored arrows and signs, greeting a passing nurse along the way.

Many people whom Alice knew shied away from hospitals, but her senses sprang to life the minute she went into one. She supposed her job fulfilled her innate need to help others. Though she only worked part-time now, she still enjoyed the thrill of rubbing shoulders with other medical professionals as they worked to provide the best possible health care for their patients. Whether busy or quiet, she truly could not complain. Besides, she had a feeling that Wilma Rinker was about to change her morning.

She stepped into the patient's room.

"This is unbelievable, Wilma. You will do absolutely anything to get out of shopping with me. Isn't that mean?" Margaret Ballard, who happened to be a guest at their inn while awaiting her sister's recovery, turned a mischievous smile to Alice. The black pantsuit, accompanied by black and silver jewelry, black shoes and black purse, looked lovely on the silver-haired woman.

Alice looked first at her patient, then back to Margaret. She held up her hands. "Oh no, you can't pull me into this. I just work here."

Margaret shrugged and walked over to her sister's bedside. A serious expression lined her face. She lifted Wilma's hand into her own. "I love you, Sis. I'm glad you're all right. The second doctor has confirmed that it was just a slight stroke. You'll probably be up and around in no time at all." Then, as if she could not stay serious too long, she added, "We'll go shopping the minute you're better."

Wilma Rinker groaned. "Well, if you love me so much,

forget the shopping. Makes my bunions hurt just thinking about it." They all laughed. "By the way, I'm hungry. When do I get to eat?" Wilma asked with a slight snap to her voice.

"Well, that's a good sign." Alice glanced at the clock on the wall. "Your lunch should arrive in another hour."

Wilma pouted like a reprimanded child.

Alice checked the I.V. fluid in the bag and then picked up the woman's frail arm to check her vitals. After she finished writing some notes on the patient's chart, Alice slid the chart holder into the slot at the foot of the bed and turned to leave the room.

"Excuse me, Alice."

Alice turned to the visiting woman. "Yes?"

"Might I have a word with you outside?"

"Certainly."

Margaret nodded. She turned to her sister. "I'll be right back, Wilma."

Wilma raised a gnarled finger. "Now don't you two go talking about me . . . and don't you think I won't be listening," she warned.

Margaret's eyebrows went up as she said in a conspiratorial tone, "I'm going to tell her all our family secrets."

Wilma brightened. "Well, remind me what they were so I can enjoy the memories."

Margaret shook her head and followed Alice out of the

room. Once they stepped into the hallway, Margaret talked in hushed tones. "I just want to know if everything is really going to be all right."

Alice tugged on Margaret's arm to pull her farther away from the door, toward the center of the hallway. She offered a comforting smile. "She will be fine. As you know, your sister has suffered a slight stroke, but the doctor has put her on a blood thinner to reduce the chance of future clotting, and he is recommending physical therapy."

While they stood talking, a gurney carrying a patient rolled toward them. Two people dressed in hospital uniforms pushed it forward while a man and woman followed closely behind.

"Let me get something to write down the phone number of her doctor's office," Margaret said. As she rummaged through her purse, a slip of paper toppled from the front pocket of her bag. She bent to pick it up, causing the gurney to halt in front of her.

Standing upright again, she saw the people waiting. "Oh, I'm sorry," Margaret said, straightening herself. She glanced at the patient. He gave her a pleasant smile. Everyone waited for her, but she seemed totally transfixed with the man on the gurney, as if she had completely forgotten all else.

"Margaret, are you all right?"

"*Hmm?*" She finally broke her gaze away from the

patient and looked at Alice as if seeing her for the first time. "Oh yes, I . . ." she stammered, almost as though she was out of breath, before she furiously stuffed the paper back into her purse. The gurney went on its way. She turned a pink face and look of confusion to Alice.

"Are you sure you're all right?" Alice asked, knowing that the poor woman had been through a lot with the news of her sister's stroke and the traveling to be by her side.

"Oh yes, I'm fine," she said, still acting a bit flustered, clutching her purse tight against her.

"Weren't you going to write down Wilma's doctor's number?"

"Pardon?" She looked dumbfounded. Then understanding seemed to dawn on her. "Oh yes, of course," she said with a laugh, then started to search for the paper once again.

Alice wondered if she should retrieve a sheet of paper from the desk and save them all some time. "Why don't you follow me to the nurse's station, and I can look up the information for you. That way if you miss him when he comes to the hospital, you can call him," Alice suggested.

Margaret nodded and followed Alice. Once they reached the desk, a nurse turned to Alice. "This call is for you," she said, holding the phone to her.

"Excuse me," Alice said to Margaret before taking the phone.

While Margaret waited, the young woman who had followed the gurney arrived at the counter beside Margaret. Alice hung up the phone and smiled at the woman.

"Excuse me," the woman said.

"Yes?"

"My name is Sherri Hanover. I'm Michael Lawton's daughter. He's the patient they just brought into the room down the hall." She turned and pointed. "I wondered if I might speak with the nurse attending him?"

"Yes, I am Mr. Lawton's nurse." Alice turned to Margaret who seemed frozen in place. "If you want to wait by Wilma's room, I'll be right with you."

Margaret nodded.

Alice watched as the young woman turned a charming smile toward Margaret. Dark brown hair lay in soft ringlets all over her head and coiled lightly upon her shoulders. Concern underlined her dark eyes. At the same time, an odd expression covered Margaret's face. She smiled briefly and headed down the hall. Alice made a mental note to keep tabs on Margaret Ballard. Perhaps the strain of her sister's illness had been too much for her.

"I'm telling you, Wilma, it's him. I know it's him," Margaret was saying when Alice entered the room.

"Here's the information you requested, Mrs. Ballard," Alice said, extending to her the paper with the doctor's name and number on it.

"Please, call me Margaret."

Alice nodded. "Margaret."

"Well, you gonna sit there all day or are you going to ask her about him?" Wilma snapped while tugging at the tape on her I.V. "Boy, I'll be glad when I can get this thing out. It's driving me crazy."

"Be careful with that or you'll pull out the needle," Alice said.

Wilma gave a grunt and folded her free arm across her chest in a huff.

Alice smiled and turned back to Margaret. "Did you want to talk to me about something else?"

"Um yes, as a matter of fact." Margaret took a deep breath. "I know this will all sound a little strange, but, well, here goes." She looked to her sister. Wilma nodded her encouragement.

"You see, the reason I got all flustered in the hallway was because the man on the gurney reminded me of someone in my past. When I walked with you to the nurse's station and that woman explained to you who she was and mentioned her father's name, I knew it was him."

Alice smiled again, wondering what all this had to do with her.

"But then I thought, how could it be the Michael Lawton I knew in high school? After all, he and his family moved to Florida. What would he be doing here?"

Alice nodded. Thinking of the valuable working time that she was losing, but not wanting to be rude, she waited.

"Um, that's where you come in." Margaret smiled sheepishly. "Is there any information that you could find for me so that I can learn whether this is the same Michael Lawton?"

Alice grimaced and shook her head. "I can't possibly do that for you, Margaret. I'm sorry, but we have privacy laws in place now, you know, and we have to be very discreet to protect our patients."

Margaret bit her lip. "I was afraid of that."

"Oh, for crying out loud, privacy, schmivacy. There has to be something you can do," Wilma said with all the charm of a drill sergeant. "Maybe check his address or next of kin."

Alice shook her head. "All I can tell you is that he was visiting his daughter in Potterston when he encountered a problem with his appendix. I'm sorry."

Margaret lifted a weak smile. "That's all right. I understand."

Still, one look at Wilma and Margaret told Alice that she had not heard the last about the matter. "The lunch trays will be here soon," Alice said to Wilma, hoping the food might keep her patient out of trouble. Alice headed out of the room, then turned once more to Wilma. "And please stop picking at that tape."

Wilma stopped mid-pick and pursed her lips into a frown. "It's like having my own jailer."

Alice turned and walked out of the room with a smile, though she knew she had her hands full with this one.

After lunch, Alice's day picked up. Between paperwork and a few demanding patients—with Wilma Rinker at the top of the list—she had all she could do just to keep up. She chuckled to herself. Alice suspected Wilma had a soft heart despite her ornery exterior.

Just before quitting time, she decided to check once more on Michael Lawton. The infection from his ruptured appendix was much better. Still, Alice thought that she would keep a close eye on things. She made her way down the hall and stopped short as she entered his room.

The patient lay sleeping peacefully, but there at the foot of his bed stood Margaret Ballard, just staring at him.

"Margaret, what are you doing in here?" Alice was shocked at the woman's bold behavior.

Margaret lifted a finger to her mouth. "I'm sorry," she whispered as she tiptoed out of his room, motioning Alice to follow her into the hallway. "I'm really sorry," she said to Alice with pleading in her voice, "but I just had to know."

Alice was speechless.

"It's him. He has the same birthmark on his neck that my Michael had. After forty-six years, I've finally found him," she said with a dreamy, faraway look in her eyes. "Michael Lawton, the man who filled my dreams my junior year in high school and for many years thereafter."

Chapter Two

*A*fter work, Alice headed home to Acorn Hill and Grace Chapel Inn. Shutting off the car engine, she climbed out of her car and walked up the porch to their Victorian bed and breakfast.

Once inside, Alice was greeted with quiet. "Hello?" she called out. Silence. She spotted Wendell, their gray and black tabby, basking in a patch of sunlight. Alice had always thought Wendell's white paws gave him the appearance of wearing boots. He gave her a weary look, moved ever so slightly and tucked his face beneath a furry paw. "Well, it's good to see you too," Alice said with a smile. She reached down to give the pet a loving scratch or two behind his right ear, causing him to tilt his head and purr. The sound reminded her of her late father's contented snoring when he had taken naps in his easy chair.

With a sigh, Alice slipped off her brown sweater and draped it across her arm before making her way into the warm and delicious-smelling kitchen. She took a seat at the table and watched Jane, her younger sister, remove a batch of cookies from the oven. Alice rubbed the back of her neck, thankful for the chance to sit down.

Jane appeared comfortable in her khaki pants and bright red cotton shirt. Her long, dark hair was pulled back in its usual ponytail and swished about as she put a pan on a cooling rack. She looked much younger than her fifty years. Alice smiled as she watched Jane do what she loved most, work in the kitchen.

Jane shrugged free from her silver baking mitts, blew a stray lock of hair from her eyes and turned to Alice with a smile. "When did you get in?"

"Just got here," Alice replied. The room was filled with the spicy scents of pumpkin and cinnamon. She lifted her nose slightly heavenward. "*Mmm*, smells good," she said.

Jane smiled. "Pumpkin bars. As soon as they cool a little, I'll spread on the cream cheese icing, and we'll have one. Be sure not to let it spoil your dinner though."

"Let me wash my hands first. I always feel better washing my hands again when I get home. Don't want to pass around germs, you know," Alice said, making her way to the sink.

"Spoken like a true medical professional."

Alice shrugged. "I try to do my part."

Jane clicked off the oven knob and looked at Alice. "Must be getting cold outside, your cheeks are rosy."

Alice dried her hands with a paper towel, then absently ran her fingers over her face. Her skin was cold. "There is a definite autumn chill to the air. I'm not complaining though. I love this time of year."

Jane smiled and stepped toward the stove, lifting the teakettle. "Just the same, a good cup of tea will warm you."

Alice nodded, thinking how her sister perked up the weariest of days with her cheerful hospitality. She walked back to her chair and sat down.

Jane filled the kettle at the tap and placed it on the stainless steel stove.

"You're having a party and forgot to invite me?" Louise Howard Smith teased, her blue eyes twinkling as she entered the kitchen. Wire-rimmed glasses dangled on a chain around her neck and mingled with the pearl necklace against her blue sweater. She maneuvered a chair her way and settled into it.

Looking on as Louise smoothed the wrinkles from her blue wool skirt, Alice thought how she loved times like this, chatting around the table with her sisters over something good to eat. When Louise looked up, Alice gave her a welcoming smile. "We are just ready to have some pumpkin bars and tea."

"Sounds lovely," Louise said, tucking back a silver strand of hair from her forehead.

"Are you finished with your piano lessons for the day?" Alice asked.

Louise nodded. "Yes, thank goodness. I am tired. I'd like to curl up in a chair and spend the evening reading a good book." Louise immediately took on the expression of one about to recite something important.

"'If only one had time to read a little more: We either get shallow and broad or narrow and deep.'"

Alice smiled, remembering her older sister's fondness for C. S. Lewis and how she often quoted him. For a few moments Alice wondered how she might approach what she needed to discuss with her sisters. Her fingers toyed absently with her wristwatch as she considered how to bring it up. After all, she did not want her sisters to think she was interfering. Her mind searched for the right words.

Clearing her throat and attempting an air of nonchalance she asked, "Our guest, Margaret Ballard, hasn't made it home yet, has she?"

Louise thought for a minute. "I don't think so. Did you see her come in, Jane?"

Jane checked the temperature of the pumpkin bars, then turned to her sisters. "I don't believe I did see her. Why?" She pulled out a chair and sat down.

Alice leaned into the table. "Well, you know her sister is one of my patients."

"How is she doing?" asked Louise.

"Wilma Rinker is doing fine," Alice said with a smile. "That woman has more sass than Aunt Ethel, I can tell you."

"Oh dear," Louise said.

"But that's another story altogether," Alice said with a laugh. "Anyway, I have another patient, Michael Lawton, who Margaret seems to know. Evidently, the two of them were quite an item back in their high school days."

"Indeed," Louise said with obvious interest.

"I found Margaret standing at the foot of his bed in his room." Alice frowned, remembering the scene.

"Goodness, did he see her?" Louise asked.

Alice shook her head. "He was sleeping. But of course, as I was about to give her a talking to, she told me she knew it was her old flame because she had seen a birthmark on his neck, and her friend had the same mark. She's convinced this is the same Michael Lawton with whom she fell in love in high school."

Like one hearing a delightful secret, Jane pulled her chair closer to the table. "Oh, how fun."

Alice loved the enthusiasm that so often lit Jane's face. "From what I've learned from casual conversation, both are widowed. He lives in Florida but is in Potterston visiting his daughter." She waited a moment before plunging ahead.

"I was wondering . . ." She hesitated. "If I should arrange a meeting between the two of them?"

Just then the kettle on the stove began to whistle. Jane held up her finger. "Don't breathe a single word without me," she said before rising to prepare the tea.

"Would you like some help?" Louise asked.

"No, I'm fine," Jane said, scurrying about the kitchen in her usual manner.

Alice and Louise talked about how nicely the weather had been holding out, and they wondered what the winter would bring. They also discussed the hospital and the challenge of dealing with difficult patients, while Jane gathered the Wedgwood, arranged the tea fixings on a serving tray along with plates and forks, and then set everything on the table.

When Jane finally sat in her chair, she looked at Alice. "Thanks for waiting. You were saying you wondered if you should arrange a meeting between your patient and our guest?"

Louise lifted a cup and saucer for herself. Always the practical one, she frowned in a big-sister fashion and said, "I'm not sure that is a good idea, Alice. Do you think you should get involved?"

Jane jumped in at once. "Oh, lighten up, Louie. I think it's a great idea. Just imagine," her eyes sparkled with enthusiasm, "you could help rekindle an old flame." Jane walked to the maple butcher-block counter and spread cream cheese icing over the warm pumpkin treats. When finished, she placed the plate of bars on the table.

Alice ventured further. "It might be a kindness to get them together. See what happens." She knew how Jane felt about the matter, but she wanted Louise's blessing, too, before she got involved. She looked toward her older sister.

"I don't know, Alice. You are too sentimental for your own good." Louise scooped a pumpkin bar onto her plate, cut a bite with her fork, then placed it in her mouth. "*Mmm*, these are wonderful, Jane."

"Thanks." Jane brought the filled teapot to the table. "Well, Alice, you can't have them meet at the hospital," she said while pouring the hot liquid into her sisters' cups. "Sterile rooms with floors smelling of industrial detergent, white scratchy sheets and cold steel machines are no place for a romance." She pulled the teapot upright and thought a moment. Her eyes grew wide as if struck with inspiration. "You could invite him here for afternoon tea and tell him you have an old friend who would like to meet him." Seemingly satisfied with her suggestion, Jane poured herself some tea.

Alice pondered the idea. She looked to Louise, who shrugged. "I suppose it wouldn't hurt to reintroduce them. Let nature take its course from there."

Just then Margaret Ballard appeared at the swinging

door. "I'm sorry to intrude, but would it be okay if I came in a moment?"

The sisters smiled in unison. "Pull up a chair and join us for tea, Margaret," Alice said, waving her in.

Alice watched as Margaret slipped onto a chair beside her. Jane pushed the pumpkin bars toward her. "Here, Margaret, have one. They're pretty good, if I do say so myself," she beamed.

Margaret reached over and used a serving utensil to lift one onto a plate. "Thank you." She took a bite. "Oh, they're still warm. Wonderful."

Jane set a cup of tea before their guest. Alice did not fail to miss the pleasure on her sister's face. How Jane loved to treat others to her culinary delights. And how people loved to be the recipients of her kindness.

Margaret turned to Alice. "I wanted to thank you for taking such good care of Wilma, and," she glanced briefly at Louise and Jane, then lowered her voice, "um, I wanted to apologize for what happened today."

Louise seemed to sense Margaret's awkwardness and started a side conversation with Jane to let Alice and Margaret talk.

"I shouldn't have been in Michael's room. I know that was inappropriate," Margaret said over Louise and Jane's soft murmurings.

Alice patted Margaret's hand. "It's all right. After you explained, I understood your reasoning." Alice ate the last bit of her treat. "I've told my sisters about your former boyfriend. You're sure it's him?"

Margaret bit her lip and nodded. "No doubt in my mind. When he turned his head and I saw that birthmark on his neck, I knew." She looked toward the window. "After all these years . . ." she uttered wistfully.

"Anyone want more tea?" Jane asked, lifting herself partially from her chair.

"No thanks, Jane," Alice said.

Louise shook her head. Jane shrugged and sat back down.

"Did you talk to him after I left work?" Alice asked.

Margaret studied her fingers and shook her head. "I just don't know how to approach him. I mean, forty-six years." Her hands absently touched the delicate wrinkles around her eyes.

"Well, it would be a shame to let your friendship stay in the past when you could catch up on each other's lives," Louise said matter-of-factly, surprising Alice.

Margaret smiled her thanks.

"Margaret, why don't you invite your friend over to join us for an afternoon tea?" Jane asked.

"Oh dear, I . . . I couldn't. Why, I wouldn't know what

to say. He might not remember me, for all I know." She held her hand near her throat as if she might choke from the mere thought of it.

Before Alice could get a word in, Louise said, "Alice can do it for you."

Margaret looked confused.

"She can ask your friend to come over," Louise explained.

Margaret appeared skeptical. "He might wonder why she would ask him."

"Well, she can tell him she has come across an old friend of his who would like to see him." Louise tipped her head abruptly as if the matter were settled.

Margaret frowned. "With a big emphasis on the old."

"It happens to all of us, Margaret. Remember, he is forty-six years older too," Louise encouraged.

Margaret smiled. "Sure, but he still looks like Michael." She stared straight ahead, her eyes far away. Then as if she had mustered the courage, she took a deep breath and turned back to Alice. "Okay, let's do it."

Jane clasped her hands together. "Go for it!"

"Let's try for an early afternoon after he's had time to adjust to being discharged," Alice suggested.

Everyone agreed.

Chapter Three

The next day Alice padded softly into Michael Lawton's room where he lay sleeping. A beam of sunlight slipped through the window blinds and waved across his sheet like a wide golden ribbon. Michael stirred on his bed, catching Alice's attention. He looked around the room a moment, then turned to Alice and offered a hesitant smile.

"You may remember me. I'm Alice Howard. Do you remember where you are, Mr. Lawton?" Alice asked, lifting his wrist to time his pulse.

Looking none too pleased, he nodded.

"You know, I just don't understand why no one is ever happy to see me," Alice teased.

"I think it's your clothes," he said with a voice groggy from sleep.

Alice shrugged. "I suppose the white does make me look a bit ghostly—"

His eyes widened.

"Or should I say ghastly?"

Michael let out a measured breath. "I think I'd better let that one slip on by."

She smiled, then recorded his vitals on the chart. After she finished the notes, she looked at him.

"They took my appendix, you know," he said with a tone that encouraged sympathy.

Typical male patient. She smiled and patted his hand, then placed the brown plastic chart holder into the slot at the end of his bed and nodded. "So I've heard. You have to watch hospitals, they're always taking things," she said in an effort to keep him lighthearted.

He mustered a stronger smile.

"We are still trying to take the infection out of you. You've been hanging on to it like a pit bull. The hospital is gaining on you though. You'll be up and running in no time."

He groaned dramatically, as if the very idea hurt.

Alice grimaced. "Oh, sorry. Maybe not running, but I think it's possible you could get out of here in a couple of days."

He didn't look convinced.

"Want some water or crushed ice?" she asked, noting that his lips were dry and cracked.

He nodded and moved his leg, then stopped abruptly.

"A little sore?"

He held his finger to his lips. "*Shhh*, don't tell anyone,

but I think the doctor might have left his tools behind. Right here." He pointed to his stomach.

"Oh dear, he loses more instruments that way," she said, lifting the gold hospital pitcher and pouring ice into a plastic cup. She liked this patient. Anyone who peppered their complaining with humor could not be all bad. "I'll see if I can get you some pain meds." She handed him the cup.

He eased himself into a different position on his bed. "You know, Alice, I'm sure you are great company, but I hope I'm not around here long enough to find out." He looked at her and gave a teasing grin.

"As you say, it's the clothes." Alice checked the fluids in his I.V. bag. "If it helps at all, they tell me you are doing much better."

"I do feel better."

Alice smiled. "Great. That's what we like to hear." She prepared to leave. "If you need anything, you just let me know." She turned to go.

He nodded. "Oh, one more thing."

She stopped and faced him.

"Have I had any visitors today, or did I chase them off?" he asked, before putting a little crushed ice in his mouth.

Alice played along and pretended to think hard on the matter. Finally, she said cheerfully, "Come to think of it, you did have a visitor."

"My daughter?"

Alice nodded. "She was here when I arrived this morning. I encouraged her to take a break and walk down the hall for a minute, get a snack. She looked a little pale. I didn't have the energy to set up another bed."

Michael smiled. "That's my girl. She's quite the mother hen."

"That she is. Just proves she loves you though."

"I suppose."

"Hi, Daddy." As if on cue, Sherri Hanover walked in and kissed Michael's cheek. "Feeling better?"

Michael waited until Alice was a few feet away. He cupped his hand beside his mouth and said in a staged whisper, "If you call feeling like roadkill better, I'm better."

"Don't think I didn't hear that," Alice said, refilling his water pitcher at the tap. She turned toward the patient and his daughter.

Sherri smiled and said to her father in a conspiratorial manner. "That bad?"

He shrugged.

"Well, not to worry. I'm here to take care of you." She straightened his pillow and began tucking in the bed sheets.

"Uh-oh, you mean to tell me we're paying these doctors and nurses a bunch of money for nothing?"

Sherri flashed a grin. "I'm afraid so."

"Listen, Sherri, I'm fine."

"I know, but Mom—"

Michael held up his hand to silence her. "Sherri, Mom has been gone for three years. I'm doing okay. Really. Don't worry. I'm not totally helpless, you know. Besides, Jeremy—"

"I see we didn't get your blood pressure earlier, so I'll need to do that now, Mr. Lawton," Alice interrupted, feeling a little uncomfortable for intruding in their family discussion.

He nodded toward her.

Alice lifted his arm and wrapped the pad around his bicep.

Sherri watched Alice a moment, then continued. "Dad, Jeremy understands perfectly. He's planning to pick up some dinner on the way home, so he's fine."

"Well, I'll tell you what. You can stay for a while, but then I want you to go home and get some rest. I'm doing fine, and I'll need to get some rest, too."

"Now, Daddy—"

"Do we have your phone number, Sherri?" Alice asked, releasing the pad from Michael's arm and lifting the chart once more.

"Yes," Sherri answered.

Alice wrote something on the chart, then looked up. "We'll call you if there's a problem. But let me assure you, he is doing fine. He just needs time to rest." Alice walked out of the room, picked up his meds and walked back in to hand them to her patient. She raised the little pill holder to him. He plunked one pink and one yellow pill into his mouth while Alice poured a cup of water for him to wash them down. With a grimace, he swallowed the pills and drank some water.

A slight frown covered Sherri's face as she considered her father's asking her to return home.

"Sherri, it's what I want you to do," Michael said in a fatherly tone.

"All right," she finally said as if the words were pried out of her. She turned to Alice. "But you promise you'll call at the first sign of any problem?"

"You can count on it, dear."

Sherri pursed her lips together but seemed to see she was outnumbered. "Well, all right, I'll go home after a little while. Once I'm sure you'll be all right." Her eyes brightened. "Hey, Dad, I brought you something to read." She pulled a book from her bag and waved it in the air.

Alice walked toward the wastebasket to throw away the pill cup.

"I hope it's not a medical thriller," he teased.

"Nope. A mystery."

"In a hospital?"

"Nowhere near a hospital."

"Good. I'll take it." Alice heard him say as she slipped from the room.

The day proved busier than the one before, and Alice's shift passed in a flurry of activity. She had barely had time to complete her tasks, let alone talk to Michael Lawton about the tea. She decided she would approach him the following day. She prepared to leave and groaned when she saw Wilma Rinker's call light flick on.

The nurse on the next shift turned to her. "I'll answer it. You go on home." Before Alice could argue, the nurse was on her way.

Alice sighed and put on her sweater. Since she had not taken time for lunch, she could hardly wait to see what Jane had planned for dinner.

The nurse returned. "Sorry, Alice, she insists on seeing you."

Alice smiled. "It's all right. Thanks, anyway." Alice trudged over to Wilma's room. "Yes, Mrs. Rinker?"

With a sparkle in her eye and a smile on her face, the old woman motioned Alice over like they were in on a huge secret together. "Did you ask him yet?"

Alice stared at her blankly.

"Michael Lawton," Wilma said, a tinge of impatience edging her voice. "Margaret told me what your plans were to get the two of them together. So did you ask him?"

"Where is Margaret?"

"Oh, she went downstairs to get a bite to eat. I made her go." Wilma sounded like the bossy sister that she was. "She was afraid you'd come in to talk to her and she wouldn't be here, but I told her I'd let her know what you said." Her eyes sparked to life. "So did you ask him?"

Alice smiled in spite of herself. How could she disappoint these women? Wilma looked almost as excited as Margaret about the whole thing. Evidently, this man had been special to the entire family, or perhaps Wilma held out hope for happiness to light upon her sister's life once again. "I'll go see if he's awake. If not, it will have to wait until tomorrow."

A slight shadow crossed Wilma's face, but it lingered only a moment. Alice shook her head and walked out the door. She stepped into Michael's room where he was sitting up, reading a magazine. "Well, you certainly look better."

He closed his magazine, turned to her, and smiled. "Thanks. I'm feeling lots better." He glanced at the clock. "I thought your shift was over."

"Yes, it is. I just, um, wanted to ask you something."

He said nothing, but merely waited for her to continue. She was beginning to think maybe this had not been such a good idea after all. *What was I thinking sticking my nose into other people's affairs? Goodness, I am behaving like Aunt Ethel.*

"Alice?"

She cleared her throat. "Oh yes, I'm sorry. I'm a little tired," she apologized. "Um, anyway, my sisters and I, well, we have a bed and breakfast over in Acorn Hill." She paused as if by waiting she might find a way out of this uncomfortable situation.

He stayed perfectly still.

"Well, we . . . that is to say, I, ran across someone who knows you, it seems, from years ago. An old friend, I guess you would say."

His eyebrows lifted. "Is that a fact? Who is it?"

Alice thought for a moment. She was not sure if she was supposed to reveal Margaret's identity. *Oh dear, now what should I do?* She had to think quickly. "Well, we thought it might be fun to surprise you. So we were wondering if after your release from the hospital you would come to our inn for afternoon tea to renew your friendship."

There. She had said it.

He stared at her in such a way, she felt silly for bringing the matter up at all. "Of course, if you would rather not—"

"Oh, quite the contrary, it sounds rather intriguing." He smiled and looked toward the window. "Just wonder who he might be."

"Oh, well, it's a . . . she."

"She?" He looked mildly shocked.

"Are you all right?"

"Oh yeah. I just hadn't considered that possibility."

"Do you still want to meet her?"

He smiled. "Sure, if you can talk the doctor into letting me out of here."

Relief allowed her to release the breath she was holding. "He'll let you go when he thinks you're over the infection."

"Okay, it's a date then," he said, picking up his magazine once again.

"What's a date?" his daughter asked.

Michael cleared his throat. He and Alice exchanged a glance. "Well, I'll see you folks in the morning," Alice said. She would leave Michael alone to explain. She felt that she had interfered enough already.

She made a hasty retreat down the hall as she wondered why in the world she was getting involved with these people. After all, she hardly knew Michael or Margaret, and yet she felt compelled to help the two of them get together once more. For old time's sake? She was not sure. *I only know that they deserve another chance.*

Time had stolen forty-six years from the couple. She thought they should have one more evening together if for no other reason than to reminisce over an old friendship.

Chapter Four

A week passed as the patients got well and autumn colors became more vivid in the foliage of Acorn Hill. Louise played another phrase on the piano and reached up with a pencil to make a notation on her music. The bell on the front desk rang. Knowing that Alice was at work and Jane had gone to the store, Louise placed the pencil on the piano and walked into the front hall. "Hello, welcome to Grace Chapel Inn," she said, smiling and extending her hand in greeting.

"Hello. My name is Ruth Kincade, and I've scheduled a stay at the inn beginning tonight." Her handshake was as gentle as her petite frame might suggest. Swept up and out in a fashionable style, her short brown hair stayed in place, no doubt, with the help of a styling gel. One look at the slight, thirtyish woman made Louise wonder how the guest would manage against a brisk wind. The woman's large blue eyes almost looked out of place among the small features on her pale face.

Louise opened the scheduling book. "Yes, I see it here.

You'll be staying in the Sunset Room." She made an entry in the book and smiled at the woman. "Would you please fill out this form?"

"Of course." Miss Kincade looked as though she was trying to appear polite, but really wanted nothing more than to go to bed.

"If you will follow me, I'll show you to your room," Louise said, reaching for one of the guest's bags.

Miss Kincade nodded and followed Louise up the stairs. Once they reached the room, Louise unlocked the door and nudged it open. She stepped aside and waited a moment for her guest to survey the interior. She watched as the woman took in the terra-cotta ragged faux paint and the impressionist prints covering the walls. With a final glance at the cream-colored antique furniture, the guest turned to Louise.

"It's lovely," she said.

"Good." Louise handed the key to her. "There is a phone downstairs if you need to make a call."

"Thank you. I shouldn't need much, really. I'm just here for some rest."

"Do you have any special needs we should be aware of?" Louise asked with concern.

"Oh no, nothing like that. I've just taken a sabbatical from teaching. I'm exhausted and trying to decide, well, what I want to do with my life." She offered a slightly embarrassed smile, as if she feared she had revealed too much of herself to a stranger.

Louise felt her motherly instincts kick in. She knew the demands of teaching could be overwhelming at times, and she wanted to encourage this young lady. She smiled warmly. "My sister has a good friend who teaches here in town. It can be a demanding job. I simply teach children to play piano and sometimes I get weary."

"Do you teach here?" the woman asked, concern in her voice.

Louise quickly assured her that the lessons were held in the parlor, a soundproof room. "I, for one, do not like a lot of noise, so we try to keep such disturbances at a minimum. You should have no problem resting here."

Miss Kincade nodded her gratitude.

"Well, let us know if you need anything," Louise said over her shoulder as she turned and headed back toward the stairway. With a quick glance at the closed door, Louise noted the "Do Not Disturb" sign already hung from the doorknob.

The following morning, well after breakfast, Jane finished wrapping dough around the last of the apple dumplings, then placed them in the oven. She took off her oven mitts and cleaned the apple peelings from the counter. Only when the kitchen was returned to its usual sparkle did Jane allow herself to fall into a chair and relax. The syrup from the apple dumplings would soon fill the inn with the sweet smell of brown sugar and cinnamon. Perfect for the autumn season, she thought with satisfaction.

Jane thought of Margaret. She seemed like such a nice lady. Her story rivaled a fairy tale, meeting an old love all these years later. Perhaps they would have a second chance at romance. Jane wondered if she would ever have that chance. Since working through her divorce, she had grown accustomed to the single life and found that it suited her now. She could not say whether she would always stay single, but she felt at peace with her life either way.

"Any chance you could use some company?" Alice asked, entering the kitchen.

Jane smiled at her sister. Always ready to help, Alice was a welcome sight at any time of day. Truly, Jane enjoyed her new life with her sisters. As different as they all were, she would never have dreamed they could live together in such harmony. "Please, come join me. Would you like some tea?"

Alice held up her hand. "You just stay put, dear. I'm a big girl, and I can put on my own tea." True to form, Alice was already filling the kettle with water.

With affection, Jane watched her older sister take over the tea preparations.

"I'm a lady of leisure today," Alice was saying, her attention on the kettle. "I switched days with another nurse. So I'll cover for her later." She shut off the faucet and turned to Jane. "Besides, you look a little tired. You feeling okay?"

"I'm fine, just taking a break."

"Whatever is in the oven smells absolutely wonderful."

"Apple dumplings."

"Oh, my favorite!" Alice said, as she put the kettle on the stove and turned on the burner. "Would you like some tea?"

"No, thanks. I've already had some."

Alice tugged on the cabinet knob. "You know, I still remember my initial hesitance about the paprika paint on these cabinets." Opening the door, she pulled out a cup and saucer.

Jane smiled. "I remember feeling it was a bit chancy, but it's a nice color for the kitchen."

"You are so good with such things, Jane. I wish I had the gift for it that you do." Alice placed her cup and saucer on the table and sat down in her chair. "But at least I have you around if I get in a decorating dilemma." She smiled. "So are we ready for the afternoon tea?"

"The food is ready, if that's what you mean. How about the guests of honor?" Jane asked.

"Well, Margaret is a nervous wreck. Michael is just plain curious—and glad to be out of the hospital. Although Margaret's sister Wilma can't make it to the tea, she is ready to, as she put it, 'get this show on the road.'"

Jane laughed. "Sounds like she and Aunt Ethel could be good friends."

Alice cringed. "Oh dear, we'd better not let them get together. I shudder to think of the ruckus the two of them could raise."

"You're right," Jane said. "From what you've told us, I'll bet Wilma was a hoot to have around the house as a kid. I'm looking forward to meeting her," she added.

"Well, you won't soon forget her, that's for sure." Alice toyed with the handle on her teacup. "By the way, did our teacher friend come down for breakfast?"

Jane shook her head. "In fact, I wondered if we should look in on her. I haven't seen her since she arrived at the inn."

"*Hmm*, that is a bit disconcerting," Alice said, her brown eyes shadowed with concern. She walked over to the whistling kettle and prepared the tea. "While the tea is brewing, I think I'll slip up there and make sure she's all right."

"I certainly hope she is," Jane called after her sister, who made a hasty retreat from the kitchen. Jane wondered if she should follow Alice to the woman's room, but then thought it best not to overwhelm the poor thing. She no doubt needed the rest.

Jane got up from her chair and decided to prepare some tea for herself after all while she waited for Alice's return. Pouring herself a cup, she had barely sat down when Alice walked in with a smile.

"She's doing fine. She brought a stack of books with her and has been reading all morning. I must say, she looks much better than the description Louise gave us over dinner last night." Alice poured some tea. "I feel better now. She said she'd join us for tea." Alice took a sip. "I think Louise had a good suggestion when she mentioned having Miss Kincade talk to Vera. I'll ask Vera about it when we go for our walk. Being a teacher herself, Vera might be able to encourage her."

Jane nodded. "It's certainly worth a try."

"Would you mind if I invited her to the tea?"

"That would be great. The more, the merrier. I figure Margaret and Michael will feel more comfortable if we have other people around." Jane shrugged. "Take some of the pressure off."

Alice agreed. "So who all is coming?"

Jane began to count on her fingers. "Let's see, we have you, me, Louise, Vera, Ruth Kincade and, of course, the honored couple."

Alice nodded and took another sip.

"You know, I certainly wouldn't want to spend my life at a job I didn't like," Jane said, looking into her cup.

"Do you like what you do here, Jane?"

Jane's head jerked up with a start. "Of course, I like it. I love it." Jane paused a moment, thinking about something but wondering if she should voice it. She took a deep breath. "Though, sometimes I wonder how, well, beneficial it is."

"What do you mean?"

"Oh, I don't know. I spend so much time in the kitchen, I sometimes wonder if what I do is worthwhile."

"You have to be kidding. With your gift of hospitality you have lightened the load for many a weary traveler," Alice said with conviction.

"Yeah, but I hope I do more than fill their stomachs, you know?"

"Oh, Jane, can't you see it? How many times have I found you on the front porch offering words of encouragement to those who pass by? Not only are you known around Acorn Hill as a wonderful cook, but also as someone approachable and friendly. You always offer a smile to others when they are down. Why, I've even heard Aunt Ethel go so far as to say, 'When life gets insane, go talk to Jane.'"

Jane giggled and shook her head. "I can always count on Auntie to come through for me." She studied her sister. Alice had a way of comforting others with her kind words. Jane felt better already. "Thank you, Alice. I hope you're right."

"I'm right," Alice said, with a reassuring pat on Jane's hand. "Did I tell you that Wilma has a daughter?"

Jane shook her head.

"Her name is Julie, and she's coming here from Georgia. Evidently, she and her mother had a falling out years ago and haven't talked since. After this shake up with Wilma's stroke, Julie has decided to surprise her mother and is coming to see her."

"Oh, how wonderful!" Jane exclaimed.

Alice nodded and smiled. "Isn't it? Margaret is thrilled with the idea of seeing them reconciled. Julie should arrive tomorrow. I hope I'm at the hospital to witness the happy event."

"It makes you wonder how families let themselves get into those situations. You know, where they're so angry with one another that they let their lives drift apart."

Alice shook her head. "I can't imagine it. We've been so blessed in our family. I don't know what I'd do without you and Louise." Once again, Alice reached over and patted Jane's hand.

"And we don't know what we'd do without you," Jane said, putting her free hand over Alice's. Jane could feel tears sting her eyes. "But before I turn into a soggy cook, I think

I'd better get up, make lunch, and then start preparations for our little tea. They'll be here before we know it."

Alice nodded and finished the last of her drink. Gathering her dishes, she took them over to the sink, rinsed them off and loaded them in the dishwasher.

"You know, I'm really excited about the tea this afternoon," Jane said, feeling like a child waiting for playmates to arrive. "I don't know. I just have this feeling that love is in the air."

Chapter Five

Though she normally worked on her ledgers in the morning, Louise had been too busy earlier, helping Jane get the Symphony Room ready for their upcoming guests. That afternoon she found herself working on the inn's business at the reception desk. Once she finished her final notation, she closed the ledger and put the book away. It always surprised her that she found such satisfaction in working with the ledgers. She smiled, thinking of Alice's distaste for such things.

Louise thought it wonderful how each sister brought her own gifts to the inn: Jane's culinary arts; Alice's warm, welcoming personality and serving spirit; and, Louise hoped, her own contribution of handling accounts and playing her music. They each played an integral part in running the business, and she breathed a prayer of thanks for the blessing of such a life. After her husband Eliot had died, she thought she would never know happiness again. But she was wrong. Though she missed Eliot deeply, she loved her life with her sisters. God was good, and they were blessed.

A glance at her watch told her she had another half hour before her next piano student was scheduled. The Burton family was due to arrive shortly. Louise mentally went through her checklist over their room. She had seen to the final preparations and felt sure she had not missed anything. She wanted to make them especially comfortable since Mrs. Burton, who had made their reservation, had indicated that their stay was partly to explore a new area of Pennsylvania, but mostly to give their daughter a chance to relax in a tranquil setting. The youngster had not been attending school because of the lingering effects of mononucleosis, and the Burtons hoped that with home-schooling and a chance for their daughter to rest, she would regain good health and return to her regular school, perhaps by December.

Before she could think on the matter further, the front door opened. In walked a man and woman in their mid-thirties, and a girl around eleven.

"Hello," Louise said, rising to meet them. "Welcome to Grace Chapel Inn." She extended her hand in greeting.

The man offered a hearty shake and his wife a warm one. The girl gave a friendly smile.

Louise went through the usual speech that she gave to the inn's new guests. She also advised the Burtons about places to visit in town, but they indicated their need to rest awhile. Accordingly, Louise showed them to the Symphony Room. As they talked, Louise noticed that the mother, Dorothy Burton, used hand gestures to talk to her daughter.

Dorothy turned to Louise. "Annie has been hearing impaired since first grade. She has nerve damage in her ears caused by a high fever. While she can hear some sounds and noises with the help of her hearing aid, and she is pretty good at lip-reading, she cannot fully make out conversations. And then there's always the matter of people turning away when they talk." She gave a reassuring smile to her daughter and signed while she said, "That's why we use sign language."

Annie smiled and looked at Louise. She made some hand gestures.

"She says she is very happy to meet you and looking forward to staying at the inn. She also wants to know if your cat likes kids," Dorothy said, pointing to Wendell, who now circled Annie's legs.

Louise laughed. "Well, looks to me like Wendell has taken an instant liking to you, Annie," Louise said, watching their cat. She looked up to see Dorothy interpreting her words to Annie. "Oh, sorry. Did I go too fast?"

Dorothy shook her head. "No, no. We use sign in our home so much that we're able to keep up with most conversations."

The Burtons talked with ease about the matter, and Louise thought that admirable. The parents' acceptance of Annie's disability also seemed to have a positive effect on the child. Having worked with children for years, Louise quickly spotted Annie's confident and positive nature.

Louise decided she liked this family very much.

Margaret paced her room. "I don't know, Alice. Maybe this wasn't such a good idea."

Though they had only known each other for a short time, Alice and Margaret had taken a rapid liking to each other. Alice felt as if she had known Margaret for years.

"Margaret, look at you. The silver pantsuit looks stunning on you. And that pin," Alice said, pointing to the sparkling cluster of diamond look-alikes on the lapel of her jacket, "is just beautiful. You look wonderful. You have nothing to worry about."

"But I . . ." She stopped pacing and looked in the mirror again. "I look old," she said, suddenly doing facial exercises as if that would erase her wrinkles before Michael arrived.

Alice had to stifle a giggle. "Relax. You're going to have a nice visit with an old friend."

Margaret let go of the breath she was holding. "You're

right. I don't know why I'm putting all this pressure on myself. I'm acting like a foolish teenager." She shook her head, then looked up at Alice. "Thank you."

"You're welcome," Alice said with a smile. Just then someone rang the bell at the downstairs desk, causing Margaret to stiffen.

She shook her head and sighed.

"It's going to be fine. You'll see." Alice gave her new friend a slight hug. "I'll see you downstairs."

When she walked down the stairs, Alice saw Michael Lawton standing there in crisp navy pants and a red-plaid shirt. His short, dark hair, with a sprinkling of gray, lay neatly against his head. When Alice came down the stairs, he looked up with a grin.

"There you are. Now I know I have the right place."

Alice gave him a kind smile and extended her hand. "You do indeed. You look so much more colorful than you did when I first met you," she said.

"It's those hospital gowns," he teased. "You know the color white just washes me out."

"*Hmm*, feels like we've had this conversation before," Alice said with a laugh. "Well, I must admit your shirt looks a bit snappier than your hospital gown."

"Yeah, I don't plan on wearing white anytime soon." He lifted his nose. "Something sure smells good."

"Oh, it's good all right. You've not lived until you've tasted my sister Jane's cooking."

His eyebrows raised. "Sounds like I've come to some-place special."

Alice watched him as he shoved a hand into his pocket and looked around, a bit ill at ease.

He leaned slightly toward her. "Since she's an old friend, what if I don't know who she is?"

Alice thought it amusing that he seemed as jittery as Margaret. "I'll make the proper introductions, so you won't have to guess," she assured him.

He sighed, and Alice suppressed a smile at the relief in it. He shuffled as if he did not know what to do with his feet. A noise on the stairway caught their attention. They both looked up to see Margaret coming down the steps. Alice moved aside to watch the couple's first meeting after forty-six years. She glanced over to find Jane, Louise and Vera smiling from the living room doorway.

Michael's eyes grew wide as Margaret drew nearer. By the time she had reached the bottom stair, he walked over to her and took her hand. "Margaret." He whispered her name as if he could not believe that she was standing there.

"Hello, Michael."

Well, it did not look as though Alice would need to introduce them. She smiled as she watched the forty-six years that had stood between this couple dissolve in a heartbeat.

Michael and Margaret appeared wrapped in the moment, as if they had stepped through a magic door and slipped into a time long ago forgotten. Silence filled the room until a tickle started in the back of Alice's throat and forced her to cough. The unexpected noise seemed to shake the couple free from their wanderings.

No one knew what to do next. "Well," Alice said, deciding to take matters into her own hands, "shall we have some tea?"

The couple turned and smiled at the others. Alice noticed that Michael continued to hold Margaret's hand as they made their way into the dining room.

Amid excited chatter the little group settled around the mahogany table where Jane proceeded to serve her guests coffee or tea and warm apple dumplings topped with a dollop of whipped cream. Vera and the sisters talked with Ruth Kincade about her school assignment while the couple reacquainted themselves with each other after so many years apart. Once everyone had finished eating, Jane told them they were free to take their coffee and tea into the parlor where Louise would be playing for their pleasure.

Outside, the weather had turned chilly, sufficient to warrant the burning of logs in the fireplace for just a little while. With the lovely music Louise provided, the warmth of the room, and the friendly chatter, Alice deemed the tea a pleasing success. Her few glances toward the couple told her things were going well and perhaps Jane's prediction about love in the air had been right after all.

The next morning at the hospital, after Alice finished talking with a doctor on the phone, she sat back in her chair and rested a moment. The desk held a few more notes that she needed to work through, but she had pretty much kept up with the paperwork.

Wilma's call light came on. The other nurses were busy, so Alice went in to check on her. On her way, she glanced at her watch. Knowing that Margaret and Wilma's daughter would arrive to visit Wilma at any minute, Alice offered a quick prayer that God would provide healing to their relationship.

Though the white-haired woman looked somewhat frail as she lay in her bed, Alice knew her looks were deceiving. Wilma Rinker had enough spunk to run the hospital single-handedly if she so desired. And, in fact, if they did not get her out of there soon, Alice felt quite sure the little spitfire might do that very thing.

Heading toward Wilma, Alice stifled a chuckle. "Did you need something, Mrs. Rinker?"

She made a face as if she had just taken a bite from a dill

pickle. "How many times do I have to tell you my name is Wilma? Call me Wilma. You make me sound like my old mother-in-law." An ornery twinkle lit her eyes. "Before she died, that is. God rest her soul." Wilma put her hand over her heart rather dramatically as if she were about to recite the Pledge of Allegiance.

"My apologies. I certainly don't want to make you feel old, let alone like your mother-in-law," Alice said, feigning horror at the very idea. "Wilma it is."

Wilma nodded once with a satisfied smile. She studied Alice for a moment. "You're all right, you know that?"

Alice was not quite sure how to answer. "Thanks . . . I think," she added with a little reserve.

"It's a good thing. I don't take to just anybody. If I take to you, that means you've earned it. And I like you."

Alice supposed she should feel special but before pride could take root, Wilma added in her no-nonsense fashion, "But don't let it go to your head."

Alice tried to hide her amusement as she watched the woman settle back into her pillow. After Wilma got situated, Alice waited for her to say what she needed, but she just lay there staring at Alice.

"Well, are you going to tell me what it was you needed?"

"I wanted to talk about Margaret and Michael's get-together yesterday."

"Didn't she tell you about it?"

Wilma shook her head. "I haven't seen her yet, and it's driving me crazy."

"Well, I'm sure Margaret would want to be the one to tell you how things went. Besides, who would know better than she?"

Wilma harrumphed. She clearly had her heart set on finding out all she could about her sister's rekindled romance, if one could call it that. Wilma crossed her arms over her chest and her lips pulled into a frown. Though she wanted to, Alice didn't dare allow herself to laugh. "Now, Mrs.—"

The woman made an animated expression.

"I mean, Wilma, if you'll excuse me, I have work to do. Besides, Margaret should be here shortly."

"She's probably shopping. That girl shops more than anyone I know. Never buys anything. Just shops. For crying out loud, what's a body to do all that time walking around in the stores? I've never seen the likes of it."

The comment struck Alice as funny. She thought of the conversation she and Jane had earlier about the similarities between Wilma and Aunt Ethel. No doubt about it, she could not let the two of them get in cahoots or there was no telling what might happen to Acorn Hill. Before Alice could think about it further, a noise sounded in the doorway, and the look on Wilma's face told Alice who was there.

For a moment, Alice wondered if the shock of seeing her daughter might be too much for Wilma. Wilma didn't move a muscle, not even the slightest twitch, which, with her disposition, was quite an accomplishment.

"Hello, Momma." The tall, thin woman looked to be in her forties. Dressed in dark green slacks, a sage green blouse and smart brown flats, Julie wore her dark hair short and flipped out at the ends. Margaret stood next to her awkwardly.

Wilma's eyes filled. Tears spilled down her cheeks, and before they could hit the blanket, Julie was at her mother's side. Raising the old woman's hand, Julie kissed it, repeating over and over through tears of her own, "I'm so sorry, Momma. I'm so sorry."

The room suddenly felt sacred. With tears stinging her own eyes, Alice gave a slight nod to Margaret and slipped quietly out of the room. She walked to the nurse's desk and pulled a tissue from the box. She loved it when God worked miracles like this one.

"Could I have one, also?"

Alice turned with a start to see Margaret standing there with tears on her face. Reaching into the tissue box, Alice pulled out a couple for Margaret.

"I never thought I'd see the day," Margaret said. "I'd given up hope."

"It is wonderful," Alice agreed, feeling excitement bubbling up from it all. Why, the more she thought about it, the more she wanted to kick up her heels and shout, "Glory!" But since she was not one to make a fuss, she would have to settle for a racing pulse.

"Julie realized she'd almost lost her mother. Time on this earth is so short. I told her now is the time to make amends. We don't know when we'll have the chance again." Margaret wiped away fresh tears.

Alice touched Margaret's arm. "It is a wonderful thing you have done to bring them together."

"It wasn't me. The Lord has been dealing with Julie's heart for some time. Wilma's stroke shook Julie to the core. She knew she had to do something and fast."

Alice nodded. "Wilma is doing well, you know. She will most likely go home tomorrow. Of course, she'll have to have physical therapy on a regular basis. Louise tells me you will be staying with us for some time?"

Margaret nodded. "Julie told me she wanted to stay over a couple of days in Potterston. Wilma only has a one-bedroom apartment at Evening Manor, so there's not much room. With the reasonable package you and your sisters have graciously offered to me, I'll have no problem staying at the inn for as long as Wilma needs me. That will enable me to transport her back and forth to physical therapy as needed without having to travel to and from Philadelphia."

"We're thrilled you can stay with us." Alice wondered if she should bring up yesterday's meeting with Michael or wait for Margaret to bring it up.

"Thank you for yesterday. Michael and I had a wonderful time. We're going out again."

"I'm so happy for you," Alice said, meaning it. Before they could talk further, the phone on the desk rang.

"Oh, I'll let you go. I need to go check on Wilma and Julie. We'll talk later."

Chapter Six

*T*he October chill crept upon the inn, and Jane decided to place some logs in the living room fireplace for a cozy evening by the hearth. One could never tell about the weather in October. Sometimes it merited burning wood, other times it offered warm evenings on the front porch.

Moving the logs into position, Jane lit the kindling. Before long the wood ignited and grew into a mesmerizing display of bluish-yellow flames, popping and crackling, and the smell of burning logs filled the room. Jane could not imagine anything more wonderful than sitting down to read near a warm fire. She picked up her cooking magazine and settled onto the burgundy sofa. Curling her stocking feet beneath her, she was flipping through the pages of her magazine when Ruth Kincade entered the room.

"Is it okay if I come in?" Ruth asked with a hint of shyness.

"Oh sure, come on in," Jane encouraged, putting aside her magazine. "Would you like something warm to drink?"

"No, thank you." Ruth adjusted herself onto an over-stuffed chair. "The fire looks and smells wonderful."

"Doesn't it, though? I love the change of seasons," Jane said, adjusting a plump pillow on the sofa. "Of course, you never know from one day to the next whether it's going to be cold or warm."

Ruth smiled. "One thing I do like about teaching is that you get to enjoy all the seasons," she said, staring into the fire. "In other jobs, I think you get so busy, you don't really pay much attention, but with teaching, you have posters to prepare, parties and such to bring the season alive—even if you live in an area where the weather doesn't necessarily change with the season."

Jane took a sip of coffee, then placed her cup back on the saucer. "I hadn't thought of that, but you're right," she said, thinking how her seasons all ran together when she worked in the restaurant back in San Francisco. "I've noticed that with Louise and her piano students. They play music appropriate to the time of year." Jane glanced at the bobbing flames. "Did you get a chance to talk with Vera at the tea?"

Ruth perked up. "Oh yes, I did. She was very encouraging. I suppose you all know I'm a little frustrated with my job."

Jane nodded.

"Don't get me wrong, I love the kids." She looked

toward the fireplace. "That's part of my problem." She stared into the flames, then turned to Jane. "See, these are inner-city kids. They have so many needs, and I feel helpless. It's hard to teach hungry, tired children. They live in a different world from the one in which I grew up." She looked at her hands for a moment. "On a teacher's salary, there's not a whole lot I can do to help."

"That is a tough one," Jane agreed, thinking of the needy people she had seen so many times on the streets of San Francisco. "Do you mind if I share this with my sisters—"

"Share what with your sisters?" Louise asked with a smile when she entered the room.

"Don't start without me," Alice added, trailing right behind Louise.

Alice's words were greeted with laughter. Jane uncurled her legs from beneath her so that Louise and Alice could sit beside her on the sofa. Both had tea.

"How lovely you started the fire, Jane," Louise said before taking a drink from her cup.

"It does feel good," Jane agreed.

"So, what were you talking about?" Alice asked, looking first at Jane, then toward Ruth.

"I was telling her what I've already told Louise, that I'm struggling with my teaching career. I don't know whether to continue in that field or to look for something entirely different to do with my life."

"Do you enjoy working with children, Ruth?" Louise asked.

"Oh yes. I love my kids." She smiled. "Well, they feel like my kids by the end of the year."

Louise nodded. "I understand."

"Do you have too many children in your classroom, or what are the things wearing on you—if you don't mind my asking?" Alice wanted to know.

Ruth shook her head. "I don't mind at all." She took a deep breath and let it out before she answered. "As I told Jane, I have inner-city children, and there are so many needs."

For the next twenty minutes, Ruth poured out her heart to the sisters on the subject of the schoolchildren and her teaching career. Always one to dig in and get to work, Jane wished she could think of some way to help.

When Ruth had finished her story, Alice was the first one to speak. "Well, I'm sure it's quite a burden to carry, Ruth. With your permission, we would like to add your concerns to our prayer list so that we might pray for your needs."

Ruth appeared surprised by that. "I would appreciate that very much," she said finally.

"Good," Alice said.

A reflective silence filled the room with the exception of the crackling fire in the hearth. "I knew there was something special about this place," Ruth said. "I felt a peaceful warmth the moment I entered."

The sisters smiled.

"Alice told me some about your minister father. I'm sorry to hear of his passing, but I'm sure he would be very pleased to see how you're taking care of your guests."

Louise gave her a questioning look.

"I mean, encouraging those who enter your home. I could have come and gone in a hundred other places, and no one would have paid much attention to me. But you are different. Thank you."

Jane looked at her sisters and could see they were as pleased as she felt by the teacher's kind words. "Now, it's our turn to say thank you."

"I was wondering if I might change my mind about something to drink and get a cup of coffee?" Ruth asked.

Jane grinned. "You certainly may," she answered, already heading toward the kitchen.

The following day, Jane dragged the rake across the last row of her garden. She had already weeded out most of what needed to be pulled and tossed, and she made sure roots were safely tucked in for the winter. A slight breeze stirred, lifting one solitary golden leaf and settling it into the garden. "Great," she said, bending over to pick it up. She glanced up at the tree. "You'll probably just drop them one at a time to keep me forever picking up leaves," she said with a pinch of consternation.

The autumn winds continually blew leaves into her garden patch. She shoved her straw hat up from her forehead and glanced around. By the looks of the abundance of leaves remaining on the trees, Jane would be cleaning the area many more times before the season's end.

"Hard to believe it's that time again," Louise said, pulling Jane out of her reflection.

She turned. "Oh, hello, Louise. Yes, it is."

"I saw you standing out here and thought I would see if you needed any help. My last piano student canceled, so I'm free for the rest of the afternoon."

"Thanks, but I'm finished here." A shift in the wind caused Jane's hat to lift a little. She reached up with her hand to hold it in place.

"It looks very tidy. All seems ready for cold weather—well, at least until more leaves fall."

Jane grew pensive. "Where does the time go, Louise? It seems only yesterday I was planting seedlings." The wind subsided, and Jane took her hand from her hat.

Louise nodded. "Seasons do seem to come and go quickly as we grow older."

"No wonder Margaret wanted to meet Michael again. If she had allowed her fears to talk her out of it, look what she would have missed," Jane said.

Louise looked at her with surprise. "Where did that come from?"

Jane shrugged. "Oh, I don't know. I've just been thinking about things. Missed opportunities."

"Anything in particular, Jane?"

"Well," she turned to Louise, "for instance, what if I had been so preoccupied with my life in San Francisco that I had decided to stay there and not come to live at Grace Chapel Inn?"

Louise frowned. "You're not trying to tell me something, are you?"

"It's just that I could have chosen a different path. Now I feel like I'm making the most of my life right here in Acorn Hill—even if it's from the kitchen," she said with a chuckle. "I'm glad I didn't miss it. That's all." She shrugged. A small bird flew overhead, catching her attention for a moment. She looked back at Louise. "Does that make sense?"

Louise's face now took on a thoughtful expression. "It certainly does."

They stood in comfortable silence. Then Jane broke free from her reverie.

"My goodness, I'm certainly thinking deep for such a brisk afternoon. Let me put this rake in the shed, and I'll be back to make us a snack."

Louise laughed. "Sounds good."

Late in the evening, Alice walked down the stairs just as Margaret came through the door. She was dressed in jeans and a white hooded sweatshirt with the words "Bernardo's Pizza" stenciled in red letters across the top.

"Oh, I see you've been to Bernardo's in Potterston," Alice said with delight, thinking how good a large pizza smothered with cheese, pepperoni and mushrooms sounded at the moment.

"Yes." Margaret closed the door behind her. She turned a smile to Alice. "It was wonderful. I think it was the best pizza I've had in a long time." She patted her stomach. "And I ate entirely too much."

Alice laughed. "Everyone eats too much when they go to Bernardo's." Perhaps she could talk her sisters into going for a pizza. No, no, it was much too late in the evening. She would gain ten pounds in one fell swoop. Alice studied Margaret. "So things are going well?"

Margaret could hardly contain her excitement. She walked over to Alice. "I feel like a schoolgirl again, Alice. I mean, it's like we've picked up right where we left off." Worry lines suddenly etched her face. "I don't mean to imply we didn't love our spouses. We did. It's just that we've both been widowed for some time now and . . ."

Alice patted Margaret's hand. "I understand, dear." And she did understand. Though spouses were never forgotten and were greatly missed, for the one left behind, life trudged forward.

Obvious relief washed over Margaret. "Thank you."

"I'm glad things are going so well," Alice encouraged.

"If things keep going this well, I'll have to tell my son. I don't think he'll mind, though he has been trying to match me up with his friend's father."

"Oh?"

"He's a nice man but, well, he's just not for me. I haven't had the heart to tell my son. I just keep making excuses when the man calls. Speaking of calls, has Julie phoned?"

Alice shook her head.

"Well, I didn't know if she would, but she's leaving tomorrow, so I thought maybe she'd call to say good-bye. I'm kind of anxious to hear how their reunion is going. I didn't want to bother them though."

Alice nodded. "I'm glad Wilma was able to go home while Julie was still in town."

"Yeah, me too. Well, I guess I'd better get ready for bed." Margaret turned to go. "Oh, one more thing."

Alice stopped and looked at her.

"Michael recently retired. He owned a computer business in Florida. I guess he customized software for companies. Anyway, he was going to bring his laptop over tomorrow to teach me how to do some things on the computer. I'm embarrassed to admit it, but I've never learned how to do anything besides a little word processing. Do you mind if we work on it in the living room?"

"I don't see any problem with that." Alice had learned how to do e-mail, though she did not have many people with whom she had to communicate online. Most of her friends lived in Acorn Hill, and she felt no need to e-mail them when she usually bumped into them several times a week.

"Great. Thanks, Alice. Who knows? I just might learn something."

Chapter Seven

By the time Louise stepped into the dining room, their guests were already seated around the table, eating breakfast and chattering happily. She greeted them, then went into the kitchen to see if Jane needed any help. Alice and Jane sat eating at the table.

"I apologize. I can't imagine what made me sleep so late this morning." Louise muffled a yawn.

"You're allowed now and then, you know," Jane said with a wink. She pointed toward an empty seat, then quickly got up and placed bacon, biscuits and scrambled eggs on Louise's plate.

"You don't need to wait on me, Jane. I'm not a guest. Your breakfast will get cold."

Jane waved off her comment. "That's what sisters are for. Besides, don't argue with me, or I'll start singing this morning."

Alice and Louise made a unified groan. The mere thought of Jane's singing made Louise uneasy.

Jane laughed. "Okay, so I'll never be famous. How is

it I'm tone deaf, and you're a great pianist, Louise? Was I out to lunch when they passed around the musical gene in our family?"

"Most likely *making* lunch," Alice said with a laugh. "You see, we could ask the same about you, Jane. Why can't we cook like you do?"

Jane shrugged and formed her bottom lip into a mock pout. "Just the same, it would be nice if I could sing while I worked in the kitchen."

"How are you at whistling?" Louise asked.

"Whistling?" After placing Louise's plate in front of her, along with a glass of juice, Jane took her own seat.

"Yes. Have you heard of that song . . . oh, I can't remember the exact name of it, but it says something about 'whistle while you work'?" Louise asked.

Alice laughed. "I think maybe that is the name of it."

"Is it? Oh well, I don't remember."

Jane seemed to think a moment, and then her face brightened. "Well, I think I can whistle a little bit."

"There, you see," Louise said with a slight nod of her head, "you are musical after all."

Jane puckered her lips and began to blow. Air. Nothing but air. She made a face. Never one to give up easily, she tried again. And again.

Louise wished she had not brought it up.

Over and over, Jane tried to blow out a whistle, but nothing came out. Finally, when she attempted to suck in some air, the wisp of a note came out. She turned to her sisters and let out a triumphant grin.

Louise gave her a cautious smile. "Well, maybe with a little practice," she said with hesitation, though trying her best to encourage her sister.

Jane flipped the cloth napkin on her lap and smiled. "I will practice." She lifted her nose slightly. "I see no reason why I can't be musical. It's in our blood, after all."

Louise decided it was best to change the subject. "I noticed little Annie Burton was teaching Ruth some more sign language at the table a minute ago," Louise said before taking a bite of her eggs.

"Annie has sure taken to Ruth." Alice said before sipping her juice.

Louise nodded. "Ruth is a natural teacher. Children are drawn to her. I have seen a couple of my piano students talking with her."

Jane took a bite of a biscuit slathered with strawberry jam and nodded. After swallowing, she said, "I saw that, too, Louise. And I agree with you, she does have a way with children. She shouldn't leave teaching. We have to help her. If we only knew how."

Finishing the last bite of bacon on her plate, Alice

said, "Well, one way we can find out how to help her is by praying."

"You're right, Alice," Jane agreed.

"Don't rush off, Alice, and we can pray together as soon as I finish here," Louise suggested, taking a last sip of coffee.

"Great idea," Jane said, jumping up with her plate and taking it to the sink. Alice stepped right behind her. Jane washed off their plates, then placed them in the dishwasher. Jane and Alice tidied the kitchen while Louise finished clearing.

She took her plate to the sink, washed it off and slipped it in with the rest of the dishes.

"Ready?" Alice asked.

The other two nodded. The sisters walked over to the kitchen table and sat down. They held hands and waited a moment in silent worship. "Father, You have blessed us in so many ways," Alice began. "May we never take your blessings for granted."

A holy hush seemed to settle over the room, as though God was among them.

"We lift up our new friend, Ruth Kincade. She has a heart for her students, Your children, Lord. Sometimes, it's less painful to look away when we see a need, rather than deal with it. If Ruth is Your instrument to make a difference in the lives of these children, then we ask that You show her, Father." Alice took a deep breath.

"'Now to Him,'" she began a favorite passage from Ephesians 3:20, and Jane and Louise joined in, "'who is able to do immeasurably more than all we ask or imagine, according to His power that is at work within us, to Him be glory in the church and in Christ Jesus throughout all generations, forever and ever! Amen.'"

They dropped hands. When they got up from the table, they saw Ruth Kincade standing in the doorway, tears streaking her cheeks. "Thank you," was all she said before she turned and walked out.

The afternoon seemed a bustle of activity when Alice returned from shopping. The parlor door was closed, which meant Louise was teaching a student. The smell of spicy chili wafted through the rooms. Chili seemed to be an especially good selection on such a breezy autumn afternoon. Walking into the living room, Alice spotted Annie Burton in one corner with Wendell perched happily on her lap. The cat's eyelids drooped and his head fell lower with every stroke Annie gave him.

That cat has the life, Alice thought with amusement.

She heard Michael's voice and turned to see him

showing Margaret something on the computer. They looked up. "Hi, Alice," they said in unison.

"I hope you don't mind me coming in here so informally," Michael said, an expression of doubt on his face.

Alice brushed her hand in front of her. "Not at all. You are Margaret's guest, and you are welcome here." Alice felt especially comfortable with Michael since she had tended to him in the hospital. She smiled and walked over to them. "So, are you learning how to get on the Internet?"

Margaret sighed heavily and shook her head. Michael patted her hand. "Now, don't worry, you'll get it."

Margaret looked up at Alice. "So much to learn."

Just then the front door swished open. Alice walked toward the foyer to see who was there.

"Yoo-hoo, anybody home?" The Howard sisters' aunt, Ethel Buckley, was turned toward the door, trying to push it closed. Alice noticed how attractive her aunt's short red hair looked in contrast with the green of her jacket.

The older woman turned around, quite out of breath. She looked up at Alice with a start. "Land's sake, Alice, you trying to scare me half to death?" Ethel held her hand to her chest as though to keep her heart from jumping out.

"I just came to see who was at the door, Aunt Ethel. I'm sorry if I startled you."

Ethel looked momentarily put out. Then with a shrug

she said, "Well, no harm done. Still, you should be careful coming around the corners like that, unannounced."

"I'll be careful," Alice said, rolling her eyes.

Her aunt leaned in, "Is that couple here, the one that Jane was telling me about—you know, the high school sweethearts?"

With a slight frown, Alice quickly put her finger to her lips and pointed toward the living room. "They're in there," she whispered.

Ethel did not seem to feel reprimanded in the least. She walked just short of the living room entrance, straightened herself, patted her hair into place much like one would tap cotton candy on a stick, and then walked in with confidence. "Hello, all," she said.

Alice stepped in behind her. She decided it would be safer for everyone if she sat in on this first meeting. She made the introductions, then offered to get everyone something to drink. Immediately afterward, she wished she had not offered. She did not want to leave Ethel alone with them for too long.

Ethel was a good woman, but, well, she did tend to have a sharp tongue from time to time. Strangers didn't know that was just her way. Alice wanted to keep things calm without the tiniest ripple of misunderstanding. On the other hand, Ethel lived in the carriage house right next to

Grace Chapel Inn, so her visits were inevitable. Might as well make the best of the situation.

With the drink offer extended and the requests made, Alice slipped from the room into the kitchen. She wondered why she had not seen Jane. Stepping over to the stove, she carefully lifted the lid on a deep pot of simmering chili. A spicy aroma lifted with a puff of steam. Alice took a deep, pleasurable whiff, and then replaced the lid on the kettle. She looked at the counter and noticed that Jane had prepared bread bowls, an old favorite of Alice's, for chili. A noise sounded in the storage room and Alice turned. Jane stepped forward.

"Hello, Alice. I didn't know you were home."

"We have company," she said. Motioning her thumb like a hitchhiker, she mouthed, "Aunt Ethel."

Understanding seemed to light Jane's eyes. "Margaret and Michael still out there?"

Alice nodded and gave a fearful glance, then started pulling glasses from the cupboard.

"Here, let me help you," Jane said.

In no time, they had the glasses filled with cider and water, and Alice carried them on a tray into the living room. As she passed them around, she watched Michael teaching Margaret how to get into a chat room. Ethel looked on with interest.

"My, my, what will they think of next," Ethel said, shaking her head.

"You've never been in a chat room, Ethel?" Michael asked.

"Oh my, no," she said with a wave of her hand, as if that was the most absurd question anyone had ever asked her.

"Well, watch carefully, and you can see how it's done," Michael said. "They are wonderful places to exchange information online with people who share a common interest."

Ethel looked at Alice and shrugged as though she did not want to be rude, and was being forced into this lesson whether she liked it or not.

Alice wondered whether Michael should show Ethel such things. Her aunt ran around Acorn Hill with just enough information in her head to be dangerous.

They all sat there for a while, watching as Margaret conversed with a woman in a gardener's chat room. They laughed over the things you could do with the little faces on the screen. Before long, Alice noticed that her aunt seemed totally enthralled with the whole thing. Never before had Ethel acted the least bit interested in learning the computer. In fact, before they had installed a computer at the inn, Ethel had referred to it as the devil's instrument on more than one occasion.

Alice turned to see that Louise and her student had emerged from the parlor. At that moment, the phone on the reception desk rang. Louise walked over to answer it. Alice continued to listen to Michael give instructions on the computer.

"Michael," Louise called from the doorway.

He looked up. "Yes?"

"Your daughter is on the phone. Sherri, I believe?"

Alice noted the look of concern that crossed Margaret's face.

"Yes, that's her. Thank you, Louise."

He got up and walked into the reception area. Alice looked over at Margaret. "I'm kind of nervous about how she feels about us," Margaret said.

"She'll get used to the idea," Alice encouraged. "It takes time for these things."

"It sure does," Ethel began, "Why, I remember when—"

Jane had just stepped into the room. "Auntie, so good to see you," she interrupted.

Ethel blinked. She looked perplexed, but when Jane walked over and hugged her, Ethel seemed to forget all about her story. While patting Ethel's back, Jane looked at Alice and Louise and gave them a wink.

Alice and Louise both blew out a sigh of relief and settled back into their chairs.

"Would you like to join us for dinner, Auntie?" Jane asked.

"Why, sure. It smells like chili from where I stand."

"That it is," Jane said with a grin, ushering Ethel into the kitchen.

Just as Jane and Ethel slipped into the next room, Michael entered the living room. All eyes turned to him. He shrugged and gave what Alice thought was a somewhat forced smile, but he said nothing.

Margaret looked to Alice for reassurance.

Alice smiled, hoping to encourage her. Still, Alice wondered if everything was all right.

Chapter Eight

*T*hat night Jane was in the kitchen, making chocolates, when she heard someone shuffling toward her.

"Excuse me, Jane, could you use some company?"

Jane looked up from stirring the chocolate in the pan to see Margaret standing in the doorway of the kitchen. Jane smiled. "Please, I was starting to feel lonely."

Margaret came forward. "How about some help? Before I quit teaching, um, about twenty-five years ago now, I was a home economics instructor, I'll have you know."

Jane stopped stirring and looked at her. "Is that right?"

Margaret nodded.

Jane thought a moment. "Well, why not? This will be fun."

"Great," Margaret said, making her way to the soap dispenser at the sink. She washed her hands and dried them with a paper towel.

"If you'll take over stirring here, I'll pull out a double boiler to melt some more chocolate."

"How many do you have to make?" Margaret asked.

"Well, I had planned on four dozen, but I'd like to make a few extra for some of the shut-ins from our church, those who can eat candy, anyway." She laughed. "I don't give them candy very often for fear their doctors will get after me, but every now and then I indulge them. Too many of the folks can't eat nuts and some of the fillings, so I just make the plain chocolates for them in different molds. They get a kick out of it."

"I'm sure they do," Margaret said. "So where did every-one go tonight?"

"Well, Alice had a special meeting at the church, and Louise is up in her room with a headache."

"Oh, I'm sorry to hear that."

Jane shook her head. "Bless her heart, she gets them from time to time. She just has to wait them out."

"Actually, I'm surprised I don't have a headache tonight."

After filling the bottom pan of the double boiler with water, Jane had put the duo of pans atop the stove and turned on the knob to heat them. Unwrapping a brick of chocolate, she cut it into pieces and plopped them into the top pan. "Really? Why is that?"

Margaret took a long-handled spoon from Jane and placed it on the stove beside the pan. "Oh, I don't know. This thing with Michael is happening so fast. In some ways it's exciting, and in other ways, well, it's a little scary."

Margaret let out a guarded smile. "I mean, he lost his wife three years ago and hasn't been active socially since that time. I don't know how Sherri feels about it all, but I remember how I felt when my mom started dating after my dad died." Margaret toyed with the spoon on the stove. "I didn't like it very much." She looked up.

"How old were you at the time?"

"About Sherri's age."

"How did you work through it?"

"Well, I can't really say it was any one thing. I just noticed how much happier Mom seemed. I hadn't seen her smile for so long after Dad died, but then when Rick came into her life, she smiled again."

Jane nodded. "It would be kind of hard to work through that, I imagine." After a while she pulled the pan of chocolate off the burner and began to pour the dark candy into molds. She resisted the urge to lick the chocolate that had trickled onto her fingers. "What about your son, has he said much about it?"

Margaret smiled. "Greg. Bless his heart. He wants me to date Roy, his friend's father. Roy is a nice enough man, but we just don't click, you know what I mean?"

Jane nodded.

Margaret checked her pan and started stirring. "I don't know. I guess I shouldn't worry about it. Time will tell if it's right or not." Her voice took on a lighthearted tone. "I think I'll just enjoy myself in the meantime and see what happens."

Jane smiled. "I think that's a wonderful idea."

"Anyway, Michael wants me to meet Sherri." Her expression showed mock fear. "I feel like I'm sixteen years old again and having to meet the parents."

Jane chuckled. "I suppose it would feel that way."

"I sure was crazy about him when we were kids," Margaret said. A shy smile touched her face. "I suppose if we don't find out now, we'll never know. It's like we're getting a second chance to see if there's anything between us, and we want to explore that possibility. The first time his parents moved to Florida, taking him with them, of course." She shrugged. "We'll have to see what happens."

Jane noticed the dreamy look on Margaret's face as she stirred the pot. "What about the distance between you now? I mean, doesn't he still live in Florida?"

A shadow crossed Margaret's face. "Yes, he does. Since I'm staying here at the inn for a while to see that my sister gets back and forth to the physical therapist, and he's staying with his daughter and her family, it will give us time to see how we feel about each other. We'll deal with the long-distance thing at that point."

Jane poured the last bit of chocolate into the mold, and

promptly walked to the sink and rinsed the pan. "So, what are your plans from here?"

Margaret considered this. "Take it one day at a time and see what happens." A playfulness touched her voice.

"Time will tell, right?"

Margaret's eyes sparkled. "Yes, time will tell."

After a nap, Louise felt much better, so she came downstairs and settled onto the piano bench. She picked up a sheet of music and straightened it against the holder. Placing her hands in perfect form upon the instrument, she moved her fingers across the keys in delicate motion as she made her way through the sonata, allowing the soft melody to calm her spirit as nothing else could. From there, she moved into another piece and then another, as the perfect blend of chords and melodies chased away the weariness of the day. Before she knew it, she had journeyed into her favorite hymns, closing her eyes, offering her voice, her hands, in musical worship to the Savior.

Completely caught up in the moment, Louise had not heard anyone enter the room. When she opened her eyes, she saw a movement in her peripheral vision. Still singing and playing, she turned to see Dorothy Burton standing before her daughter, Annie, who was sitting on the chair.

Dorothy's hands and arms swayed and flowed with the words and music in one of the most beautiful forms of art that Louise had ever seen. Songs of the rugged cross and the Savior's love echoed through the room as Louise sang from her heart and Dorothy seemed to lift her words with the greatest of ease and translate them into beautiful music that made Annie's eyes sparkle.

Seeing the words of the song played out before her through Dorothy's hands touched Louise's heart. They went through several songs before Louise came to a stop. After a moment, she turned to Dorothy and Annie. "Thank you. I've never seen the beauty of music expressed in such a way."

Dorothy walked over to the piano. Placing her hand on Louise's shoulder, Dorothy said, "It's the only way Annie can truly 'hear' the music."

Louise nodded.

Annie joined them and signed to Louise.

"She says, thank you for sharing your beautiful music," Dorothy said.

Touched in a profound way, Louise knew that her world of music had opened to a place where she had never been before.

The following day, after church, lunch and a Sunday nap,

Alice walked into the living room to find Ethel, of all people, sitting alone on the sofa with Michael's laptop computer resting on her legs. Her gaze was fixed on the screen as her fingers pecked along on the keyboard. She did not seem to notice Alice had entered.

Alice eased around the back of the sofa to sit on a chair. "Hello, Aunt Ethel."

Ethel jumped so hard, the laptop almost fell off of her. "Land's sake, Alice, there you go again," she said, steadying the laptop on her legs, "scaring a person half to death. You could jar a woman's teeth right out of her head, sneaking up on her like that." Ethel frowned.

Alice resisted the urge to dwell on that image.

Ethel promptly closed the laptop. "Michael shows me how to use this laptop, how to plug it in and store it, and you act like I shouldn't even be touching it."

"Well, silly me. You need not stop on my account, Aunt Ethel," Alice said.

"No, no, that's all right. Wasn't anything important anyway."

Alice eyed her with suspicion, wondering what her aunt was up to. "So, what does the mayor think of your taking up with the computer?" Alice asked.

Ethel's frown melted into a smile and she let out a slight chuckle. "He's getting a kick out of it. Never figured I'd try it, I guess." A hint of pride touched her voice. "He says I'm finally getting with the rest of the world." She turned her head and stared directly at Alice. "That's not why I'm doing it, mind you," she said.

Alice smiled. "Of course not." She knew her aunt would not be forced into an activity. "So how are you and Lloyd getting along these days?"

Ethel always brightened with the mention of Mayor Lloyd Tynan, her *special* friend. She sat a little taller on the sofa. "We're doing just fine." Her fingers reached up to smooth her hair into place. Then she glanced at her watch. "Speaking of Lloyd, I'd better get home and get cleaned up. We're going to dinner tonight in Potterston." Ethel leaned over and placed the computer on a nearby table. With a heave, she pushed herself up from the sofa, picked up her handbag, and hurried out the front door.

No sooner had the door closed than it opened again. Alice got up to see who was calling. As she walked into the foyer, Vera Humbert and Ruth Kincade stepped inside the inn.

"Hello, Alice," Vera said, straightening her hair from the wind's assaults.

"Well, hello." Alice noticed a pink glow in Ruth's cheeks. "It appears you have enjoyed yourselves."

"We had the greatest time," Ruth said, holding up a bag

of assorted goodies. "We went to a couple of garage sales, and I discovered some wonderful bargains."

"She is the bargain queen, I assure you," Vera said with a laugh. "I've never seen someone with such an eye for things."

"Well, we'll have to take you shopping in Potterston so you can help us find some good bargains," Alice teased.

"I would love to," Ruth offered, her eyes sparkling. She glanced at her treasures. "Well, I'd better get these up to my room."

By the time Ruth reached the top step, Vera whispered to Alice, "What a gift she has, Alice. She has such a good eye, and she can bargain as well. If only we could have that gift work for her in some way."

Alice considered Vera's comment and looked toward the stairway, her mind searching for ways to help the struggling teacher.

Chapter Nine

I love late autumn afternoons," Alice said to Vera Humbert as they took a stroll through Acorn Hill, crunching fallen leaves underfoot, releasing their pungent aroma to mingle with the cool October air.

"Oh, I know. I try to never take them for granted. I especially enjoy walking on a beautiful day like this after being cooped up in a classroom with twenty-five rambunctious students."

The two friends strolled down Chapel Road and turned onto Berry Lane, passing Nine Lives Bookstore. The owner, Viola Reed, was outside sweeping the walk. They waved at her. Viola stopped swinging her broom a moment. "Lovely time for a walk," she said.

"It sure is," Alice called out. Vera nodded.

Viola smiled and started sweeping once again.

The two walkers journeyed on past the town hall. A customer left the Time for Tea shop, causing the bell on the door to jangle. Alice shaded her eyes. Leaves of orange and yellow lighted by the setting sun glowed through the oaks and maples along the street.

"Look at that sunset," Alice said, pointing.

"God's creation never ceases to amaze me. Who, but God, can paint a picture as lovely as that?"

Alice shook her head. "It's times like these when I feel blessed beyond measure. So often I take for granted my sight, the use of my limbs, my hearing. Annie Burton has helped me to remember to be grateful."

Vera nodded. "That child is a wonder. It's unusual to see one so young take such a positive attitude. She seems determined to make the best of her situation."

"I agree. She's an example for us old folks, too." Alice chuckled.

"That's the truth." They walked a little farther. "My students seem to love this time of year about as much as I do," Vera said almost with a pensive tone.

"What special plans do you have for Fred this year?" Alice teased, referring to Vera's husband, who helped out in Vera's classroom from time to time. Alice remembered how one year he dressed like Ben Franklin and gave a speech on US colonial history.

"No plans for Fred this year, but I might have Clarissa Cottrell come over from the Good Apple bakery and talk about the tasty things made with apples. Afterward, we could play some games, bob for apples, and finally eat a caramel apple on a stick—or a pastry from Good Apple."

"Boy, I wish I'd had a teacher like you when I was a girl. No wonder the children love you."

Vera shrugged. "I can't deny that I enjoy what I do. Besides, I like to eat the treats as much as they do."

Alice laughed. "Ah, the advantages of being a teacher."

"Exactly."

A slight breeze rustled around them, twirling a scarlet leaf or two overhead, then dropping the leaves, slowly and gently, to the ground.

"If only we could help Ruth get that same enthusiasm back for her students," Alice said.

"Oh, she has the enthusiasm, she just doesn't know what to do about it. It's like trying to feed all the hungry people in the world. The difficulty of the task sometimes seems too much. We have to work at things a little at a time."

Alice nodded.

They walked on in comfortable silence. "So how are Margaret and Michael getting along?" Vera asked.

"They seem to be doing fine." Alice and Vera turned down Acorn Avenue. "I think Margaret is a little concerned about their children, though."

Vera turned to her. "Oh? How so?"

Alice explained Margaret's worries.

"Well, these things have a way of working themselves

out," Vera said. "They're such a nice couple. I hope their children don't ruin their chance for happiness."

After turning from Acorn Avenue onto Hill Street, they headed back toward Grace Chapel Inn. "How are Polly and Jean doing?" Alice asked.

At the mention of her daughters, who were away from home, Vera's face brightened. "They're doing very well. Jean's classes are going well, and Polly and Alex are happy," Vera said. "I can't wait till they all come home at Thanksgiving. I miss them." Alice noticed how her eyes lit up when she talked about her two daughters and her son-in-law.

"I miss them too," Alice said with a smile.

"Thanksgiving seems like such a long time, but here it is October already, so it will be upon us before we know it."

Alice and Vera finally arrived back at the inn. "Thanks for the walk."

"My pleasure. See you next time." Vera waved at her friend and headed for home.

The next morning, Jane slung the strap of her purse across her shoulder and called out from the foyer, "We'll be back sometime this afternoon."

Louise walked out of the living room. "I'll hold

down the fort. Everyone will be out today anyway. Should be quiet."

"Let's hope so," Jane said, smiling.

"You and Ruth go on to Potterston and have a good time shopping. Alice said some student nurses were coming in for training, and she might get off work early today, so I doubt that I will be here for very long without someone. Besides, even if Alice has to work her full schedule, there isn't that much going on that I can't handle it myself."

"Thank you, Louise. We'll be back before too long." Jane gave her sister a hug.

"I hope you'll have a peaceful day," Ruth added.

"Don't think for a moment I will be slaving away while you two are off shopping. Quite the contrary, I will be sitting comfortably at the sofa in the living room knitting happily away on my afghan." Louise laughed.

"Good," Jane said, adjusting her shoulder strap. "See you later." With that, she and Ruth headed out the door.

Though Jane had wanted to spend the day alone, she felt she should ask Ruth to come along. The teacher had not made any plans for the day, and Jane thought perhaps Ruth might be tired of reading and would enjoy getting out.

Once they were in Jane's car, Ruth said, "I really appreciate your inviting me along, Jane. I wanted to get out, but since I don't know my way around, I wasn't sure where to go or what to do."

"Oh, it's my pleasure, Ruth. I think you'll enjoy Potterston. They have some nice little shops."

"Did you have something in particular you needed from there?"

Jane thought a moment. "I'm not sure. Let's just say, I'm thinking about something, and I wanted to check it out."

Ruth looked at her with a grin. "Oh, a bit of a surprise, eh?"

Jane laughed. "I guess you could say that." She nodded. "Yes, I guess you could say that."

The sisters had decided to have a little gathering for tea, so after returning from her trip to Potterston, Jane brought tea on a tray to the porch and served her guests. Margaret and Michael, whom Jane affectionately called "the lovebirds," sat in the swing while Vera Humbert, Dorothy Burton and Louise sat on chairs. Ruth and Annie perched themselves on the porch steps. Fred Humbert and Doug Burton squared off in a game of checkers.

"Are those yearbooks from your high school days, Margaret?" Jane asked, as she passed them their tea.

Margaret's face fairly glowed. "Yes, Wilma had them

stored away. Michael and I both are pictured in here. In a couple of the photographs, we're together. We were dating at the time," she offered, with a shy smile. She turned to glance at Michael. He smiled at her and Jane noticed he squeezed Margaret's hand.

Jane looked down at the picture on the opened page. "Is that you?"

"What do you think?" Michael asked.

Jane studied the photo a moment. "I think it is."

He grinned. "You're right."

"Oh my, you were young," Jane exclaimed.

Michael and Margaret laughed. "That we were," he said.

"Here, you can look through this one, if you want," Margaret said, handing another yearbook to Jane. "We've already looked through it. See if you can find us in some other pictures," Margaret challenged with a giggle.

Jane took the red yearbook with large white letters naming the school and year across the front and walked over to her seat. She glanced at Louise, who sat with her glasses poised on the end of her nose as she worked the next row of knitting in her afghan. Vera and Dorothy were having a discussion about schoolchildren and the challenges of teaching in today's world.

On the porch steps, Annie sat teaching Ruth how to make signs with her hands. Then Annie mouthed the words, saying them as best she could. They laughed together as Ruth fumbled through the signs with her hands, and Jane could see that Ruth had the heart of a teacher. She communicated easily with children.

"What is that sign?" Vera asked when she looked up to see Annie's thumb stroking the side of her chin, then coming down to poke her chest bone while her fingers spread apart.

Dorothy looked at Annie. "Oh, that's the sign for woman. All the signs having to do with females—grandmother, mother, daughter, sister, girl, woman and so forth—those signs are all located near the mouth. Signs having to do with men—grandfather, father, son, brother, boy, gentleman and so on—those signs are located near the forehead."

"Oh, I get it," Fred said. "The mouth is because the women are busy talking all the time, and the signs near the forehead are because we men are thinkers." Doug Burton extended a high five, and the guys smacked their hands together in victory.

Moans and groans erupted from the women.

"Fred Humbert, you're just asking for it," his wife warned.

"Aw, Vera, you know I'm just having some fun."

"Actually, the signs are located where they are because women used to wear bonnets and the ribbon came down around the mouth and chin area. Men wore hats—without ribbons, by the way—and thus their signs are near the fore-head around the brim of the hat," Dorothy informed them.

"I like my version better," Fred said, pretending to duck from anything Vera might throw.

Everyone laughed. Soon they drifted back into their own conversations.

The chattering of the others faded as Jane quietly viewed the yearbook. Times had changed so much that the people's clothing and hairstyles in the pictures looked quite out-of-date in comparison with current fashions. Still, books like these were nice for remembering days gone by. Each picture represented a cherished memory for someone, somewhere. One by one, Jane flipped through the black and white pages that depicted the high school days of yesteryear.

Finally, Jane came upon a couple that she thought resembled the young Margaret and Michael. She glanced first from the couple on the page, then to the couple on the porch swing. The man had the same smile as that of the boy. The woman had the same shy presence. Though their hairstyles had changed, and the years had given their skin a natural maturity, Jane felt sure that the couple on the page was Margaret and Michael.

She got up and walked over to them. Pointing to the page she said, "Is this you?"

Michael nudged Margaret lightly. "See, I told you she would find it."

Margaret laughed. "I am amazed that you were able to pick us out after all these years."

"Wasn't hard," Jane quickly asserted.

"Of course not, you're as beautiful as the day I met you, Margaret," Michael said with affection.

Not wanting to intrude, Jane slipped back to her chair. Sometimes she wished she had taken better care of her pictures. With her move to San Francisco and then back to Acorn Hill, she had been careless with her things. Though she did not think she had lost many photos, she cringed at the thought of those tossed about in a box in one huge heap. Maybe, one of these days, she would get organized.

"Yes, I won!" Fred shouted with gusto. Doug sat grinning like a good sport.

"Well, Fred, I must say winning a game of checkers certainly seems to boost your energy. I hope you're not gloating," Vera said dryly.

"Heck, no," he said, "but when you beat the best, it's time to celebrate."

Jane went back into the house to get refills. Louise walked in to help her.

Filling the mugs, Jane asked, "Louise, did you keep many pictures from your childhood?"

Louise picked up extra napkins. "Well, I suppose I have a few of them. Why?"

Jane shook her head. "Oh, no reason, really. I was just thinking how all my pictures are in a disorganized mess. Looking through the yearbook made me see how important it is to treasure those memories. Like, well, I wish I had more pictures of Father. To be honest, I'm not even sure what I have anymore."

"I have some photos in albums, but I have some thrown about in a box in total disarray as well. There never seem to be enough hours in a day," Louise called over her shoulder while carrying a tray outside.

Jane followed close behind. She did not want to forget times like these. Before going outside, she laid down her tray and ran up to her room to fetch her camera. In a few minutes she returned quite out of breath carrying the tray of drinks to the porch. This time, though, her camera dangled from her neck.

The others were absorbed in conversation and had barely noticed when she passed out the drinks. But when she called out, "Everybody look this way," they turned to her. "Smile!" she said.

And in a flash, with a click of her finger, Jane Howard snapped a memory.

Chapter Ten

"*hew!*" Ethel said as she pushed the inn's front door closed. "That wind is sharp, I tell you." She shivered a moment in her jacket. "Hard to believe we had such nice weather last evening."

"Good morning, Aunt Ethel," Louise said, coming down the stairway.

"Winter is coming, you mark my words, Louise." Ethel said lifting a crooked finger in the air to make her point. "It's turning mighty cold for autumn." Ethel poked her head through the living room entrance and looked about. She turned back to Louise. "Is Jane around? I could sure use some hot tea."

"I think she went to the grocery, but I can make you some."

Ethel appeared satisfied with that. She followed Louise into the kitchen. "I probably shouldn't have it this close to lunch, but I'm chilled to the bone."

Louise poured water from the tap into the teakettle.

"Why, I'm surprised you didn't hear my teeth chattering."

"My ears would have to be pretty good to hear you halfway up the stairs."

Ethel chuckled. "I guess they would at that. Say, I picked up some flowers from Wild Things a little while ago, and who do you think I ran into?"

Louise put the kettle on the stove and turned on the heat. "I'm sure I do not know."

"Michael Lawton and some woman."

Louise turned to her slowly. "You mean, Margaret?"

"No," Ethel said, pursing her lips like she wanted to let the juicy news squeeze through a little at a time.

Her aunt loved to make people work for the details.

"Okay, Aunt Ethel, what did you see?" Louise took the teacups and saucers from the cabinet. She placed them on the table. Taking the kettle of hot water from the stove, she poured it into the teapot.

Ethel released a breath as if she had thought that Louise would never ask. "Well," Ethel said, smacking her lips like she had just sampled the tastiest of treats, "the woman looked young. Long dark, bouncy curls on that head of hers. A real beauty, that's what she was," Ethel said with a snap. "He was handing her long-stemmed red roses when I started to walk in."

"Did he say anything to you?"

"No, he didn't see me. I turned away so he wouldn't notice me. Didn't want to embarrass him."

Louise was actually quite impressed that Ethel had

thought to do that, though she wondered if Ethel secretly wanted to spy on them a little longer. "Well, I am almost sure there is a simple explanation. Michael seems quite smitten with Margaret."

Ethel raised her eyebrows as though she were not convinced. "You can't tell about some old codgers."

"Aunt Ethel," Louise said with a hint of rebuke, "I don't think I would classify Michael Lawton as an old codger."

"Well, whatever he is, you know what I mean. Some old men prefer them younger chicks nowadays."

Surprised by her aunt's choice of words, Louise drew in a quick breath.

"Well, that's what they call them."

"Good morning, Louise. Ethel," Margaret said, poking her head into the kitchen. "Could I drink a cup of coffee or tea with you? My nerves could use it."

Before Louise could utter a word, Ethel was already in motion, "Absolutely, dear," she said, taking Margaret by the hand. "You come right in here and tell us all about it. We'll help you get through it." Ethel looked positively giddy at the prospect of learning more about this highly suspicious situation.

Once the raspberry tea was ready, Louise poured everyone a cup. She did not want Margaret to feel pressured into sharing her concerns. Louise glanced at Ethel, who sat on the edge of her seat with wide-eyed anticipation. She reminded Louise of Wendell when he spied a bird on the porch.

"So, Margaret, do you have any plans this afternoon?" Louise asked, hoping to change the subject from where she felt sure Ethel wanted it to go.

Margaret took a deep breath. "As a matter of fact, I do." She took a drink with a trembling hand, then placed her cup back in the saucer a little too hard, causing the tea to slosh about. "Oh, I'm sorry. That was clumsy."

Louise got a napkin and handed it to her. "No harm done. Are you okay?"

Margaret dabbed at the spilt liquid and looked up at Louise. "It's just that Michael is due to come over any minute with—with his daughter Sherri."

With the wind taken right out of her sails, Ethel sat back in her chair with a thump.

"Are you all right?" Margaret asked.

"Yes, I'm fine." Ethel said the words like a child who had just opened a gift box that contained a winter coat when she had hoped for a cuddly doll.

"I truly don't think you have anything to worry about, Margaret. Sherri will love you instantly," Louise encouraged.

"I don't know," she said, biting her lower lip. Just then they heard the doorbell ring. "That's him . . . I mean . . . them." She looked worried.

Louise patted her arm. "You'll see, things will be fine. Let's see who's here."

Margaret swallowed hard.

Louise noted that Ethel had already left her seat and was leading the way.

Together they walked into the foyer. Louise opened the door. "Hello, Michael. You don't need to ring when you come here. You are practically one of our guests," Louise said with all the charm of a good hostess.

"Well, I'm certainly here as often as a guest," he said with a slight apology in his voice.

"Not at all. Come on in." Louise stepped aside.

"Hi, Michael," Margaret said, giving him her prettiest smile.

Louise noticed how handsome Michael looked and how he lit up when he saw Margaret. His daughter was indeed beautiful, just as Ethel had said, although Louise thought she noticed a slight hesitation on Sherri's part at the sight of Margaret.

"This is my daughter Sherri. Sherri, this is Margaret."

"Hello," Sherri said in a polite, yet somewhat formal tone.

"Sherri, so good to meet you. I've heard wonderful things about you," Margaret gushed.

"Thank you." Her lips curved into a slight smile.

"Oh, and this is Louise and her Aunt Ethel," Michael blurted.

"Hello," Sherri said, revealing a beautiful smile. There was a definite difference in her greeting to them and the one she had offered Margaret.

An awkward silence followed. "Oh, uh, these are for you," Michael said, handing Margaret a cluster of long-stemmed red roses.

"Oh, Michael, thank you. They're my favorite," she said, taking a whiff of the scented flowers.

"They were my mother's favorite, too." Sherri said with a hint of sadness.

Louise did not miss the frustrated glance Michael gave his daughter. "Well," Margaret said, "I should put these in a vase of water."

"Let me do that for you," Louise interjected. "I will put them on your dresser so you can enjoy them when you get back."

"That would be wonderful. Thank you, Louise," Margaret said.

Michael turned to Margaret. "We're dropping Sherri off in Potterston to meet her husband. Then we'll go on to lunch from there. Will that be all right?"

"Oh, that's fine. Though it would be wonderful if you and your husband could join us for lunch, Sherri," Margaret said, showing her gracious spirit in spite of Sherri's reserve.

Sherri seemed caught off guard for a moment. No doubt the invitation surprised her. "Thank you, but we need to pick up our daughter from his parents' house in Potterston, and then go on a few errands."

"I see," Margaret said, looking a bit dejected.

"Perhaps another time," Sherri offered. Her voice held more warmth this time.

Margaret seemed to notice. She smiled. "That would be great."

When they had left, Ethel added her two cents about the matter, but Louise paid little heed. She watched Margaret, Michael and Sherri walk down the inn path. All the while, Louise prayed that things would indeed be wonderful for their families in the days ahead.

Arriving at the inn after work, Alice heard muffled notes coming from the parlor, telling her that Louise was in the middle of a piano lesson. Alice took off her jacket and headed for the kitchen for a snack before dinner.

The news anchorman talked softly from the TV in the kitchen. A faint scrubbing sound caught Alice's attention, and she turned to see Jane leaning into the refrigerator. "What are you doing?"

Jane bumped her head as she pulled out of the refrigerator.

"Oh, how very graceful of you."

Jane pulled off her rubber glove and gingerly rubbed the top of her head. A sheepish grin played at the corners of her mouth. "That's what I get for being too engrossed in my work."

"Why are you doing that now?"

"I found a container holding something that would definitely qualify for a science experiment."

Alice laughed. "I guess time does get away from us."

Jane stretched her back. "Actually, you arrived just in the nick of time."

"Oh?"

"Yeah, my back is starting to hurt. Time to quit."

"I'm glad I gave you an excuse then."

"Fortunately, I was finished anyway." Jane pulled the bucket of soapy water from the fridge and placed it on the floor. She then turned the cooling button back to its original position. "Goodness, if you're home, that means I'm running behind on dinner." Jane closed the refrigerator door, picked up the bucket, and poured the water from the bucket into the kitchen sink, and then wiped the sink clean.

"I'm a little hungry. Thought I might snitch something before dinner."

Jane frowned. "Did you skip lunch again?"

Alice remained silent.

"Alice, you need to take care of yourself. Take a granola bar to work if you must, but eat something to give you nourishment throughout the day."

"Okay, Mom, I promise to do better tomorrow," Alice said with a salute.

Jane acted as though she wanted to play the part. She placed balled fists on her hips. "Well, what have I told you about proper nourishment?"

"You're absolutely right. I appreciate your concern, Jane, I really do. Now, how about a snack?" Alice wiggled her eyebrows.

Jane laughed. She walked over and pulled out chunks of cheese and some party crackers. "Will this do?"

Alice nodded. "Wonderful. I just want something to carry me through to dinner."

Jane arranged the snack neatly on a plate and handed it to Alice. "Have you heard how Margaret's sister is getting along?"

Alice offered a short prayer over her snack and looked up. "Oh, Wilma is doing great. She loves being out of the hospital, and her therapist says that her sessions are going very well."

Jane's eyes widened. "Oh, that's terrific. She bounced back pretty quickly."

"Yes, she did. She was one of the lucky ones. Wilma

didn't actually have a permanent stroke. She had something called a 'transient ischemic attack.'"

With her own plate of crackers and cheese, Jane sat across from Alice.

"These are episodes where the patient experiences symptoms of a stroke, but then the symptoms disappear within a short period of time. TIAs can be a warning, though, of a future stroke, so they're taken quite seriously."

Jane munched on a cracker. "Poor Wilma."

"Margaret must continue taking her to the hospital for a while, but other than that, her life will be much the same."

Jane finished the last of her cheese. "Well, I'm just thankful everything turned out all right and she's doing so well."

Alice shook her head and laughed. "Believe me, I think it would take a lot more than rehab to keep Wilma down. That woman is a wonder."

"How do you mean?"

"Um, let's just say that she would make a great marine."

Chapter Eleven

*A*fter dinner, Alice went to the parlor and joined Louise, who was playing Beethoven's *Moonlight Sonata*.

Relaxed by the music, Alice had practically melted into her chair by the time Jane walked in carrying a tray with bowls of warm apple crisp topped with vanilla ice cream, along with a pitcher of steaming decaf and a pot of apple-cinnamon tea.

Alice rubbed her stomach and sighed. "A wonderful dinner and now this."

Louise stopped playing and walked over to her sisters and sat down.

Jane smiled. "My sisters are worth it," she announced happily. It was then that Alice noticed that Jane had changed into khaki pants and a purple blouse. "You going somewhere?"

Jane set down the tray and turned to Alice. "Uh-huh, I'm running over to Potterston to meet some friends. We've decided to get together a couple of times a week."

Louise and Alice exchanged a glance, then turned to Jane.

"Really?" asked Louise with an arched brow.

"This should take care of you until I get back," Jane said, pointing to the dessert.

Jane's secrecy was making Alice curious. "You never said how your time went with Ruth at Potterston the other day," she said.

"Oh, it was great. We had a wonderful time. She's a wise bargain shopper, I can tell you that," Jane answered.

Alice nodded. "That's what Vera said too."

Jane adjusted the band on her ponytail. "Well, it's true. She can make a penny squeak louder than anybody I know. Father would have loved her."

Alice chuckled, remembering how frugal their father had been.

"Well, I'll see you soon." Jane waved, her ponytail bouncing with every step.

Once the door closed, Alice turned to Louise. "What do you suppose that is all about?"

"I have no idea, but whatever she's doing, she seems to be excited about it."

"I noticed that too." Alice thought a moment. "Though I can't help wondering what she's up to."

"Who knows," Louise commented between bites of apple crisp. "She doesn't get out much. Her work here keeps her pretty busy. I think it is good for her to get together with friends now and then. I am quite sure she misses the big city life in San Francisco."

"I suppose so," Alice agreed.

After they had eaten dessert and cleaned up their dishes, Alice and Louise settled in the parlor once more. Before long, the Burtons and Ruth Kincade joined them.

The group exchanged pleasantries, and finally Louise again settled onto the piano bench where she began to play through various melodies. When she happened upon songs Dorothy knew, Dorothy signed them to Annie. When the music stopped, Annie told her mother she wanted to sign a song for everyone. Dorothy asked if that would be all right. Everyone quickly expressed delight.

Annie walked toward the front of the room and stood before the group. She began to sign the words her mother lifted in a beautiful soprano voice, "I Heard the Voice of Jesus Say." When they got to the words "behold I freely give," Alice was filled with wonder as she watched little Annie bend to the floor, touch her hands to the ground, then bring her palms toward her body, as she began to rise, then up and out toward the audience by the time she was standing.

In that one beautiful expression of the word *give*, Alice caught the full impact of everything that Jesus had given for her.

Once the song was over, everyone sat spellbound. No one moved or uttered a sound as the truth of those words impressed all present. Finally, Ruth Kincade started clapping, and the others joined in.

After a few more numbers and some conversation, they called it a night, and as Alice was leaving the room, she heard Ruth say to Dorothy, "Please thank your daughter for me. She's made me see that I cannot stop teaching. I'm not sure, but I know I will do whatever it takes to make a difference in their lives."

⌒

Jane almost said, "Well, look what the wind blew in," when Ethel came through the back door the next afternoon, but the pained expression on her aunt's face stopped Jane in her tracks. "Why, Auntie, what's the matter?"

"Oh, that cold weather is going to put me six feet under," she grumbled, rubbing her arms to warm herself. With a dramatic sneeze, she pulled out her handkerchief and patted the end of her nose. "See what I mean? Now I've gone and caught a sniffle."

Jane stepped closer, put her arm around Ethel, and walked her into the kitchen. "You just sit down, and I'll pour you some spiced cider."

Ethel's mood seemed to brighten instantly. "I thought

I smelled something good in here. Course, your kitchen always smells good."

Jane mimicked a curtsy.

After sitting down, Ethel rested her chin in the palm of her hand and thought a moment. "How am I going to the harvest party with a cold? That's what I want to know."

Jane stopped pouring the cider and looked at Ethel. "Harvest party? Oh, I had forgotten about that."

"Then you need an update. Samuel and Rose Bellwood are having a town harvest party out at their farm. We're supposed to bring hot dogs, buns, marshmallows, chips, and any desserts we want. They'll provide the drinks." Ethel's finger tapped her cheek, and her gaze went to the ceiling. "Um, hot and cold apple cider, soda, coffee, hot chocolate." She hesitated, then added, "I think that's it. Is that what she told you?"

"That pretty much covers it. What fun!" Jane said, rubbing her hands together. She turned her attention back to the cider, finished pouring Ethel a cup, and walked over to the table.

"Isn't it, though? They're going to provide a hayride, games, songs around a roaring fire, just like when we were kids." Ethel laughed. "Like I can remember that far back."

"What about when we were kids?" Louise asked with a muted yawn as she entered the kitchen.

"Louise, you yawning in the middle of the afternoon? Didn't you get your beauty sleep last night?" Ethel asked.

Jane chuckled to herself thinking how Ethel never had a problem speaking her mind. "Now Auntie, you know Louise works hard around here. Alice and I have been encouraging her to get more sleep, and even take an afternoon nap if necessary."

Louise offered Jane a grateful smile.

"Well, I guess you're right." Ethel tapped her spoon against the rim of her cup. "I've been telling her she needs to slow down."

"You all are fussing far too much about me. I didn't just wake up as you might suppose. I have been in the parlor doing paperwork. I decided to take a break." She lifted a cup from the cabinet and turned her head toward the stove. "Is that cider I smell?"

"Yes, it is. Would you like some?"

Louise held up the palm of her hand and edged toward the stove. "You stay put, Jane. I can get it myself." Once her cup was full, Louise took a chair at the table. "Now, what were you saying about when we were kids?"

"Oh, I was just telling Jane here about the Bellwoods' throwing a town harvest party, complete with hayride, hot dogs, marshmallows and hot apple cider. Just like when we were kids," Ethel said, grinning from ear to ear.

Jane smiled at Ethel's enthusiasm. She was certain that Ethel was as excited as she was about the upcoming party.

"You started to tell us about that last week, Jane, and we got interrupted." Louise made a face. "I think I would rather not ride in a wagon and get all that hay on my clothes." She paused a moment. "But it might be nice to attend the party for the fellowship."

With a mug in her hand, Jane sat down filled with all the excitement of her youth. "I can't remember the last time I went on a hayride or sat around an open fire. We'll have such a good time."

Ethel chimed in. "I suppose people will come dressed in overalls or some such nonsense."

"Oh, absolutely," Jane countered. "And straw hats." Jane's mind was already off and running as to what she might do to prepare for the event.

Louise laughed. "Uh-oh, Jane has that faraway look in her eyes. That can only mean one thing."

"We're in trouble," Louise and Ethel said together.

After drinking hot cider, Ethel and Jane walked into the living room, while Louise went back into the parlor to wait for one of her piano students.

"Jane, since Michael left his computer and Margaret is out, I think I'll kick around on it a little bit," Ethel said.

"Help yourself. Michael told me you were welcome to use it whenever you came over," Jane said, lifting a gardening magazine from a nearby basket.

"He's a nice man." Ethel clicked the computer on and waited for it to boot up.

"Yes, he is." Jane flipped through the first couple of pages of her magazine. "You know, Auntie, they have some fun gardening sites and recipe sites, too, if you would like me to show you."

Ethel's eyes lit up. "Sure, come on over here and show me what to do," Ethel said, patting the seat next to her.

Jane sat down beside her aunt, and the two of them spent the next hour or so surfing the Web for different food and gardening sites. Finally, they stumbled upon eBay, the online auction site. Time got away from them as they opened windows for all sorts of products, chatting excitedly about all the items they might like to bid on.

"See how much fun this is, Auntie?" Jane could hardly believe they had spent so much time surfing the Web. It was like opening an endless book.

Ethel chuckled. "I have to admit it is kind of fun getting on this thing. Opens a whole new world."

"Hi, what are you doing?" Ruth asked as she entered the living room.

"Hi, Ruth," Jane said. "Come on over and join us. We're just looking at stuff on eBay."

Ruth walked over to look. Before long, she joined the conversation, pointing out good buys and things that were not so good for the prices being offered.

Jane was impressed with the teacher's knowledge of merchandise and of fair prices.

"Oh no, I wouldn't offer that much," Ruth said about a Coach handbag on which someone, she felt, had bid too high. "You can get one at the outlet for much less than that."

Jane looked at her. "You are quite the shopper, you know that?"

Ruth shrugged. "What else do I have to do with my time?" She smiled.

They surfed a little longer until Jane finally said, "I'd better get dinner started." She arose from the sofa.

"And I need to go home and get ready for Lloyd. I'm supposed to meet him for dinner," Ethel said. "Would you like to look some more, Ruth?" Ethel asked, holding out the computer.

"Sure. Thanks." Ruth pulled the computer onto her lap. Ethel followed Jane into the kitchen and went out the back door. Jane started dinner preparations by arranging the ingredients for a new salad recipe. She chopped away at celery, carrots and onions while her mind tangled with thoughts of Ruth Kincade, her teaching dilemma, and eBay. Jane felt certain that an answer was right under her nose.

She momentarily buried her face in the crook of her arm. Then again, it might just have been the onions.

Alice held her ANGELs meeting each week in the basement of the church during the midweek service. On this night, however, the seven middle-school girls met at the inn so that they could work on their project in the cozy environment of the inn's kitchen.

One by one, they entered. Alice brought in extra folding chairs for them. Once they all were seated around the table, Alice started their meeting with prayer.

"Did you all bring your cleaned pumpkin seeds?" Alice asked after prayer.

The girls nodded and held up plastic bags of washed seeds.

"Great."

"Miss Howard, did you notice I have braces?" Ashley Moore asked, smiling proudly as she revealed the shiny metal brackets on her teeth.

Turning to Ashley, Alice said, "I hadn't noticed. How nice for you."

"My mom says I can wear black and orange spacers for Halloween."

"Sounds like fun."

Alice glanced around the room, and in an instant she could detect a hint of dissension among her girls. It seemed quite obvious Sarah was poking fun at Ashley about her braces. Though Ashley had attempted to take it good-naturedly, Alice thought she had seen a flicker of embarrassment flash across the young girl's face.

With a quick prayer for wisdom, Alice said, "Well, back when I was a kid, they didn't wear braces much. Today, people have beautiful smiles because of such advances in dentistry."

Ashley showed a grateful expression.

Sarah smirked and nudged Jenny Snyder. Jenny kept her eyes fixed on Alice, saying nothing.

Perhaps Alice would talk to Sarah later, but for now, she thought it best to change the subject. She took out a large mixing bowl. "Okay, girls, let's pour our seeds into this bowl."

Each girl emptied the seeds from their plastic bags into the bowl.

Bringing the saucepan to the table, Alice dropped some butter into the pan. "We're going to melt the butter in the pan, then add the seeds and these spices, garlic powder and seasoning salt, which I've already premeasured." The girls looked on as Alice took the pan to the stove. "Now after this butter melts, I want to start with you, Ashley, and have you get a scoopful of the seeds from the bowl and drop them into this pan. I'll stir them around in the butter, then Jenny, you go next, then, Kate, until all the seeds are in the pan. Afterward, I'll toss all the seeds with the butter, sprinkle on the spices, and toss them about to coat them well. Understand?"

The girls nodded.

Linda raised her hand.

"Yes, Linda?"

"Do we get to taste some, Miss Howard, or are we giving them all away?" Linda asked.

"Of course, we'll taste some. You know our rule—"

"'Don't muzzle the ox as he treads the grain,'" Sissy Matthews recited with pride.

"That's right, Sissy," Alice said with a chuckle.

The butter quickly melted. The girls did as they were instructed, and before long the pumpkin seeds were seasoned and spread upon several large cookie sheets, then placed in the oven.

"Now, while those are baking, we can work on our jelly jar lid covers. I have brought different colors of material to cover the lids of your jars." Alice laid out an assorted mix of calico print fabrics. Each girl touched and examined the pieces carefully until she found the perfect fit for her own jar.

"Here are some pinking shears," Alice said as she set them on the table. "I don't have enough for everyone, so you'll have to take turns." She reached in her box and lifted up several cardboard circle cutouts. "These are patterns for your fabric," she explained. "You place the cardboard over your material, use the sewing marker to trace around it, then use your shears to cut around the mark you made."

Alice watched as the girls eagerly set to work on their projects, and she felt pleased with their enthusiasm. As they worked together, she wondered why Sarah would try to make Ashley feel bad. They had always been the best of friends. It seemed out of character for Sarah to act that way.

Oh well, Alice figured they would soon forget the whole thing. Young girls could be like that. Sometimes they would have little tiffs like this, and then by the time the parents got wind of it, the children had totally forgotten the matter. That was probably all this was, just a little tiff. They would be over it by the next meeting, no doubt.

Once the girls had cut out the material and covered their lids, the pumpkin seeds were toasted. Together, they ate some of the seeds and then filled their jars with what was left. They attached ribbons with gift cards to each jar and, of course, they signed them ANGELs, since their work was usually anonymous.

Finally, the girls took turns individually quoting their memory verses to Alice. She passed out angel pens to those who quoted their verses correctly.

The girls then prepared to leave. As they filed out, Alice frowned as she watched Sarah walk out with Jenny and Kate, making it obvious that they purposely left Ashley behind.

Alice shook her head. She could not imagine what Sarah was up to, but whatever the problem, Alice hoped that they would resolve the matter before the next meeting.

Chapter Twelve

On Thursday afternoon, Alice noticed that the mail had not been picked up for the inn. She went over to retrieve the white envelopes and a large manila one stuffed in their box. She eyed the bigger package with interest; it was addressed to Jane with no return address. *How curious.* Gingerly fingering the package, she squeezed a little here and there, but all she could feel was the bubble wrap inside. Not that it was any of her business, but she could not for the life of her figure out what was in it. Well, after all, Jane had a right to her privacy. It seemed Alice had to keep reminding herself of that fact lately.

The air smelled damp. Alice glanced at the heavy gray clouds that hung low over the town. They were in for a downpour by the looks of things. A gust of wind swished by, stinging her face and neck. Alice adjusted her jacket, making it snug against her, and hurried toward the house in hopes of arriving before the clouds erupted.

The mail slipped in her arms. Once she reached the porch, she stopped to readjust it. While doing so, she

thought of how Jane had been acting, well, a little mysterious recently. Alice could not quite put her finger on it.
She shrugged. Perhaps she could chalk it up to reading
too many mystery books. Still, she decided she would
discuss the matter with Louise and get her take on
things.

Alice stepped into the inn and turned to close the front
door just as the rain started to pour. She went over and laid
the mail on the desk, her gaze lingering a moment over
Jane's package.

"Is something wrong?" Louise asked as she walked into
the foyer.

"*Hmm?*" Alice looked up. "Oh no. I was just thinking
that maybe I should bring this package to Jane's attention."

Louise studied Alice, then walked over and looked at
the package with obvious interest. "No return address.
That seems rather odd these days."

"I thought so too."

Louise shrugged, as if the matter was of no concern to
her. "Well, you will find Jane in the kitchen."

Jane had just finished making their lunch of Omelettes
Lyonnaises, warm croissants and orange slices, and she was
placing it on the table. "That looks wonderful," Alice said
upon entering the room.

Wiping her hands on her white chef's apron, Jane

turned around. "Oh, hi," she said with a satisfied smile. "It is pretty good. I must confess I did sneak a little taste before you got here." Jane looked at the package in Alice's hand. "Is that for me?"

The question brought Alice back to her reason for entering the kitchen. "Oh yes," she said, "I almost forgot why I came in here." She handed the package to Jane and hesitated just a moment to see if Jane would open it or offer any explanation.

"Thank you," was all she said, plopping the package on the counter before she went back to her meal preparations.

Alice looked on with a sigh. She wondered if Jane thought it odd that there was no return address on the package. Alice debated about asking her, but then thought that Jane might know perfectly well who had sent the package but preferred to keep the matter to herself. Oh well, if Jane refused to talk about it, there was little Alice could do. With a touch of disappointment, Alice dismissed the mysterious package and walked into the dining room, where she saw the dishes stacked at the end of the table.

"Are we eating lunch in the dining room today?" she called over her shoulder. She could hear the open and close of the oven door just before Jane appeared in the dining room.

"Yes. It just felt like an eat-in-the-dining-room kind of day," Jane said with a chuckle. "Do you mind?"

"Not at all. I like doing things out of the ordinary. We're too young to get stuck in our ways."

"Absolutely."

Alice began to assemble the place settings. Jane reached over to help and together they had the table set in no time.

"Have you talked with Margaret today?" Jane asked, scrutinizing the table.

"No. Have you?"

Jane shook her head. "Just a minute." She stepped into the kitchen, then came back with a lovely candle center-piece. Placing it on the table, she said, "There. That's what it needed." She looked back toward Alice. "I saw Margaret this morning and she looked a little, well, unsettled. I wondered if it had anything to do with their children. Do you know how they're accepting things?"

Alice pinched her lips together. "I'm not really sure. I know Margaret is a little concerned about it. I'm sure their children want what's best for their parents, but regardless of how they feel, they have to know their parents have their own lives to live."

"I hope you're right, Alice."

"We need to pray for them. I'm sure everything will

work out fine," Alice said, believing it. After all, their children were adults. They would understand.

∽

After lunch and kitchen clean-up, Jane retrieved her package from the countertop and headed for her room.

"Aren't you going to join us in the parlor, Jane?" Louise asked.

"In a bit," Jane replied. "First, I'm going to put this in my room and make a quick phone call. Then I'll join you."

Louise looked at her with curiosity for a moment. Jane merely smiled, turned and climbed farther up the stairs. She knew her sisters were starting to suspect something, with her going to Potterston twice a week, and now the package. She did not know how much longer she could keep it from them, but she had to, at least for a little while. They would understand soon enough.

Once she reached her room, Jane securely closed her door and flopped on the bed, tearing open the package. The contents were exactly what she had wanted. She looked through the items, studying each one with great care. Finally, she stuffed everything back into the package and placed it on a shelf in her closet. Closing her closet door, she walked back over and opened the drawer of her nightstand. There on white notepaper was the number she needed. She tucked it in the pocket of her black pants and went back downstairs.

Once in the foyer, she could hear the others in the parlor. She walked over to the desk and picked up the phone. Punching in the numbers, she waited for an answer.

"Hello?" said the voice on the other end of the line.

"Hi, it's me," she said, cupping her mouth near the phone. "Thanks for sending that stuff. I got it today. I'll study the information and get back to you on it."

"Fine. It should answer most of your questions. Let me know if you need anything else."

"I might need more, but we'll see."

"Have you told them?"

"Remember, I wanted to wait until everything was completed before I told them. I think they're getting a little suspicious of my running off to Potterston," Jane whispered, looking around to see if anyone could hear her. "I don't like keeping things from them."

"I know. But it will be worth it in the end."

"I sure hope you're right. For now, I have to keep quiet about it."

"Well, think of how delighted they will be."

"Okay, talk to you soon."

"Bye."

Jane hung up the phone and sat still for a moment. She

did not want to cause her sisters anxiety over this whole matter. She hoped that, in the end, they would decide it was worth it.

 ⌒

Margaret and Michael returned to the inn with Wilma after they had taken her to physical therapy. Margaret thought that Alice might enjoy a visit from her former patient.

"Wilma, so good to see you," Alice said when she walked into the foyer. Alice gave Wilma a hug. "Here, let me take your jacket." Alice helped her as she struggled with her outer wraps.

"I'm colder than an iceberg and twice as brittle," Wilma said.

Alice looked at Jane, who stood smiling in the living room entrance. "See, she's not nearly as tough as she pretends."

Wilma raised a gnarled finger under Alice's nose. "Now, don't you go ruining my perfectly good reputation, Nurse Alice."

Jane extended her hand toward Wilma. "Don't you worry, your secret is safe with me." She gently shook Wilma's hand and gave her a welcoming smile. "I've got some logs burning in the fireplace, so you can warm yourself in here," Jane offered, stepping aside so they could enter the living room.

"Thank you, Jane." Margaret walked behind her sister, Alice and Jane as they helped Wilma into the room.

"Margaret, I know you want to change your clothes, so you get on up there. I can take care of myself. But I can tell by the way everyone is fussin' over me that I won't get a minute's peace."

"That's right. I didn't take all those nursing classes for nothing," Alice teased.

Jane and Alice walked Wilma to a chair by the fireplace. "Boy, that does feel good on these old bones," Wilma said, easing into her chair with a sigh as if she had just settled into a steaming tub of water.

"Good. Now how about I get you something warm to drink?" Jane suggested.

"Are you all this nice around here?" Wilma scanned the room. "If you are, I'm going home to pack."

"Oh, I don't think that would work out, Wilma," Margaret said with a laugh.

"You don't?"

Margaret shook her head. "They drink tea."

Wilma scrunched up her nose. "Tea drinkers, huh?"

"I'm afraid so," Alice said.

"Oh well, guess I'll have to stay put." Just then

Wendell happened along and seeing Wilma, jumped up on her lap.

"Well, looky here," she said with a chuckle. Wendell hardly paid her any attention as he worked his paws around her dress, trying to make a comfortable bed for himself. "I'm afraid it will take you a spell to find a soft spot on these bony legs." Wendell circled for the last time and spilled in a heap on her lap. Before Wilma could say another word, the tabby lapsed into a rhythmic purr.

The others looked on and laughed.

"So did you have a nice time with your daughter, Wilma?" Jane asked.

Wilma beamed. "The best. I never thought I would see the day. Well, I'm downright thankful, that's what I am."

"We're so happy for you," Jane said.

"Julie seems like a lovely young lady," Alice said.

"You know, she did turn out pretty good," Wilma agreed.

"If you'll excuse me, I think I will run upstairs and change my clothes," Margaret said.

"You still never told me if you want something to drink, Wilma."

"No, thank you, Jane. Between this here cat and the fireplace, I'm getting toasty warm."

Later, when Margaret came downstairs, Alice overheard

Michael say to her, "How about I take you and Wilma for dinner in Potterston?"

"That would be great," Margaret said.

"You mean to tell me I gotta get back up after me and this here cat just got comfortable?" Before anyone could answer, Wilma nudged Wendell off her lap and then pushed herself up with a grunt.

Everyone watched. Once she had risen to her feet and smoothed her dress, she looked up. "Well, what are you all gawking at? Let's go eat. I'm hungry," she said, poking her finger in the air for emphasis.

Alice glanced around and everyone started laughing—including Wilma.

Alice walked them to the door. "It was great seeing you again, Wilma. Come back when you can stay longer," she teased.

"I'll be back, you can count on it."

"Is that a promise?" Alice asked.

"A warning, a promise, you take it however you like," Wilma said with a snap.

Alice chuckled and waved good-bye. She closed the door behind them and headed for the kitchen, thinking of how thankful she was that Margaret and Michael—yes, and even Wilma—had come their way.

Chapter Thirteen

W hat has caught your attention so early in the day?" Louise asked the next morning when she walked into the living room and found Ethel and Jane peeking out the window.

They turned with a start like two kids caught snooping in their big sister's diary. A crimson stain made its way up Jane's cheeks, a sure sign of getting caught mid-snoop.

"Michael's daughter just showed up," Ethel announced as if the citizens of Acorn Hill should clear the streets. "He went out to talk to her and Margaret came inside. Must have gone to her room."

Louise acted nonchalant. "Have you seen my book, Jane?" Louise asked.

Jane looked as though she had expected a reprimand instead of a question. She relaxed a little and thought a moment. "I think I saw it in the library when I was putting something away this morning."

Louise brightened. "That's right. I forgot I went in there last night. Thanks." Louise started to leave, then turned around as the "snoop sisters" fell back into place at the window. "You two behave yourselves," Louise said with as much reproof as she could force into a whisper.

Leaving the room, Louise shook her head. Sometimes she did not understand her aunt at all. Always tying herself up with other people's affairs. And Jane? What could she be thinking, letting Ethel get her involved in the mix? Upon stepping into the library, Louise heard something. She turned with a start to see Margaret sitting on a chair.

"Margaret, are you all right?" Louise asked.

Margaret twisted a handkerchief in her hands. "I don't feel good about this. Instead of making Michael happy, I fear I am causing problems between him and his daughter. I don't want to do that. We invited Sherri and her husband to go to lunch with us today. I suppose she's talking to Michael about that. Jeremy is not with her. They're not coming, I just know it. She was very aloof with me just now. That's why I came in. Sherri made it obvious she wanted to talk to her father alone."

"I'm sure there is a reasonable explanation," Louise said, patting Margaret on the shoulder. "I am quite sure Michael can handle the situation."

"I hadn't expected our children to be so concerned about Michael and me getting together. It's a puzzle to me."

"Well, puzzles can be pieced together, you know. I wouldn't give up just yet." Louise smiled.

Margaret took a deep breath. "Well, we'll just have to wait and see what happens. We've committed it to prayer, and now we need to wait on the Lord to direct us."

"That is the best thing to do." Louise assured Margaret.

Just then they heard the front door swing open. Margaret looked at Louise. "Guess it's time to face the music." She managed a smile.

"As you know, I happen to think music can solve many of life's problems," Louise said with another smile.

"Let's just hope there's harmony in the next room."

Together they walked into the foyer to see Michael standing there—alone.

Later that afternoon when Louise came into the kitchen, she saw Jane carrying groceries into the pantry.

"I see you've been to the General Store. Would you like some help?" asked Louise, already lifting a sack from the counter and making her way to the pantry.

"Sure, thanks. We needed a few things for the weekend," Jane said. She reached into the bags and started pulling things out to place on the shelves. "I ran into Rose Bellwood while I was there."

"Oh?" Louise carefully stacked the new cans of tomato sauce, chicken broth and various soups onto the shelves.

"She came into town to pick up something at Nine Lives Bookstore and thought of a couple of things she needed for dinner. So she stopped at the General Store."

Louise nodded.

"Anyway, I offered to help decorate for the harvest party tomorrow." Jane adjusted a few of the cans on the shelves, then plucked more cans from the sacks.

"Did she need help?" Louise asked.

"Yes. She was planning to do everything herself—well, with Samuel's help, of course," Jane said, referring to Rose's husband. "So she was thrilled that I offered." After placing the last can on the shelf, Jane twisted from her waist, first to the left, then to the right, to work out some kinks. Then she turned to Louise. "I think it's going to be such fun. It's been a long time since I've been to a harvest party."

Louise smiled. "I think you're right. It should be delightful." When they stepped out of the pantry, Louise went over to put some water in the teakettle and turned the stove's burner on. "Are you going to help with any of the food?"

"I thought I might bring some kind of apple or pumpkin dessert to go along with the fall theme. I haven't decided which one, yet. I'll look through my cookbooks and see what I can come up with."

Louise nodded. "Are you planning much in the way of decorations?"

"We'll hang up some streamers in the barn, decorate food tables, that kind of thing. Nothing fancy. She wants to focus on the fellowship," Jane said.

"That sounds like a good plan. Let's hope that the weather will be nice."

"They're predicting a nice crisp, fall evening for tomorrow," Jane said, eyes sparkling like a hopeful teenager's. "It was nice of them to host this gathering."

"They are very giving that way."

"Well, Rose says, 'What's the use of having a big old farm if you can't share it?'"

Louise smiled. "That sounds like something she would say. Wonderful people, the Bellwoods."

Jane nodded, already pulling down cookbooks from the cabinet.

The teakettle whistled, prompting Louise to pour the water in a pot so the chamomile tea could begin brewing. "Would you like some?"

"No thanks. So what are your plans this afternoon?" Jane asked.

"My lessons don't start until three o'clock, so I thought I would have some tea in the living room and maybe read a little in my C. S. Lewis book." She stopped and looked at Jane. "Unless you need me to do something?"

"Oh no. We've finished the laundry, so we're in good shape. But thank you for offering."

"Are the guests all out?"

Jane flipped open one of the cookbooks. "I think the Burtons are here somewhere. I saw their car just a few minutes ago."

Louise carefully poured her cup of tea. "Well, I will leave you to your recipe browsing. I will be in the living room if you need me."

"Okay, Louise," Jane answered without looking up. "Enjoy your book."

Louise smiled and slipped through the doorway. It amused her how absorbed Jane could get within the pages of a cookbook. One would have thought she was caught up with the most riveting reading material. But then to Jane, Louise supposed, it was interesting reading. Settling onto her chair with a contented sigh, she opened her C. S. Lewis book. "Now this is reading," she said to Wendell, who took her comment as an invitation to come over and join her. Louise laughed as the tabby worked his head underneath her book and finagled himself onto her lap.

No sooner had she read through the first paragraph than the Burtons entered. "Good afternoon, Louise, mind if we join you?" Doug Burton asked.

"Not at all, come in." Though Louise had hoped for a

moment to herself, she truly enjoyed visiting with the Burtons. "How are you today?" Louise asked.

"We're doing well. We've been walking the streets of Acorn Hill, sampling goodies here and there in the Coffee Shop and, of course, the Good Apple bakery," Dorothy said.

"They are hard to resist. Though, I confess, with Jane around we eat just as well in our own home."

"I don't doubt that," Doug said.

They settled into general conversation about the weather and how the Burtons were enjoying their stay in Acorn Hill. Ruth Kincade entered the room and soon their discussion turned to Annie's world of sign language. Before long, Louise and Ruth found themselves learning parts of the sign language alphabet. Annie and Dorothy helped Louise and Ruth form the different letters with their hands. Louise thought it all fascinating.

"Seems like it would take forever to spell out a word. How do you decide when to use a gesture for a word and when to use letters to spell it out?" Ruth asked.

"That's a very good question," Dorothy said. "Using one letter at a time to spell out a word is called finger-spelling. You might use that for a company name, let's say, for which you would have no particular sign or gesture, or perhaps you would use it to spell a word for which you don't know the sign. As a hearing person, I'm still learning signs for various things. If I'm talking to someone who knows a sign that I don't, and I fingerspell it, they show me the sign, and then I use that sign from then on when referring to it."

Louise shook her head. "So much to learn."

Dorothy interpreted their conversation for Annie's benefit. Annie smiled at Louise's comment and signed a response. "Annie says it's not hard once you get the hang of it."

"Does everyone use the same signs no matter where they live?" Ruth wanted to know.

"That's another good question," Dorothy said, while signing the inquiry to Annie. "Actually, some signs are specific to certain regions. For the most part, though, there are three types of sign languages. There is American Sign Language, or ASL, as it is commonly called. This is known as the true language of the hearing impaired. It's a little tricky because the sentence structure is different from the English language. This is what many adults in the deaf community use."

"I think I've heard of that," Ruth commented.

Dorothy nodded. "Now, in a public school setting, an interpreter would most likely use Signed English. It's structured much like the English language, and is basically just signing how you and I talk. This makes it easier for the hearing-impaired children to communicate through letter writing, etcetera, because they have a grasp of our syntax."

Louise nodded and sipped her tea. She was truly impressed.

"The third language is called Pigeon, and that's basically a combination of ASL and Signed English. That seems to be used quite often, depending, of course, on where you are and with what community."

"I had no idea," Louise said, placing her cup back on the saucer.

"Our lives were pretty miserable before we learned sign language as a family. We were all so frustrated in trying to communicate with one another. We wrote endless notes." Dorothy chuckled with the memory. "I'm glad that's behind us."

Annie nodded vigorously and everyone smiled.

"Annie's friends all know some sign and use it regularly with her. She's touched so many with her patient and understanding ways. She is a wonder," Dorothy said, signing the words to her daughter and smiling.

Annie gave a shy smile.

A short time later, Louise's piano student arrived, and she went into the parlor for her next lesson, all the while thinking how much she enjoyed having the Burton family as guests at the inn.

Alice had spent some time shopping for new jeans in Potterston and was tired by the time she got home. Shopping was not her forte. She much preferred being home instead of sorting through racks of clothes, most of which never seemed to appeal to her. At least today she had success in buying a new pair that seemed suitable, and a couple of comfortable tops to match.

With a tired sigh, she put her clothes away and sat a moment on the edge of her bed. She glanced around at the buttery yellow walls, the patchwork quilt on her bed, and matching braided rug on the floor. She liked this room, and often placed a vase of cut flowers on her dresser; the color and scent enhanced the charm of her retreat. She had been too busy lately to purchase flowers, but she remembered the lavender spritz Jane sometimes sprayed on her sheets to make them smell good. Maybe she could borrow that until she could buy some for herself.

Alice thought that she had heard Jane in her room. Stopping for a brief glance in the mirror, Alice fluffed her hair, then headed toward her sister's room to see if she could borrow some of the lavender spray. She tapped on the door, but did not hear Jane's response, though she could hear Jane moving around. Alice knocked once more, then opened the door.

"Jane, I wondered if—"

Before Alice could open the door wide, Jane stepped forward, blocking Alice's entrance. "Oh hi, Alice, I was just coming out," she said, though Alice was not convinced.

"I'm sorry if I bothered you," Alice said, feeling a bit curious about Jane's reaction. She wondered why Jane would not want her in the room. "I had hoped I might borrow your lavender spritz for my room."

Jane thought a moment. "Oh dear, I'm not sure where I've placed it just now. Can I get it for you another time? I'm really late for dinner preparations, and I must get started soon or we'll all go hungry tonight."

Alice studied her. "Sure, that would be fine."

"Great." Jane flashed a huge grin. "Can you help me set the table since I'm running late? I'm making apricot-glazed chicken."

"Sounds wonderful. I'm starved," Alice said, her hunger almost making her forget her curiosity about Jane. Almost.

Chapter Fourteen

You know, I'm a little concerned about my ANGELs. Sarah has blown this thing with Ashley's braces out of proportion, and now the girls are picking sides," Alice said with a sigh as she and her sisters sat around the kitchen table for a midmorning break on Saturday. "I'm not quite sure how to handle it."

Jane lifted her coffee cup and shook her head. "That's a tough age, no question about it. Junior high girls seem to go through these kinds of things all the time. I wouldn't worry too much, Alice. I'm sure it will pass in no time."

"That's what I thought, too," Alice said, "but now things are worse than before. I have to do something. I just don't know what."

"Well, we believe what James 1:5 says: 'If any of you lacks wisdom, he should ask God, who gives generously to all without finding fault, and it will be given to him,'" Louise quoted in her practical manner. "Let us pray about it together."

Alice nodded. "I would appreciate it. I want to do the

right thing and handle it in such a way as to help the girls grow, not hinder or hurt them in any fashion."

"Sometimes answers come unexpectedly." Louise took a sip of her tea. Then with a slight frown, she added, "Have you talked with their mothers?"

Alice shook her head. "Not yet. I was hoping not to have to do that. Sometimes it stirs things up more when the parents become involved." Alice looked toward the window. "I can't imagine why Sarah is acting this way. It's just not like her."

"You're right, it's not like her," Jane agreed.

Alice reached over, held her sisters' hands and began praying.

During that morning prayer, Alice felt Heaven touch earth, and she knew in her heart the answer was on its way. Though she could not know from where the answer would come, she knew that God had heard the plea for wisdom. And that was enough.

After prayer, Jane poured herself a fresh cup of coffee, and Alice and Louise refilled their teacups.

"Yoo-hoo, anybody home?" Ethel called from the back door.

The sisters exchanged glances and smiled. Ethel came into the kitchen. "Well, good morning. Looks like I arrived right at break time."

Jane laughed. "That pretty much sums it up. What are you up to today?"

"Oh, I, uh . . ." Ethel hesitated, "I was thinking I might play on Michael's computer a little bit." She looked at them with a start. "He did leave it, didn't he?"

"Yes, he said he would leave it for you and Margaret to fiddle with." In an effort to hide her amusement, Jane pressed her lips together.

Ethel showed obvious relief.

Alice was sure that Ethel had been thinking most of the morning about the prospect of coming over and getting on the computer. She, too, hid a grin.

"By the way, are you ready for the big party?" Jane asked.

"Oh yes." Ethel's arms flailed with animation. "Of course, I've made some peach tarts, and I've got hot dogs and other such things."

"Is Lloyd taking you?" Louise asked.

"Yes. You know Lloyd would never pass up a get-together with the townsfolk."

Alice wanted to chuckle, knowing the same was true of Ethel.

"Would you like some tea or coffee before you get on the computer, Auntie?" Jane asked.

Ethel waved her hand. "No thanks, I had some coffee

before I came over here. It's too chilly not to have something early to warm these old bones," she said, her voice wavering between a complaint and stating a fact.

"Is it really cold out?" Jane asked.

"Oh, you know me, I'm always cold," Ethel said, as if to cut the conversation short. It was obvious she was on a mission to get to the computer, and without further ado she made her way toward the living room.

After more comfortable conversation, the sisters finished their drinks and scattered to work on their agendas for the day. Louise left first, heading for the parlor to meet her next piano student.

"Would you like me to help with the desserts, Jane?" Alice asked, knowing Jane needed no help whatsoever when it came to cooking. Still, Alice did not want Jane to think she had to do everything herself.

"Thank you, but I'm fine. I love whipping up special desserts, and I'm already in the festive mood. I think I'll listen to some radio music. You just may find me twirling around the kitchen as I concoct something delicious for the party."

Alice chuckled. "Well, if you're sure."

"I'm sure."

"Be careful you don't hurt yourself, Twinkle Toes," Alice added before leaving the kitchen.

Wondering how the Lord would answer their prayer for the ANGELs, Alice stepped into the living room where Ethel sat staring at the computer screen in deep concentration. Her aunt did not so much as blink an eye or look up when Alice entered the room. Not being very computer savvy herself, Alice wondered what could be so interesting. She stepped around the back of the sofa and peered over Ethel's shoulder. To Alice's astonishment the screen said, "Over-Seventies Chat Room." Alice could scarcely believe her eyes. "Aunt Ethel, you're in a chat room?"

Ethel jumped. "Land's sake, Alice, there you go again. I told you to stop scaring the daylights out of me."

"I'm sorry, Aunt Ethel, I thought you heard me come in. I wasn't trying to scare you. I just wondered what you were doing on the computer. I figured you were looking at garden things or something. I had no idea you were . . . I mean, I'm just surprised that . . . um . . ."

Aunt Ethel's face turned a rosy pink. It was one of those rare moments when she actually seemed at a loss for words.

It did not last long.

"Well, I'll have you know, Alice Christine Howard—"

Alice grimaced. She knew when her aunt used anyone's full name in that tone of voice, it was time to look for a hiding place.

"Whether I want to be in a chat room or in a garden

room, what does it matter?" she asked, eyes flashing. "I may be old, but I'm not dead." She pursed her lips and lifted her chin.

Alice knew that she had done it. She had ruffled Ethel's feathers, and everyone knew her feathers were better left alone.

"I'm sorry, Aunt Ethel. I didn't mean to upset you," Alice soothed, "and you're absolutely right. You may look at whatever you wish. It's none of my affair." Alice patted her aunt on the shoulder, trying to calm her down a trifle. "I'm really sorry," Alice assured her once again.

Ethel tapped her foot and shook it with a vengeance, showing her irritation.

Alice waited.

Finally, Ethel's tapping stopped and she said, "Well, okay, but just see that you don't do that anymore."

"I'll be careful," Alice said, giving Ethel a hug. Alice tiptoed out of the room before she could get into more trouble. *Aunt Ethel in a chat room. "What was the world coming to," as Ethel would say*. No doubt, before Alice could climb the stairs her aunt would be back in the chat room.

Alice still wondered if that was cause for concern.

In the early afternoon, Ruth and Alice joined Vera for a

walk. After Alice's run-in with Ethel, she was thankful for the chance to get out of the house.

"Do you smell that?" Vera asked as the three of them walked down Berry Lane.

"What?" Alice asked.

"Fall," Vera said with appreciation. "I think fall has a special scent to it. Like, oh, I don't know, burning wood."

Alice laughed. "It's probably because someone is burning wood in their fireplace," Alice said, pointing to smoke rising from a chimney.

They laughed.

"I think fall smells like toasted marshmallows and apples," Alice said.

"That's because your sister is a cook," Vera teased.

"I think fall smells like sharpened pencils, glue, and crisp, new books," Ruth said with a smile.

Vera looked at her kindly. "You're a true teacher, Ruth."

"I guess I am. I guess that's why I came here. I had to know for sure. Now if I could only figure out how to help those kids in a new way."

"Well, Ruth, Jane and Vera both have told me how good you are with bargains," Alice said.

Ruth shrugged. "Yes, but even at bargain prices, I can't afford to get much for the students. As Vera knows, teachers aren't exactly in the upper tax bracket."

Alice nodded. "I understand. But Jane had mentioned to me something about a place on the computer, um, what was it now, e-something. A place where you buy and sell things."

"Oh, eBay?" Ruth asked. She crunched a brittle leaf in her path.

"Yes, that's the one. Anyway, she wondered if you might be able to do something with that. She knows what a clever shopper you are, and thought that you might be able to apply that gift on the Internet."

Vera got excited. "Now, there's an idea."

"But how do you mean? What would I do?"

Alice was stumped. She did not know enough about computers or that Web site to give advice. "Well, I don't know exactly. Why don't you talk to Jane about it? She's creative like you. Surely, between the two of you, you'll think of something."

Ruth seemed to mull that over. "You might have something there. I'll ask her when we get back."

"Say, are you ready for the party tonight?" Vera asked.

"Pretty much. Jane is diligently working on her desserts at this very moment."

"Are you going, Ruth?"

Ruth nodded. "The Bellwoods were kind enough to invite all of the inn's guests. Sounds like a lot of fun. I haven't been on a hayride in years."

"We are going to have a wonderful time. Looks like the weather is even cooperating," Alice said.

Amid sunshine and a town displaying a palette of russet, gold and scarlet leaves, Ruth, Alice and Vera continued their pleasurable walk absorbed in the comfort of camaraderie and fellowship.

By the time she arrived back at the inn, Alice planned to tidy her room and possibly squeeze in a moment or two to read a little more of her book before she had to start thinking about getting ready for the party.

Once her room was straightened, Alice retreated to the living room to relax. Jane had finished her desserts and gone to the Bellwoods to help decorate for the party. Louise had gone upstairs to her room to rest before the evening gathering.

Alice had barely stepped into the fictional world of her book when Margaret and Michael entered the inn.

Michael looked in to see Alice sitting in the living room. "Good afternoon, Alice."

"Hello. Is it turning cold?" Alice inquired, wondering if she should wear something warmer to the party than she had originally planned.

"Oh, it's not bad. It's just the right touch for a fall party," Michael said, as if he had read her mind. He glanced at his watch and rubbed his hands together. "Anybody up for a good game of checkers? I've brought my own," he said with a laugh.

"Don't get roped in, Alice," Margaret warned.

No one volunteered. "I guess my reputation precedes me, eh?" He wiggled his eyebrows.

"Oh, okay, I'll play you. Again," Margaret offered with a teasing lilt to her voice.

Michael cupped his hand around his mouth and turned to Alice. "She's afraid I'll beat her. Again."

Michael and Margaret sat in a corner of the room at a table that Alice had set up for them earlier.

"So, how are things going with you two?" Alice asked, watching as they placed the board on the table and put their checkers in place.

Margaret and Michael exchanged a glance and a smile. "We're doing great," he said. "If I could just get that stubborn daughter of mine to stop playing the mother hen."

"Oh?"

"It's not that she doesn't like Margaret." He looked at Margaret and smiled. "She just seems to be protective . . . or something. I can't quite put my finger on it." They took a couple of turns moving their checkers, and barely into the game, Michael jumped one of Margaret's checkers with his own. She made a face at him.

"She'll come around. These things just take time." Alice

glanced at Margaret and could see she was not so easily convinced. "You'll see."

Margaret nodded but said nothing. They sat a moment in silence until Margaret jumped three of Michael's checkers and he howled in disbelief. "Hey! Where did you learn how to do that?"

"I've had a good teacher," she said, amusement and pride all over her face.

Alice thought the two made a lovely pair. They seemed so happy together. She only hoped that Michael was right, that with time Margaret's son and Sherri would come around and accept their parents' relationship and allow them to have a life of their own.

Chapter Fifteen

That evening, Jane stepped out of the car and opened the trunk to get her desserts. Alice and Louise walked to the back of the car to help her carry things. Though Alice often wore jeans around the house, it tickled Jane to see her sister wearing bib overalls, a crisp white cotton blouse, and a straw hat, and to see Louise dressed in a long denim skirt. Louise said that she could not quite bring herself to put on a straw hat. All three sisters wore sweaters over their outfits.

"Since we seem to be the first ones to arrive, I think we'll walk up to the house and let the Bellwoods know we're here before we go out back," Jane said.

The sisters agreed.

Jane ducked her head to keep her own straw hat from falling off as she reached into the trunk. "Isn't it just a perfect night for this?" she asked, while lifting pumpkin pies, pumpkin bread and apple dumplings from the car.

Alice smiled, taking the pies Jane handed to her. "I have to admit that I have been concerned about the weather.

Though it's somewhat chilly, it does seem the perfect autumn night."

Jane heard other cars pull up to the farmhouse. Ethel joined the sisters a little out of breath. "You need any help?"

Jane took out the last container. "You could carry the apple dumplings, if you don't mind, Auntie. I'll just get my camera," she said as she closed the lid of her trunk.

Ethel nodded and reached for the apple dumplings.

"Oh, I'm glad you brought your camera, Jane. That was a great idea," Alice said.

Jane smiled. "I wanted some remembrance of the evening."

"It's cold out here. I'll be glad to get close to the bonfire," Ethel said with a shiver. Jane looked over to see her aunt in bib overalls, a red-and-white checkered cotton blouse and a straw hat. Ethel snuggled against the chill within a navy blue jacket. Dark, round freckles trailed over her nose and across her cheeks.

"Why Aunt Ethel, you look positively festive," Jane said, reaching over to give her aunt a hug.

Ethel perked up as if she had been waiting for someone to notice. "Do you like my freckles?" she asked, pointing to her face.

"Love them. Did you dot them on with eyebrow pencil?"

Ethel nodded and stretched a little taller as though she thought herself ever so clever.

"Well, I think they look wonderful," Jane said.

Alice and Louise agreed.

"So where is Lloyd?" Louise asked as they walked the cobblestone path to Samuel and Rose Bellwood's two-story white farmhouse.

"He's coming with my peach tarts. Fred Humbert called to him when we got out of the car, so Lloyd stopped to talk."

"Oh, I didn't notice Vera and Fred had arrived." Alice looked back for their car.

When they reached the house, Jane knocked on the door. Once it opened, a petite woman dressed in jeans and a colorful shirt with a matching bandana around her neck greeted them. Dark brown braids circled her head like a tightly woven crown.

"Hello, Rose. We wanted to let you know we were here before we traipsed to your backyard," Jane said with a smile.

"So good to see all of you," Rose said, looking over the small group that had gathered. "I'll be around back in a moment. You know the way, Jane," she said.

Jane nodded, then led the others toward the back. Samuel had strung big lights outside the barn, illuminating the yard. Jane looked around with satisfaction at the streamers draped heavily across the front of the red barn and swagged across the front of the food tables, which were covered with white paper. Pumpkin centerpieces adorned the middle sections. Pumpkins, corn husks, and bales of hay were placed about the area for an autumn feel. Just beyond the barn, bales of hay were arranged in a circle around an open campfire that was already working up to a good, steady flame. Jane clicked her camera here and there, taking snapshots of the decorations.

"Oh, it looks lovely," Louise said.

Alice agreed.

"Why, this is so much fun," Ethel said, clapping her hands together.

"Are Margaret and Michael coming, Alice?" Jane asked, looking like a tourist with her camera hanging from her neck.

"Yes, they'll be a little late, though. Michael had to rush off to his son-in-law's office to try to fix an ailing computer."

"Well, I'm glad they can come," Jane said, adjusting her pie plates on the table.

"Glad you folks could make it," a powerful voice called out. The group turned around. Samuel Bellwood stood tall and imposing behind them. The sheep farmer's kind eyes and gentle smile softened any intimidation his size might cause. The family dog, a black-and-white Sheltie named Missy, stood protectively at his side, her tail wagging a bit cautiously.

Soon greetings rang out from one to another as friends and neighbors of Acorn Hill, dressed in relaxed country attire for the occasion, sauntered into the yard for a night of food, fun and fellowship.

Jane helped Rose dish out the desserts and chatted with her neighbors as they dropped by. She and Rose caught up on the latest happenings. When the guests had been tended to, the women mixed in with the others. Jane thought the night perfectly wonderful. She glanced up. Twinkling stars poked through the velvety sky like tiny diamonds. Taking a deep breath, she offered a prayer of thanks for nights such as this one.

She looked over to see Louise and Alice talking together. A pleasing warmth ran clear through her. She loved her sisters. God had been good to her. As she watched her sisters, her thoughts flitted to her secret. One thing was certain: She could not keep the reason for her trips to Potterston from them forever.

Alice picked up a mug of tea from one of the tables and took a moment to look around the yard. She noticed that all of her ANGELs had made it to the party. Her gaze traveled to where Ashley Moore stood with her parents, away from the other girls. Alice grew concerned, wondering if the girls had snubbed Ashley. Once again she breathed a prayer.

If only she could fix things. She stood there awhile, trying to work through the problem, but she just could not come up with a solution.

"They're getting ready for a hayride, Miss Howard. Will you come along?" Linda Farr, one of the ANGELs, asked, quite out of breath.

"Well, I don't know—" Alice began, scrambling for an excuse not to go.

Before she could produce a satisfactory one, Linda said, "Oh, come on," taking hold of Alice's hand on one side, while Lisa Masur took Alice's other hand. Together they laughed and giggled their way to the wagon, pulling along a reluctant Alice.

Once inside the wagon, Alice decided to make the most of it. Perhaps Ashley would join them, and she would have another opportunity to reconcile the ANGELs. As the girls scrambled in and everyone got settled, Alice realized that all the ANGELs but Ashley and Sarah were present. The other ANGELs, however, gave her little time to consider it. They were already singing as the wagon started moving.

Alice leaned back against the wooden wagon and pulled a blanket up on her lap to shield her from the evening's chill. With a resigned sigh, she decided she had no other recourse than to settle in and sing along.

Alice thought that the ride down the quiet country roads with the full moon sailing overhead was marvelous, and it did much to calm her worries and concerns.

When they returned, she had forgotten about Ashley and Sarah. After warming herself by the fire, Alice took another mug of tea and headed toward the main barn. It had been a while since she had been to a large party, and the idea of a little solitude appealed to her right about now.

Slipping into the barn, she peeked in at the stock horses and the three milk cows. She knew the Bellwoods kept their sheep in another barn. The animals appeared totally unimpressed with her presence, though they watched her curiously as she walked past them. She did manage to pet the nose of one horse who stretched his head out to have a look at her. Only when she stopped to pet the horse did she hear a rustling sound nearby. She listened intently. It seemed to come from behind her. She turned around in time to see two girls leaving the barn, each going her own way once they exited the building. It was then she recognized them: Sarah and Ashley, her troubled ANGELs.

When Alice rejoined the gathering, she found that Margaret, Michael and Ruth had joined the party and stood talking with Ethel and Lloyd. Alice noticed how Michael and Margaret practically glowed with happiness. Alice felt sure they had rekindled the love that they once had for each other. It was written all over their faces.

"Alice," Margaret said as soon as she saw her, "what a wonderful gathering."

Michael nodded.

"It is fun, isn't it? Though I'm afraid I'm a mess after the hayride," Alice said with a chuckle, picking flecks of hay from her bib overalls.

"Oh my, you need a good brushing-off," Ethel said, her tone implying disapproval.

Alice sighed. "I'm afraid you're right. The ANGELs coerced me into it." Alice knew her aunt would never go on a hayride. Why, it would mess up her hair and clothes. Alice realized that she should probably behave in a way a little more befitting a woman in her sixties, but when she thought of how the ANGELs seemed to enjoy having her along, she decided it was worth losing a little dignity.

"Oh, I had hoped to go on a hayride," Ruth said.

"Well, they're gearing up for another one. So you might

want to hurry over there and climb aboard," Alice said with a laugh.

Without hesitation Ruth was on her way. The others watched after her, then lingered awhile longer in conversation.

After a time of singing around the campfire, toasting marshmallows, and eating an endless supply of other treats, the guests started to disperse.

Samuel got to his feet. "Don't anybody move," he bellowed suddenly. Those who had started to rise from the hay bales sat back down, looking at him quite seriously. "I want to grab one more piece of pumpkin pie before you start taking the delicious food away."

The crowd relaxed, and a ripple of chuckles made its way around the circle as Samuel ran over to the table where Alice was already clearing things away. She stopped so that he could help himself. Jane stepped from the house with her camera dangling from her neck. Seeing Samuel hovering over the last few slices of pie, she lifted her camera, pointed it toward him and clicked the button.

No doubt about it, this would be a night they would long remember. Jane patted the camera in front of her. Yes, she would see to that.

Chapter Sixteen

O n Sunday afternoon, the sisters invited Margaret, Michael, Ethel, Lloyd and Rev. Kenneth Thompson over for dessert and coffee. Ruth had gone with the Burtons to Potterston for the afternoon.

"Jane, this is absolutely delicious," the mayor said after swallowing his first bite of apple crumb cake.

Others around the table agreed.

"Thank you," Jane said appreciatively. Through the clink of silverware, she explained how she had decided to fix more apple and pumpkin dishes to help her to celebrate autumn.

"I would weigh fifty extra pounds if I ate your cooking all the time," Rev. Thompson said with a chuckle.

"That's how I am with Ethel's peach tarts," Lloyd said as he patted his slightly paunchy midsection and winked at Ethel.

Ethel laughed and waved at him as if to brush the matter aside, though Alice knew her aunt liked people to rave about her tarts. Not that Alice blamed her: They were marvelous.

"Well, most days I try to watch the fat content of our meals and try to keep us eating healthy," Jane said.

"She does indeed," added Louise. "She will not let us get carried away."

Alice nodded in confirmation.

"Oh, I don't mean because what you serve is bad nutritionally, but rather that it's so good, I would struggle to stop eating," Rev. Thompson said.

Chuckles and agreements rippled around the table. The group continued with their dessert in comfortable discussion about the morning service and how well things were going at church.

The weather had been mild for the past couple of days, so after dessert the group decided to retreat to the front porch and enjoy the last days of warmth before the season became frigid. Jane brought out more hot tea and coffee to take away the slight chill that greeted them on the porch.

"Well, Margaret and Michael, it has certainly been a pleasure to have you join us at Grace Chapel," the pastor said.

A shadow crossed Margaret's face. Alice surmised that the prospect of leaving had brought it on.

"We've certainly enjoyed it," Michael said. "I'm involved in my church back in Florida, but I must admit I'll miss Grace Chapel when I go home."

Alice saw him squeeze Margaret's hand.

Ethel leaned in as if she was about to receive a juicy bit of gossip. "Oh, will you be leaving soon?"

He looked at Margaret.

Margaret answered. "I'm not sure exactly. I don't know how much longer Wilma will need physical therapy, but she's improving every day. When she is finished with her physical therapy, I won't need to take her to appointments anymore, and then I'll head back to my home in Philadelphia."

"I guess that's when I'll head back to the sunny state," Michael tried, but failed, to say lightheartedly.

Everyone seemed to sense the couple's struggle. Ethel looked like she wanted to say more, but after seeing the others grow quiet, she kept silent.

"Well, we've sure enjoyed having both of you around here," Alice said.

"Thank you, Alice," Margaret said with emotion in her voice. "My stay here has been like a dream come true."

Alice knew that Margaret had enjoyed her stay at the inn, but Alice also knew Margaret's dream had more to do with Michael.

Ethel, it seemed, had kept silent quite long enough. Never one to beat around the bush, she piped up, "Are the kids accepting things between you two?"

Margaret gave a half smile. Michael jumped in before she could say anything. "Well, I finally found out that

Sherri is struggling with the idea of a 'new mother,' as she puts it. I think Margaret's son worries simply because he doesn't know me. He doesn't want his mom to get mixed up with the wrong person. I can't fault him for that. The kids mean well, they're just a bit overprotective." He paused a moment. "Funny how life turns around when you're older. Now we're the teenagers, and they think they're the parents."

Ethel and Lloyd nodded as though they understood exactly what Michael meant.

Margaret shifted a little in her chair. Alice wondered if she felt uncomfortable talking about their relationship with everyone. "Well, I don't know about the rest of you, but I think I'd like another piece of that crumb cake," Alice said. "Would anyone else like more coffee, tea or crumb cake?"

Jane released a smile that said she understood Alice's change of subject. "Let me help you, Alice." She turned to the others to take their orders.

"Jane, you stay put. Let us take care of everyone and you relax," Louise offered.

Jane smiled. "Why, thank you."

Alice and Louise turned and went inside the house. While in the kitchen, placing more slices of cake on dessert dishes, Louise told Alice how she and Ruth were learning sign language from Annie. "I will hate to see that family leave tomorrow," Louise said with a sigh. "That child is truly something special." Louise poured more coffee in the carafe. "I mean, despite her disability, she makes a difference wherever she goes. Most people would say, 'If I get better, I will do this or that.' Annie is doing it now."

Alice had placed dishes on her tray and started walking. She turned with a start. "What did you say?"

Louise carried a tray of drinks. She stopped. "Which time?"

"Something about Annie making a difference now?"

"Yes. I said Annie isn't giving an excuse to do something later. She is doing it now."

Alice stared at her a moment.

"What is it?" Louise asked.

"I think you've just solved my problem with the ANGELs."

Knowing that the guest speakers whom she had invited for the ANGELs meeting would leave town the next day, Alice had rescheduled her Wednesday meeting with the girls to Sunday night. In the assembly room of the church, Alice waited for everyone to get settled into chairs.

Alice noticed Sarah and Ashley. There seemed to be a hidden line drawn between the girls. Alice had to put an end to this childish behavior once and for all. Silently, she said another prayer for guidance.

"Girls, so glad you could come tonight. Instead of making something as we usually do, tonight I've brought in two special guests," Alice began.

The girls looked around for a new face, as if wondering whom Alice had meant.

"They're not here yet. They'll come after our lesson. So let's start right now with prayer."

The girls bowed their heads and Alice prayed to the Father that He would guide them to people who needed help and encouragement. As she prayed, her heart also whispered silently that the girls would see themselves in tonight's message.

When the girls looked up, Alice could not help the squeeze in her heart. She loved every one of these girls, and she could not bear to see them at odds with one another. She passed out Bibles. "Let's turn to Hebrews 3:13, please." Alice waited patiently during the rustling of pages as the girls attempted to find the correct place. Once she felt sure everyone had found the verse, she looked at Sarah. "Would you please read for us, Sarah?"

Sarah nodded. "'But encourage one another daily, as long as it is called Today, so that none of you may be hardened by sin's deceitfulness.'"

Alice could tell by the look on her face that Sarah had merely read the words without taking them to heart. "What could that mean?" Alice asked.

Lisa Masur sat on the right side of the table, the same side as Sarah. Her hand shot up.

"Yes, Lisa?"

"I think it means, um, we need to encourage people every day so they won't get discouraged, maybe?"

"That's good, Lisa," Alice said, noticing the smile on Lisa's face. "Anybody else have an opinion about the verse?"

Linda Farr, sitting next to Ashley on the left side of the table, raised her hand.

"Yes, Linda?"

"It means to encourage all people every day, not just some people, sometimes, but everyone we meet every day," she said with a glance at Sarah and a hint of reproof in her voice.

Alice was impressed with Linda's insight. "I think that's right, Linda. We are to encourage everyone." Alice paced in front of them a moment. "If you've had a bad day at school and when you come home your brother picks on you some more, how does that make you feel?"

"I don't have a brother," one called out.

"Makes me want to deck him," another said.

"Not good."

"Bad."

"Sad."

"Sometimes when we hurt someone else, it hurts us too, but we just don't recognize it. Deep down, we don't want to be that way, but sometimes we get grumpy and lash out without thinking, and we hurt others." Alice waited a moment for that to sink in. "What we do affects others too. It's wonderful to influence those around us with good things, helping them to be kind by our examples, but wouldn't it be awful if we caused others to be in a bad mood because we were mean? That's like stealing from someone when you take away their joy, did you know that? The funny thing is we do it sometimes to the people closest to us."

The room was so quiet Alice could only hear some faint breathing. She had their attention. *Thank You, Father*.

"Some people make a positive difference in the lives of other people. And some people make a positive difference even when their lives are less than perfect. That's where our guests come in."

Alice walked over to the stairway to find Dorothy and Annie waiting. She motioned for them to come forward. "You're sure this won't be too tiring for Annie?"

"Not at all. She has been feeling stronger, and she's looking forward to this opportunity."

Alice smiled at Annie and walked her and her mother to the center of the room.

"ANGELs, this is Mrs. Burton and her daughter Annie." The girls smiled at them. "They are staying at the inn right now, but they are leaving tomorrow. I have seen Annie carry out this verse. She encourages people all around her. Some people might not be so kind if they were in Annie's shoes. I'll let Annie share her story." Alice stepped aside and sat down in a chair.

Annie looked at the girls and smiled. She lifted her hands and began to tell the story of how she used to hear just like them until one day when a high fever finally left her and took her hearing along with it. Her mother relayed the story as Annie's hands flew with detail and expression. She explained how other kids made fun of her because she communicated with her hands and her speech sounded different from that of hearing people because she could not hear herself to form words correctly.

The girls sat spellbound as Annie told how God helped her to forgive those who hurt her feelings and made her feel *different*. She discovered the best thing she could do was teach those who did not understand and to encourage those who suffered the same persecution.

Alice just then saw Ashley and Sarah exchange a glance. For a moment, hope filled Alice as she witnessed a look of sorrow flash upon Sarah's face. Then Sarah quickly turned away.

Annie shared with the girls that life could change at any moment, and they needed to be found doing good for others. "We may not always have the chance to extend a kindness," she told them. "But we can encourage one another daily, as long as it is called 'Today,'" she said. Annie then went on to teach the girls some common signs, which they seemed to enjoy learning.

Finally, Annie signed with gusto the song her mother sang joyfully from her heart, "Make Me a Blessing."

At the close of their meeting, Alice saw the girls scoot from their chairs and gather excitedly around Annie. Everyone but Sarah, who quietly slipped on her jacket and walked up the stairs.

Chapter Seventeen

Though it was something they normally didn't do, the sisters joined their guests for breakfast on Monday morning. Alice looked around at the group and marveled that she and her sisters had developed such a special relationship with the Burtons, Ruth Kincade and, especially, Margaret Ballard. All raved about the sausage-and-egg quiche that Jane had prepared for them.

As he was finishing his meal, Doug Burton said, "Jane, I can't remember when I've had such a splendid meal." He looked at his wife, who was frowning, and quickly inserted "Not counting my wife's good cooking, of course."

Jane smiled. "Well, I'm glad you liked it, but we're not finished yet." She carried a tray with dishes of fruit and cream over to the table and passed them out. Then she refilled empty cups.

"I'm getting spoiled staying here," Margaret piped up. "I dread going home to my own cooking."

"We are fortunate to have our Jane cooking for us day after day," Alice said, looking at her younger sister.

"Yes, and we plan to keep it that way," Louise said with a stern voice, but adding a smile that belied any harshness.

"Goodness, all this praise will go to my head if you aren't careful," Jane teased. She sat down at the table to join the others.

"By the way, I thought you had to work today, Alice," Margaret said.

"I normally would have worked today, but I switched days again with another nurse who needed to get off work later this week."

Margaret nodded.

"Hey, wasn't the party the other night great?" Jane asked.

Comments floated around the table about the events at the harvest party at the Bellwoods' home.

"I got some outstanding pictures," Jane said. "I'm looking forward to getting the film developed."

"The Bellwoods sure are nice people," Margaret said.

Everyone agreed.

The phone rang as they continued to discuss the party at the Bellwoods' home. Louise got up to answer it and returned a few moments later.

"Excuse me," Louise said to the group. They looked up. "Margaret, your son is on the phone for you."

"Oh, thank you," Margaret said, excusing herself from the table and making her way to the front hall.

With others rising from the table, Alice excused herself, collected her dirty dishes, and carried them into the kitchen. Once the dishes were stacked in the washer, Alice wiped off the counters. Since her day was free, she wondered what she might do. After drying her hands, she walked through the dining room. Louise was gone. No doubt she was in the parlor getting ready for a piano lesson. As the guests mingled, Alice went into the parlor and found Margaret standing there alone. "Margaret, are you all right?"

Margaret nodded, but her expression didn't look convincing.

"What is it, dear?"

"It's my son Greg. I told him I wanted him to meet Michael, but Greg is reluctant to do so. I know it's because he wants me to get together with Roy." She paused, then looked back at Alice. "Why, that boy is becoming more protective than my father ever was."

Alice almost chuckled, then thought better of it. "The good news is that God sees your needs, and He will show you what to do. Remember Proverbs 3:5-6, 'Trust in the Lord with all your heart and lean not on your own understanding; in all your ways acknowledge him, and he will make your paths straight.'"

Margaret nodded. "You're right, of course."

"May I pray with you, Margaret?" Alice asked.

"Please," Margaret said.

Together, in the quiet of the parlor, Alice lifted her friend's needs before the Father, trusting that He was more than able to see Margaret through whatever the future held for her and Michael. When the prayer was over, Margaret gently squeezed Alice's hand.

"Thank you, Alice. I have found a treasured friend in you." The two embraced, and Alice felt sure that God had heard and would answer their prayer.

An hour after breakfast, Ruth Kincade joined the sisters in the living room. Ruth sat down and announced that she had something that she needed to share with them.

Louise looked up from her knitting. Jane stopped reading her cooking magazine. Alice put her bookmark in place and closed her book, wondering what the teacher had decided.

Having gained their attention, Ruth began. "I can't begin to tell you ladies how you have influenced my life. My stay at Grace Chapel Inn has been, well, a divine appointment, I believe."

The sisters smiled. Alice could not help thinking that their father would be pleased.

"When I arrived here, I was exhausted, distraught, and without any desire whatsoever to resume teaching." She paused a moment. "But you have changed all that." Turning to Louise, Ruth said, "Your example of interacting with your piano students spoke to me in volumes. My heart melted as I saw the love in your students' eyes toward you and you toward them." She swallowed hard. "That's how I feel about my students."

Louise gave Ruth a tender smile.

Ruth then turned to Alice. "And your example of always reaching out to help people in any way you can amazes me. I've seen you put your own needs aside to help others. Thank you for introducing me to your friend Vera. She has helped me in so many ways. I'm indebted to you both."

Alice felt too choked up to say anything herself.

Ruth turned to Jane. "And you encouraged me to take advantage of the world of eBay. That's something I would never have thought of on my own."

Jane grinned.

"I've come to a decision," she announced. "When I go back home, I am going to ask a couple of my colleagues if they will join me to form a committee. As a group, we will bargain shop at garage sales, eBay, wherever, and as we see the students' needs, we will keep a ready supply of clothing, canned goods, whatever, on hand. We may find some things that our students might not use but that we can sell on eBay to make money to buy the things our students will be able to use. In other words, I'm going to set up a little business. I hope that the principal will allow us this opportunity, and grant us the use of an empty storage room to stash our items. I know it won't be an easy task, but certainly it will be a worthwhile one. I feel this is my calling, and this is what I will do. I would never have known had I not come to Grace Chapel Inn. This place really is a mission field."

Alice was deeply touched, and she saw that her sisters were also affected. Each one got up and walked over to Ruth, hugging and congratulating her.

Alice walked away from their time together more energized than ever before. God was working in them and using Grace Chapel Inn as a means to help others. She had never before thought of their inn as a mission field, but if God chose to use them to encourage the hearts of their guests, the sisters were truly blessed. And Alice felt sure their earthly father, and their Heavenly Father, could not be more pleased.

Someone knocked at the front door. Louise got up from her chair. "That is probably my piano student." She made her way to the door while Alice and Jane stayed in the living room. She had been gone only a few minutes when she returned. "Alice, Sarah Roberts is at the door for you."

Alice could see concern on Louise's face and feel uneasiness within herself as she rose from the sofa. She walked toward the entrance, and Louise patted her arm as she went by. Once she reached the foyer, she saw the youngster. "Hello, Sarah."

"Hi, Miss Howard." Sarah looked down, tapping the toe of her shoe on the floor.

Alice waited. "Sarah?"

The girl looked back up and swallowed hard. "We remembered that you said you'd be home today. Um, we were wondering . . . I mean, me and the ANGELs, um, we were wondering if we could come and see you here at the inn this afternoon around two o'clock?"

Worry touched Alice's heart, but she responded with a gentle smile, "Certainly, Sarah."

Relief seemed to wash over the girl. "Okay, I'll let the others know," Sarah said as she reached around to open the door.

"Sarah?"

She turned back to look at Alice.

"Is there anything you want to tell me before the others get here?" Alice asked, hoping Sarah would give her some clue as to what was going on.

Sarah shook her head. "We'll tell you together, Miss Howard, if that's okay?"

Alice forced a smile. "Sure, Sarah, that will be fine. I'll see you at two o'clock."

Sarah nodded and left the inn. If only Alice knew what was going on, she might be able to head off some problem. Suddenly, the verse from Proverbs 3:5-6 that she had shared with Margaret came to her: "Trust in the Lord with all your heart and lean not on your own understanding; in all your ways acknowledge him, and he will make your paths straight."

"Lord, I'm listening," she whispered. Her job was merely to be available and obedient to whatever He called upon her to do. She had to trust Him with this, no matter what the future held.

Perhaps that was why Margaret's son and Michael's daughter were struggling. They had to let go of their parents, allowing them to go their own way, not knowing what they would choose. Letting go was not easy, but following God's plan was always the best choice.

Louise stood beside her sisters in the foyer to say their good-byes to the Burtons.

While Louise searched for the words to tell this family how they had touched her life, Alice spoke up first.

"Annie," Alice began as Dorothy signed for her, "Thank you for talking to the ANGELs. I believe your talk had a real impact on them."

Annie smiled.

Though not one normally given over to shows of emotion, Louise walked over to Annie and pulled the child into a hug. When they parted, Louise held Annie at arm's length and looked her full in the face. "You are a very special young lady, and I will never forget you."

"Now cut that out or you're all going to make me cry," Doug Burton said, easing the sadness of the moment. "Annie's had time to rest and she is feeling much stronger. We owe our thanks to you for making her stay a blessing."

"We'll be back to visit," Dorothy said with a wink. "You can count on that."

After their final good-byes, Jane closed the door behind the departing guests and turned to her sisters. "You know, we are truly blessed."

"Blessed and soggy," Alice said, wiping tears from her eyes.

When the ANGELs arrived at the inn, Alice led the girls into the parlor, where she had set up some extra chairs.

Alice noticed the girls were extraordinarily quiet. She took a deep breath and braced herself. "Okay, girls, what is this urgent matter you needed to see me about today?"

The girls all turned to Sarah.

"I've been wrong." Sarah hung her head and waited.

Alice wanted to help her, but she knew she had to let Sarah do this on her own. Sarah lifted a sorrowful face. "I don't like my teeth. I asked my parents for braces and they said I don't need them."

Knowing it took great courage for Sarah to admit that, Alice wanted to hug her. Instead, she merely listened.

"So when Ashley showed up with braces, I was . . ." she swallowed hard, "um, jealous." Sarah fidgeted with her fingers. "That's when I started making fun of her. I pulled the other girls into it. At first, I thought it was funny. Then when I saw that I hurt Ashley," she looked over at Ashley's downcast face, "well, it made me feel bad, but I didn't know how to get out of it." She stopped and waited a moment. "Until Annie came and talked to us. When she said how bad it made her feel when kids made fun of her, I knew how badly I had hurt Ashley. I didn't want to do that. Ashley has always been my best friend."

Alice watched as Sarah looked at Ashley. Ashley displayed a forgiving smile. The other girls sat perfectly still, heads somewhat bowed.

"I wanted everyone to come today so I could say I'm sorry. I couldn't wait until our next ANGELs meeting. I had to make things right today." She turned to Ashley. "I'm really sorry, Ashley. I hope you will still be my friend."

Ashley nodded.

"Well, I think this calls for a celebration," Alice said with a clap of her hands.

The girls turned to her.

"When God teaches us a valuable lesson like this, it's always cause to celebrate. I think we've all learned something here. We've seen how jealousy can hurt us and hurt others too. But I'm so proud of you, Sarah, for being brave enough to admit your wrongdoing and to make things right. That shows me you want to please God and do the right thing."

Sarah walked over to Ashley and extended her arms. The two best friends fell into a hug. Without hesitation, the other girls walked over to them and threw their arms around them. They all huddled in a huge group hug. Alice eased her way into the group and joined them.

After the embrace, they grinned at Alice. She chuckled. "Well, that's better. Let's go into the kitchen. I believe Jane has prepared some raisin cookies for us."

The girls smiled and started talking excitedly, looking much relieved to have the matter resolved. Alice followed them into the kitchen.

On the way to the cookies, Alice's heart swelled in praise to the God who had made everything right. Things had turned out so much better than she could have hoped, and the girls had learned a valuable lesson, a far better lesson than she could have taught them by herself.

Chapter Eighteen

*L*ouise sat brushing her hair before bed. Her thoughts and emotions tangled together. Whether it stemmed from spending time with Michael and Margaret, she did not know, but lately she had found herself thinking more and more about Eliot. Maybe it was the season. She and Eliot had always enjoyed autumn. She supposed it had something to do with students being back at school, and education being such a huge part of their own lives.

She put her brush down and studied her face in the mirror. Where had the time gone? She hardly knew this woman who stared back at her. If Eliot could see her now, would he still think she was beautiful? She traced the fine wrinkles. *Road maps, Eliot called them*, she remembered with a smile.

She had complained to him one day about the wrinkles forming around her eyes. "My dear, the lines tell us where we have been, whether to valleys of deep sorrow or to rivers of joy. You've been to places of joy. Be glad for them," he had said before planting a kiss upon her forehead. Her hand absently touched the place of his kiss.

Though she missed Eliot deeply, she would not linger in sorrow. They had shared a wonderful life together, and she would not allow the loneliness of their separation to take that away from her. Besides, she knew she would see him again one day.

She retraced the wrinkles around her eyes. "You have certainly enjoyed where you have been, Louise Smith," she said to her reflection, with a forced chuckle. She reached over and opened her jar of face cream and smoothed it over her face and neck. "But honestly," she spoke to her reflection once more, while working the cream into her skin, "you don't have to let everyone know how long ago you were there." She finished her ritual with the face cream and put the lid back on the jar.

Still feeling rather nostalgic, she decided to pull out her picture album. Going through their photographs and reliving their days together always brightened Louise's mood when she missed Eliot. She went to her closet and found the album. With her treasure in hand, she walked over to the bed and eased onto it, preparing herself for a stroll down memory lane.

One by one, she flipped through the photos, thinking on days gone by. She hoped Eliot had thought her a good wife, and that Cynthia thought her a good mother. She had always tried to do her best. Glancing through the photos, she felt that she had spent her life well.

She was getting close to a favorite snapshot, one where she and Eliot posed with a four-year-old Cynthia on a blanket at the park where they had been picnicking. A stranger had snapped the memory for them. And to think Louise had tried to talk Eliot out of it because she disliked having her picture taken.

As Louise flipped through the album, she came upon the page that had always held that very picture, only to discover an empty spot where the picture had been.

"What on earth," she said out loud. She flipped through page after page, trying to see if it had fallen out somehow. She discovered other bare spots in her album where pictures had fallen out or had been removed. But why would someone take her pictures?

Quickly, she rose from the bed and walked over to her closet, checking the shelf and the area beneath the shelf to make sure that the photos had not fallen on the floor. Maybe they had fallen in with some of the other things in her closet. She did not feel up to it now, but she would search out the matter another time. *No need to get yourself worked up*, she told herself. *They have fallen from the album and have somehow managed to get mixed in with some other items.*

Walking back to her bed, she closed her album. She felt sure that she would find those missing pictures before long.

The next day, after helping Jane clean and prepare the Burtons' former room for the next guest, Louise went to the living room to work on her afghan. There she found Margaret relaxing with a magazine.

"Anything interesting?" Louise asked.

"Not really. Michael will be here shortly, and I was just killing time."

"Things seem to be coming along with you two," Louise commented.

"We are happy. I haven't been this happy since . . . since . . ." Margaret's voice trailed off.

"Your husband was alive?"

Margaret stared at her folded hands and nodded.

"I understand," Louise said finally, laying aside her afghan. "I miss my Eliot. I went through some dark days after he died, but I must confess I am happy here with my sisters."

"You have a lovely family," Margaret agreed. "I get along well with my sister, but I couldn't see us working together. We'd probably strangle each other." She laughed.

"Well, as a matter of fact, we were not sure how it would work either. We are all so very different, but somehow it has worked. I can't imagine doing anything else now."

"Tell me about Eliot. Did he share your love for music?"

"Oh my, yes. In fact, he was my music theory teacher in college."

Margaret giggled as if they were in high school sharing a secret. "Really? That's romantic. So he was older than you?"

Louise nodded. "By fifteen years."

"Didn't you say you have a daughter?"

"Yes, Cynthia. She is a children's book editor in Boston."

"You must be very proud of her."

"Indeed, I am," Louise agreed.

"Well, I don't know where this thing is going with Michael and me, but I want to give it a chance and see what happens. We have been granted this moment now. We may not have another opportunity."

"I agree wholeheartedly, Margaret."

Ruth poked her head through the living room entrance. "Am I interrupting anything?" she asked.

"Not at all. Come on in, Ruth," Louise said. When she stepped into view, Louise saw the luggage in her hand. "Ruth, I have dreaded this moment," Louise said, feeling a slight lump in her throat. She had developed quite a fondness for the struggling teacher who now stood before her so full of hope and determination.

"I hate to go, but I'm ready to get back and get to work," Ruth said matter-of-factly.

"Excuse me, Margaret," Louise said as she got up and walked out to the desk to finish up Ruth's final paperwork as the two guests wished each other well.

A few minutes later Ruth turned to Louise and Jane, who had joined her sister by the front door. "Remember what I've told you. I will never forget you," she said, with a wide smile. "I can hardly wait to start on my new mission."

Jane hugged her. "You are a wonderful teacher, Ruth."

Louise hugged her next, "Come back any time you need a rest, dear."

"Thank you all so much for your encouragement and your help."

"Our pleasure, Ruth," Jane said. "Send me an e-mail and let me know when you post on eBay. I'll be sure to watch for you."

Ruth nodded. "Tell Alice I'm sorry I missed her today."

After Ruth finished saying her good-byes, Jane and Louise watched as their new friend walked out the door of the inn, determined to be a better teacher than ever before.

"Dinner was wonderful as usual, Jane," Alice said, dabbing at her mouth with a napkin.

"Jane, I certainly agree," Louise said, looking quite contented.

"You spoil me with your compliments, but I thank you," Jane said, bending down to give them a hug as they sat in their chairs. "Now you stay put while I bring on the dessert."

"Oh dear, I don't think I can eat another bite." Louise patted her stomach.

Jane frowned. "Well, I can set it aside for later if you would prefer."

"Would you mind?" Louise asked.

Alice shook her head. "I'm pretty full myself. I would rather wait, and there is no doubt it will be worth waiting for."

Jane laughed. "It actually tastes rather light. It's a lemon mousse."

Alice and Louise groaned in unison.

"If only I had saved more room. You should have told us, Jane," Alice admonished.

Jane put the dessert back into the refrigerator. "It will keep till you're ready." She brushed her hands together, then took off her apron. "But I'm afraid you will have to get it yourself when you want it. I'm off to Potterston tonight."

Louise and Alice exchanged a glance.

"Well, you certainly seem to enjoy yourself when you go there," Louise said with a bit of prompting in her voice.

"Oh, I do enjoy myself." Jane pulled on her jacket and then grabbed her purse and keys. "Now, you two behave yourselves while I'm gone." She smiled and waved, then headed out the back door.

"There she goes again," Louise said.

"It's a mystery, that's for sure."

"Well, you read mysteries, do you think you could figure this one out?"

Alice looked at Louise to see if she was teasing. She was not. "Wait a minute. Wasn't it you who said Jane is a grown woman and we need to trust her?"

"Oh, I suppose. But are you not the least bit curious?"

"Well, of course I am, but what can I do, short of following her to Potterston?" Alice asked. Her eyes widened at that notion.

"No, Alice. You are absolutely right. She is a grown woman, and we need to let her be to do the things she wants to do without our interference. Father would want us to handle it this way."

Alice grimaced. "Oh, why did you have to make me feel guilty by bringing Father into it?"

When Jane returned home, she joined Alice and Louise in the parlor for dessert.

"I know it's none of my business," Alice began, "but I can't help being a little concerned over Aunt Ethel's visits to those chat rooms on the computer." She shook her head. "It just doesn't sit well with me." Alice took a bite of the lemon mousse. "Exquisite, Jane."

"Thanks." She frowned with thought. "I really don't think you need to worry about Aunt Ethel, Alice. She's just having a little fun," Jane offered, before taking a bite of her own dessert.

"Well, they were talking at work the other day about a woman meeting a man on the Internet and running off and marrying him. A total stranger, mind you." Alice placed her cup back on the saucer. "Why, he could have been a murderer for all that woman knew."

"This dessert is heavenly," Louise whispered with her eyes shut. After she had finished the treat, she said, "What you say is certainly true, Alice. One cannot be too careful. I would hope Aunt Ethel would have sense enough to be cautious about such things."

"You are forgetting that Aunt Ethel already has a special someone. Lloyd, remember?" Jane asked.

Alice thought a moment. "That's true, but another man could turn her head if she's not careful."

"I must say that I am a bit worried too," Louise said, stirring her decaf.

"Well, one thing's for sure," Jane said, putting her coffee cup and dessert dish on the tray, "if you make a big deal about it, Aunt Ethel will be all the more determined to do it." Jane looked at them with an expression that said that they better be cautious about how they might handle this situation.

Alice rolled her eyes. "That's true. The woman is a bit, well, stubborn." She thought a moment. "I could ask Michael to take his laptop back," Alice said, feeling a little devious.

Jane shook her head. "If she wants to do it badly enough, she can find a computer. They're everywhere today, even in the libraries."

"Better she does it here where we can keep an eye on things. Then we will be able to talk to her about it now and then," Louise said like a wise, older sister.

"She'll get tired of it, and it will all be over," Jane encouraged. "You know Aunt Ethel. She goes from one thing to the next, like a butterfly flitting from flower to flower. As soon as something else catches her fancy, she'll be off and running."

The sisters smiled.

"Now, I'd better get these things cleaned up," Jane said, standing and picking up the tray. "That trip to Potterston wore me out tonight."

Alice watched after Jane as she left the room. "Why is it I feel like I don't know anything that's going on around here?"

Louise laughed. "Join the club."

Chapter Nineteen

As Alice walked to the mailbox after work, the autumn chill nipped at her exposed skin, causing her to snuggle into her coat. She could definitely tell winter would soon arrive. Wasting no time, she reached in and pulled out the envelopes, not bothering to look through them as the cold encouraged her to go inside. Practically running to the porch, she tripped on a step and dropped an envelope. She bent over to pick it up and saw that it was addressed to Jane from her former employer in San Francisco. Quickly, Alice stuffed it back into the pile with the other mail and entered the inn.

Once inside, Alice laid the mail on the desk, sneaking a peak at Jane's letter once more. Jane's secrecy lately, her trips to Potterston, and now a letter from San Francisco—what could it all mean?

"Oh, there you are," said Jane, causing Alice to stiffen. Jane laughed. "I'm sorry. I didn't mean to startle you."

"It's all right. I'm just a little jumpy." Alice turned to Jane. "Have you had a nice day?"

Jane shrugged. "Not bad. Louise and I spent the morning cleaning the Sunset Room for the guests who are scheduled to arrive today." Jane reached for the mail.

Alice pulled off her coat. "Were you expecting something in the mail?"

Jane shrugged. "Oh, one never knows," she said rather casually.

Alice pretended to fuss with her coat, but watched Jane when she spotted the envelope. Once she saw it, Jane quickly glanced up at Alice, catching her looking on. Alice coughed and folded her coat. "Well, did you get anything good?" She finished smoothing her coat and looked at Jane.

Jane wrinkled her nose. "Doesn't look like much," she said, tapping the envelope on her palm, as if there was nothing special at all about the contents.

Alice supposed she should let the matter drop, but all this secrecy was beginning to gnaw on her nerves. "I noticed you got a letter from San Francisco." Alice felt ashamed of herself right after she spoke the words. She knew better than to pry.

"Yeah, probably wanting one of my recipes," Jane said, already making her way back to the kitchen, leaving Alice to watch her go.

Try as she might, Alice could not figure out what was going on with her sister. She finally shrugged. No use worrying about it, she would find out when Jane was ready to let them know and not before, unless of course, Alice stumbled upon the answer herself.

∽

After changing from her work clothes into jeans and a sweatshirt, Alice walked into the living room and found Jane sitting beside Ethel on the sofa.

"What are you two doing?" Alice asked as she sat down with her mystery book in hand.

Jane laughed. "I'm watching Aunt Ethel in this over-seventies chat room. It's a hoot."

"Well, you wait till you're seventy, young lady, you won't think it's so funny then," Ethel said with a tinge of defensiveness.

Alice sat aghast. *Aunt Ethel in the chat room again? Should she be going there so often, visiting with strangers?* Alice wanted to warn her aunt of the dangers but knew Ethel would not take kindly to being told what to do.

"You're in a chat room?" Louise asked, joining the others. Her eyebrow rose in that special way of hers when she had a matter of concern on her mind.

Ethel rose to the challenge. "Yes, I am in a chat room. Now don't you start acting like Alice," Ethel said before Louise could comment. "It is perfectly acceptable for me to visit such a place." Her words held a measure of propriety, and her rigid stance said she was in no mood to debate the issue. "I'm meeting nice people and learning about today's world," she quipped.

Alice waited for Ethel to add, "So there."

"Why, I know some people my age who never touch a computer. I say pish-posh." She waved her hand. "We need to be informed. Live in the real world, not hide our heads in the sand."

Jane tried to cover her amusement, but failed miserably. Louise bit her lower lip as if she too was trying to hide a smile. Alice still felt a little uncomfortable with the whole matter. It just upset her for Ethel to converse with total strangers. Of course, she herself was not one to fiddle with computers, other than what she had to do at work, so perhaps she was the one hiding her head in the sand when it came to learning new things. "How does Lloyd feel about you visiting the chat room?" Alice asked, trying to appear casual about the entire affair.

"I haven't told him," Ethel said, lifting her nose slightly. The sisters looked at her.

"Well, after all," she said as she smoothed her skirt, "he doesn't have to know everything I do, does he?" Ethel stared at them. "A woman has a right to her privacy, and I aim to have mine." She jerked her head forward and went back to looking at the computer screen.

Jane patted Ethel's shoulder. "You are absolutely right, Auntie. You are entitled to your privacy, and you don't have to tell Lloyd if you don't want to." Jane looked up at her sisters and winked.

Ethel nodded her head in an "I-told-you-so" fashion to Alice.

Realizing she was getting nowhere with this discussion, Alice decided to pull the bookmark from her mystery and start reading. No sooner had she read through a couple of sentences than someone came through the front door. "I'll get it," she said to Louise who started to get up.

Alice stepped into the foyer to see an older-looking couple standing before her. The man was tall and skinny with a shiny bald head. The plump woman beside him came to just under his shoulders. Short salt and pepper hair curled toward her round, rosy cheeks and fringed just above her twinkling eyes.

"Hello," Alice said, extending her hand to them. "Welcome to Grace Chapel Inn."

"Thank you," they said in unison. The man continued, "We are the Stanfords. I'm Ralph and this here is my wife Bernadine," and he broke into a wide grin.

"Nice to meet you."

"We're on our honeymoon," he said with the utmost pride as he placed his thumbs under the lapels of his coat.

"Well, congratulations. What brought you our way?" Alice wanted to know as she walked over to the desk to check them in.

"We live down south and we read about your town . . ." he scratched his head a moment, and his eyes grew wide with remembrance. "'Quaint,' that's what they called it on the Internet. Bernadine wanted to check it out." He looked at his bride and gave her a squeeze around the shoulders. She looked at him and flushed.

"Good, we're glad you came." Alice handed them their key to the Sunset Room. "I'll show you to your room, and if you would like to come back downstairs after you settle in, I'll introduce you to my sisters, and serve you some tea."

"Oh, I would like that," Bernadine said to Alice and then flashed her husband a cheerful smile.

"Good. Follow me." Alice took them upstairs and opened their door. "If you want to step inside and look around, I'm sure you'll find everything satisfactory. If you should need anything, though, please let us know, and we'll be happy to assist you."

"Thank you. Your home is lovely. I love old Victorian houses. They're kind of, oh, I don't know, mysterious," Bernadine said with a slight giggle.

Alice smiled. "Thank you. I hope you enjoy your stay with us."

Once Alice walked into the living room, the sisters and Ethel looked up.

"Apparently, our guests have arrived." Then after thinking a moment, Louise said, "The Stanfords, I believe?"

Alice nodded. "Yes. Seem like a very nice couple. They're here on their honeymoon."

Louise looked over with surprise.

"Well, how nice they chose to stay here," Jane said.

"That's a shocker," Ethel said. "Most young people want to be where the action is, and well, let's face it, Acorn Hill doesn't have a whole lot of action—unless, of course, you count our festivals. We can throw a party with the best of them during a festival."

"Well, this isn't exactly a young couple," Alice advised, gathering everyone's full attention. "I'd say they look to be in their seventies."

"Hey, maybe they've been to your chat room," Jane said with a nudge to her aunt.

Ethel let out a smile herself.

"I guess I'd better get us some sandwiches before you have to go to church for your ANGELs meeting," Jane said.

"I don't have ANGELs tonight," Alice said. "I can stay home and help look after our guests."

"Oh good. Did you offer them tea?" Jane asked.

"Yes, I did. I believe they'll be down once they settle in."

Louise picked up her knitting. "I will look forward to meeting the Stanfords."

"You know, Michael and Margaret might enjoy meeting them," Jane said.

Alice looked up from her book. "I think you're right. What is Margaret up to today, does anyone know?"

"I believe I heard Margaret say they were going to spend the day in Potterston, doing some shopping or some such thing," Louise said as she worked away on her knitting.

"Perhaps she'll return while the Stanfords are joining us for tea."

Jane nodded. "Speaking of which, I'd better get in there and pull something together, or none of us will eat." She jumped up from the sofa and headed toward the kitchen.

"Do you want some help, Jane?" Alice asked.

"No, thanks, I've got it covered," Jane called over her shoulder.

Alice slipped into the world of her mystery, Louise clacked away on her knitting, and Ethel went back to her chat room while Jane gathered the refreshments. The fireplace crackled with dancing flames and warmed the room, giving it a homey feel. The wind howled outside, occasionally rattling the windows, making Alice want to cuddle into a blanket. So cozy. Contentment filled her. She could remember so many times like this before with her father.

Daniel Howard would bring a book from his study and join her in the living room. Alice would be lost in her mystery, while he studied commentaries on the Scriptures. The same fireplace that warmed the sisters now had warmed Alice and her father many days ago.

She still found it hard to believe he was gone. So many times she expected to see him come around a corner or pull a book from a shelf in his study. How she missed him.

"What are you thinking about?" Louise asked, her knitting needles lying silent in her lap.

Alice glanced up. "What?"

"You have not turned your page for some time, so I assume you are thinking about something. Are you all right?"

Alice smiled at her perceptive sister. "Yes. I was just thinking about Father."

Louise smiled. "Times like this make me think of him too. Remember how we all used to gather around and have checkers tournaments?"

Alice nodded. "I remember. Father always won," she said with a mock frown.

Louise chuckled. "He could beat the best of them, that is certain," Louise said, no doubt referring to the men who bravely took up the challenge of playing their father in a game of checkers.

"So is that where I get my talent?" Jane asked, entering the room with a tray full of tea fixings and pound cake.

Louise raised her eyebrows. "And you believe you are now the new checker champion, is that it?"

Jane shrugged. "Well, I hate to brag, but I have won a number of games."

"*Two* is a number," Alice replied.

"Your mother used to get stirred up when she would play checkers with Daniel. Most times she couldn't beat him, no matter how hard she tried," Ethel said with a laugh.

A noise behind her caused Alice to turn and look. The Stanfords walked into the room. The new bride wore a contented smile that echoed the one on her husband's face.

"Hello, everyone," Ralph Stanford said good-naturedly.

Alice got up and walked over to them. She made the introductions and everyone settled down for refreshments.

"So when did you get married?" Ethel asked.

Bernadine smiled and blushed at her groom, waiting for him to answer. He finished a bite of his cake and said, "We were married three days ago."

"Good for you," said Ethel.

"So tell us your story. How did you two meet?" Alice asked, then thinking herself too bold, quickly added, "If you don't mind telling us."

The couple fairly beamed with delight. "Not at all,"

Ralph said. "We met at Bernadine's church. I was visiting my cousin, who lived a couple of hours from my home. He introduced us and we hit it off. Dated a couple of months and here we are." The ladies must have shown their surprise for he promptly added, "When you're our age, you don't have time for long engagements."

Everyone laughed.

Ralph squeezed Bernadine's hand and smiled. "We couldn't be happier."

"Well, I practically had to hog-tie him to get him to ask me," Bernadine said with a nudge to Ralph's side.

Ralph rolled his eyes and smirked. "I asked her to marry me *two months* after we met. Would you call that being hog-tied?"

Alice enjoyed their lighthearted bantering.

Bernadine smiled. "Well, you see, I knew he was going to ask me, because he had told my brother, and my brother told me."

"You just can't trust the in-laws," Ralph interjected.

"So, I kept waiting and waiting. He'd come close once or twice. Then he'd back away. So I finally said, 'Ralph, are you going to hem and haw all day, or are you going to ask me to marry you?'"

Ralph shrugged. "I guess you can see I finally gave in."

Alice chuckled along with the others.

"Do you have grown children?" Ethel asked, seemingly not worrying in the least about prying into their personal lives.

They both nodded. A shadow crossed Ralph's face. "Yep, those kids sure gave us a struggle at first." He scratched his bald head. "They sure did. But once they realized they couldn't change our plans, they stopped trying to fight us, and now they have accepted our marriage. They all showed up for the wedding. We weren't at all convinced that was going to happen. Gave us lots of hugs and kisses. One of the best days of our lives, I expect," he said, pausing a moment.

Bernadine nodded in agreement.

"It was just the gift we hoped for," he said smiling once again at his bride.

Alice thought of Margaret and Michael. If their relationship happened to grow to that point, she hoped their children would give them the same assurance.

"Well, enough about us. Tell us about your inn and how you decided to start a bed and breakfast," Ralph said before taking another bite of his treat.

Louise explained their story of Daniel's passing and the sisters having to decide what to do with the house, and how the whole concept had evolved from there.

"So you gave up your chef's job and moved here from San Francisco?" Bernadine asked Jane.

Jane nodded with a smile.

"And you moved from Philadelphia?" Bernadine asked Louise.

Louise nodded.

"Sounds like you've had some upheaval in your lives too," Bernadine said.

"And some people say older folks can't change. I think we've all proven them wrong," Ralph said with a laugh.

"Life doesn't stop just because we're older. There is no time like the present to live," he said, looking to Bernadine. "And that's exactly what we're doing."

Chapter Twenty

Glancing at her watch the next day, Louise pulled off her glasses and folded away her afghan and knitting needles for the time being. She had a piano student due to arrive soon, and she decided to make her way to the parlor. Rising from the sofa, she walked through the foyer, where she met the Stanfords as they were leaving. "Going out?" she asked in polite conversation.

"Yes, we're going to Potters—" Bernadine seemed to search for the town's proper name.

"Potterston?"

"Yes, that's it," Bernadine beamed. "We heard it's a nice town fairly close to here, so we thought we would check it out."

"What that means for me is a day of shopping," Ralph said with a playful groan.

"I am sure you will have a lovely time," Louise encouraged. She smiled as she watched them walk out of the inn together. *They are a sweet couple.*

Louise slid onto the piano bench. Her fingers danced

across the keyboard in a light melody, which then built into crescendos and decrescendos as her heart dictated. Though there was no denying that she often missed Eliot, when her fingers drifted along the keys she could almost imagine him by her side on the bench, eyes closed, his expression caught up in the mood of the music. Yes, as long as she had her music, Eliot would never be far away.

As the melody filled the parlor, Louise failed to notice when her student entered the room until the child tapped Louise on the shoulder. Louise's fingers stopped abruptly.

"I'm sorry, Mrs. Smith, I called out to you, but you didn't hear me," the little girl said.

Louise held her hand to her chest. "That is perfectly all right." She waited a moment to catch her breath, then scooted over on the bench to allow her student to sit.

Louise waited while her student put her music book on the piano and turned to the appropriate page. Louise smiled to herself. Yes, she was thankful for her music and for her memories.

"I'm glad you like the shrimp bisque, Michael," Jane said, ladling a second helping into his bowl.

"It's delicious." Michael took another spoonful. "I'm delighted that you invited us to dinner. Not that I mind eating out once in a while, but I sure enjoy a home-cooked meal." He looked at Margaret and she smiled.

Jane wondered if Margaret liked to cook, but she did not want to be so bold as to ask.

"Have you had a chance to get to know the Stanfords?" Jane asked Michael and Margaret, who had met them earlier in the day.

"Yes, wonderful people," Margaret said.

"Real nice folks," added Michael.

"They should be getting back here soon. Perhaps they could join all of us for dessert in the parlor. That is, if there is enough?" Louise looked at Jane.

"Oh sure. I just made some cookies. There's plenty for everyone. You know I always make extra," Jane said with a wink.

As if on cue, the Stanfords came through the front door. Jane met a blast of cold air as she walked out to greet them. "Hello," she said, rubbing the chill from her arms.

"Good evening." Bernadine shivered slightly, then fluffed her hair back into place. "It's really windy out tonight."

"And cold. I could hear the wind howling. I suppose we're working our way into winter." Jane said, still rubbing her arms.

Ralph winced. "Oh, don't say that. Remember, we come from the South. Course, we get snow every now and then, but it's pretty rare. It sure is nothing compared to Pennsylvania."

"I suspect you'll want to fly south before it gets too cold up here."

"Oh well, the Mrs. here can keep me warm," Ralph teased, giving Bernadine a sideways hug.

"Ralph!" Bernadine said, pretending to scold him. She hit him playfully on his arm. He winced and held it as if in great pain.

Bernadine showed Jane a what-can-I-do look and let out a laugh.

Jane smiled. "Hey, we're getting ready to have some cookies and coffee or tea in the parlor and wanted to invite you folks to join us in, say, fifteen minutes, if you would care to."

Ralph looked at Bernadine who nodded. "Sounds good to us," he said with a wide grin.

"Great, we'll see you then." Jane turned and joined the others in the dining room.

Alice helped Jane get the tea and coffee ready for their guests. Once Jane was satisfied with the arrangement of peppermint snowball cookies on a decorative plate, she placed it on a tray. Then she and Alice headed toward the parlor.

"Oh, those look delicious, Jane," Alice said as she carried the tray.

Jane looked at the cookies, feeling pleased with how they had turned out. "I have to admit I snitched one, and they are pretty good," Jane said.

"Thanks for joining us," Jane said to the Stanfords when they entered the parlor. Once Alice set the tray down, the sisters went to work serving cups of coffee or tea, along with dishes of cookies.

Jane glanced around the room. It did her heart good to see people enjoying her cooking efforts. She knew God had given her the gift of hospitality. There was nothing she enjoyed more than sharing her culinary treats with others.

"So how long have you two been married?" Ralph asked Michael.

Jane felt a little uncomfortable for Michael and Margaret, though she thought Ralph's assumption an easy one to make.

Michael cleared his throat while Margaret fidgeted with her fingers in her lap. "Um, we're not married."

Ralph looked surprised. "Oh, sorry, you just sort of had that look about you, like you were real happy together and all."

"Oh, we are that. Happy, I mean," Michael said with a twinkle in his eye as he looked toward Margaret.

Ralph and Bernadine smiled. "Well, don't wait too long or she might get away," he warned. Ralph reached over and squeezed his wife's hand.

Michael smiled and Margaret blushed.

Jane thought both couples perfectly charming.

Bernadine turned to Louise. "I was noticing the books you have in your study. Alice told us about your father being a minister and all. He's sure got a lot of good books."

Before long, the ladies started talking about books, and then their conversation drifted to crafts and knitting. Louise offered to show some of the inn's special items, and Margaret and Bernadine accepted her offer, leaving Michael, Alice, Jane and Ralph together.

"So what are you waiting for?" Ralph grinned at Michael.

Though the question seemed to surprise Michael, without hesitation, he answered. "The kids."

Alice and Jane shared a glance. Alice looked as uncomfortable as Jane was beginning to feel.

"The kids?" Ralph asked. "Don't tell me your kids are squawking about the two of you the way our kids did about us."

Michael shrugged and threw him a what-can-we-do-about-it look.

Ralph straightened himself on his chair. "Now, lookey here, these kids need to know it's your life. Do you love her?" His question was straightforward and to the point.

Jane looked at her nails, and Alice flushed. Jane wondered if they should excuse themselves so that the men could talk alone, but the timing felt a little awkward, so she stayed seated and pretended not to pay attention.

Ralph must have noticed their uneasiness. He rubbed the back of his neck and said in his slow, slightly Southern drawl, "There I go again being too nosy. Bernadine's trying to teach me about those things." He took in a deep breath. "I grew up in a family where we didn't beat around the bush. If we had a question, we asked it." He shrugged, then added, "I'm sorry if I'm out of line."

Jane felt a sense of relief that Ralph had clarified things, though Michael did not seem to mind at all.

"No, that's fine, Ralph. And the answer to your question is yes, I do love her. I hadn't really called it that until this very moment. The idea scared me a little bit, I guess." He stared into his coffee cup. "But I can't let her get away from me again."

"Then you'd better not let those kids tell you what to do, or you'll regret it all your days."

Michael looked almost relieved. Jane thought perhaps it was just what he needed to hear, when she noted that a look of determination had washed over him.

"You are absolutely right. I can't risk losing her just to keep them happy. They have lives of their own, and, well, I'm not dead, so why can't I enjoy the years I have left?"

Ralph slapped his knee. "Now you're talkin'," he said with a laugh.

"Talking about what?" Bernadine wanted to know when the three of them came back into the parlor.

"Well now, dear, there are some things a man's just gotta keep to himself," Ralph said with a wink.

Alice and Jane laughed along with Michael. Jane saw Michael and Margaret exchange a glance, and she wondered if Margaret realized fully how Michael truly felt. *Does Margaret know he loves her and might ask her to marry him? Will their love help them overcome any conflict their children could, and most assuredly would, put in their way?* For their sakes, Jane hoped so.

She offered a silent prayer for the couple that she had grown to consider true friends. Her prayer also covered their children, asking God to help them to look at their parents' situation without regard to themselves. She prayed that God would help them to see where they needed to change. She knew it was a tall order, but after all, God was in the business of changing people. Her own life was proof of that.

Chapter Twenty-One

The next day, after finishing some paperwork, Louise stepped out onto the porch into the sunshine. She regretted that Alice had to fill in at work on such a beautiful autumn day, washed clean by the rain of the previous evening. Louise stood on the porch and looked around. As far as she could see, Acorn Hill fairly sparkled beneath the blazing light of the sun.

Without another thought she slipped into the house and pulled a light jacket from the closet, then walked back outside and sat on the porch swing. Perhaps she would go in to get some tea later. For now, she listened to the bird-song that called from their maple tree in the front yard. She closed her eyes, relishing the moment of solitude, wondering why she did not take the time more often to do this very thing.

She rocked the swing gently back and forth. Jane was right. Time did slip by quickly. It seemed only yesterday that she and her sisters had run through this same yard, laughing and playing as little girls. Her heart warmed with the memory of her mother and father together on the porch swing.

More birds gathered in the maple tree, chattering most likely about the need to move south before winter. Louise smiled.

She thought of Ruth Kincade. Like Ruth, Louise wanted to make her life count for something. Even little Annie Burton was making a difference in her world. Louise wondered about herself. Was she making a difference? Oh, she helped around the inn and she worked with children, but was that enough? She prayed so.

A woman in her sixties, she had been around to see many changes in the world, some good, some not so good. But what about her small corner of the world? Did it matter that she had passed through it? Had she hugged enough? Loved enough? Laughed enough? In her heart she felt like a young woman, still full of life, still wanting to offer much to the world in which she had been placed. But her body told her what her heart refused to believe. She was not young anymore. Was she too old to offer anything significant?

A rustle in the tree caught her attention. She turned her gaze toward the bird that left the moving branches, watching as the tiny creature glided happily along on a breeze, then, when the wind died down, pumping its wings to hold steady, swooping and dipping here and there until it finally fluttered out of sight.

That was like her life. She slipped into this world, carried along by her Heavenly Father's strong hand, holding her steady when needed, using her to touch a life here and there, to make a difference, until one day she would flutter out of sight.

That was the key. As long as it was called "Today," no matter how old one might be, there was time to make a difference. Doing the best one could with the gifts God had given was all anyone could do.

"There you are," Jane said, stepping onto the porch, rousing Louise from her mental wanderings. "I looked everywhere for you and couldn't imagine where you had gone."

Louise flashed a smile. "I am sorry. The sunshine called out to me this morning."

Jane walked over and joined Louise on the swing. "I understand," she said rather pensively, looking out on the grounds. "It is beautiful," she added almost in a whisper.

The two sisters rocked gently, each lost in the wonder of the season, the quiet of the moment and the comfort of one another's presence.

The sound of a car engine caught their attention. Louise turned to see that a black utility vehicle had pulled up to the inn. "Do we have new guests coming?"

"No, not for a couple more weeks," Jane said.

"I wonder who could be calling."

"Well, there is one way to find out," Jane said, rising from the swing.

Louise followed suit as two men approached the inn.

"Hello," the younger one said, as they climbed the steps. He pumped Louise's hand with gusto. "My name is Greg Ballard, and this is my friend Roy Ingram." The sharp-looking young man stood before her dressed in crisp khakis and a blue oxford button-down shirt with a maroon V-neck sweater over it. The older man beside him was dressed in a denim western shirt complete with silver snaps instead of buttons, and a pair of jeans. His features made Louise think of Colonel Sanders of Kentucky Fried Chicken fame.

"Hello. May I help you?" Louise asked. Jane stood at her side also greeting the men.

"My mother is staying here as one of your guests, and we wanted to speak with her."

Louise was puzzled. "Your mother . . ." then as if a light bulb had turned on, she realized that this was Margaret Ballard's son. Oh dear, she hoped that this was not a bad sign. "Of course, please follow me. I believe she is in." Louise led the way. "If you will wait a moment, I will check to see if she is in her room."

Jane ushered the two men into the living room as her sister made her way up the stairs.

She tapped on the door a couple of times and waited. Footsteps made their way to the door. Margaret looked surprised when she opened the door. "Hello, Louise."

Louise took a deep breath, not knowing if what she was about to announce would be good or bad news. "Margaret, your son Greg is here to see you."

Margaret's eyes grew wide. "Greg? Here?" She bit her lip and thought for a moment.

"He has someone with him."

Margaret's gazed darted to her. "A man?" She looked worried.

"Yes, a Mr. Ingram?"

Margaret groaned. "Oh, why is he doing this to me?" She stared at the floor, then looked back at Louise. "Will you come in here a moment, Louise?"

Louise stepped inside Margaret's room.

"Roy Ingram is the man I've been telling you and your sisters about, the man with whom my son is trying to set me up." Margaret began to pace the floor. "What should I do? I don't want to make a scene with my son and this man. He's nice and all, but I love Michael." She stopped in her tracks as if the impact of what she had said hit her cold. She turned to Louise. "Yes, I love Michael." A broad smile covered her face. "I've never said that until this very moment—well, except for when I was seventeen."

Louise smiled at Margaret, understanding her precisely: Louise had once gone through the same thing with Eliot, not realizing she was in love, though her heart had tried to convince her that it was true.

Margaret took a deep breath. "Well, I guess I have to face the music. I love my son, but, well, he'll just have to get used to the idea that I'm in love with Michael."

Louise patted Margaret's shoulder. "I'll be praying for you, dear."

"Thank you, Louise." Then after a moment of hesitation, Margaret blurted, "Will you stay in the room with us, Louise?"

Louise felt uneasy with Margaret's request. "Well, Margaret, I—"

"Please, I don't want to be alone. It's all so awkward."

The look on Margaret's face softened Louise, though her better judgment urged her to go upstairs to her own room. She let out a sigh. "Well, if you really think that is best. I will feel terribly in the way, I am afraid."

Margaret touched Louise's arm. "Oh, not at all, you'll be with me, my support. Your being there will make all the difference."

Louise groaned inwardly. *I want to make a difference, but do I have to do it right this minute, Lord? Like this?*

Margaret seemed to feel much better after Louise had agreed to stay with her. Louise wished she could feel the same. *Well, if I tried harder, maybe I could be a little more helpful in this making-a-difference process. After all, I may not always see how God is using me. I mean, it is not necessarily in ways I plan. The important thing is for me to be obedient to the Lord's inspiration.*

The two made their way down the stairs, Louise lost in prayer, and Margaret no doubt wondering what to say to her visitors.

Once Margaret stepped into the living room, Greg stood up to meet her and Roy followed Greg's example.

"Hi, Mom," Greg said, his smile wide and charming.

"Hello, Greg." Margaret placed a kiss on her son's cheek. "Hello, Roy." Her voice was cordial but not overly so.

Roy responded with a shy smile and a nod.

"Might I bring you gentlemen some tea?" Louise asked.

Margaret threw her a don't-be-gone-long look. "I think a glass of water would be fine for me, Louise, thank you."

The men also wanted water.

Louise, thankful for the brief reprieve, headed to the kitchen. She wondered where Jane had disappeared. As Louise gathered the glasses and filled them with ice, Jane stepped out of the pantry.

"There you are."

Jane smiled. "Just putting some things in order."

"Do you know who that man is with Margaret's son?"

Jane shook her head.

"He is the man she told us about, the man who her son is trying to get Margaret to date."

Jane's mouth formed a perfect O.

Louise winced and nodded. "Exactly." Louise retrieved a pitcher from the refrigerator and poured water into the glasses.

"Did they ask for something to drink?" Jane asked.

Louise nodded.

Jane perched her fists on her hips. "Well, how do you like that? They told me they didn't want anything."

Louise shrugged. "I guess they worked up a thirst waiting for Margaret." Louise placed the cold glasses on a tray. "And do you know what else?"

Jane shook her head.

Louise turned to her and whispered, "To make matters worse, Margaret wants me to stay in there with her."

"Oh, I'm sorry, Louise."

"Just pray," Louise said, as she carried the tray into the living room.

"I guess you're wondering why we're here," Greg said, rubbing his hands together like a little boy about to reveal a secret.

"Well, the thought had crossed my mind, Greg," Margaret said. The tone in her voice held a hint of warning, which her son obviously ignored.

"Roy had mentioned to me the trouble the two of you had been having getting together, and I thought since your schedule is a little more relaxed while you are here, maybe today would be a good day for you to visit awhile. He had the day off and it seemed like a good idea. I'll just go into Potterston for the day. I have some things I want to do there, and that will you give you two time to get to know each other." Greg flashed his mother another big smile while he reached for a glass from the tray Louise held out to him. "Thank you."

Margaret looked first at Roy, who had unsnapped the flap of his shirt pocket and began to flip it back and forth between his fingers. She looked back at Greg. "I feel bad that you have made the trip here, Greg, because I'm really quite busy today."

"Surely, you can afford a few hours for Mr. Ingram since he made the effort to come here, Mother," Greg said. "The drive from Philadelphia does take time." It was hard for him to conceal his impatience.

Louise tried to busy herself with her knitting, but she could definitely sense the manipulation Greg was using on his mother. It seemed Margaret could see through him too.

Roy now looked over at Margaret, hopeful, his eyes almost puppy-dog-like, his fingers still holding his pocket flap for moral support. Louise did not miss the exchange. She feared that Margaret would lose her nerve.

Margaret sighed. "I can spend a couple of hours over lunch, Mr. Ingram, but I'm afraid that's all I can spare. I have to take my sister into physical therapy, and afterward, I have plans with another gentleman friend."

Louise looked up in time to see Greg run his hand through his hair. He let out an exasperated sigh. Margaret gave him an apologetic look, but her expression also indicated she would stand her ground. Louise felt a degree of compassion for Mr. Ingram, who seemed to be unaware of the emotions passing between mother and son. He could not stop fidgeting with the flap on his shirt pocket, as if that was the safest place for his attention at present.

"I really think you should call off your other plans, Mom. After all, Mr. Ingram and I have taken time from our busy schedules."

"Greg, I so appreciate you and Mr. Ingram taking the time to come and see me," Margaret said with sincere sweetness in her voice, and a renewed strength, "but as I said, I do have plans through this evening. I would love for you both to meet Michael if you can stay."

Greg would not budge from his position. It was obvious he had a mission, and he did not want his plans altered in any way.

"Is that your final answer on the matter, Mother?"

"I'm afraid so, Greg."

"Come on, Roy," Greg said in a none-too-happy tone.

Roy smoothed the flap on his pocket, snapped it back, and rose from the chair. He nodded when he walked past Margaret, saying nothing.

"Where are you going, Greg?" asked his mother. "Are we going out for lunch?"

"Sorry, Mom. It appears your schedule is pretty full today, so we'll just head back. I'm sorry we bothered you."

Oh, good use of guilt manipulation, thought Louise.

He turned to Louise, "Thank you, ma'am, for the water."

Roy turned and smiled at Louise, then hurried to catch up with Greg.

Margaret held herself perfectly still until the car pulled away from the inn. Then she released a frustrated sigh. Louise went over to comfort her. "Things will be all right," Louise said, praying it would be true.

"Why can't he understand? I don't want to hurt Greg and that nice Mr. Ingram. Why is he forcing me to do this?"

"Just remember what Mr. Stanford told Michael. You

have to follow your hearts and live your own lives. Your children cannot run them for you," Louise said.

They talked awhile longer, trying to sort through the matter, until they heard the back door open and shut, and soon Ethel stepped into the room. Louise looked at Margaret, and both seemed to agree that it was best to drop the matter. The last thing they needed was to fuel Ethel's curiosity with more gossip material. After all, Ethel's audience had grown from Acorn Hill to the World Wide Web.

Chapter Twenty-Two

After running several errands in the afternoon, Louise made her last stop at the post office, where Lloyd Tynan came up to her. Dressed in a gray flannel suit and red bow tie, Lloyd cut quite a dashing figure.

"Louise, I need some advice. Luckily, I spotted you coming in here. You've got to help me," he said between short breaths.

"What is it, Lloyd?"

"Well," he checked the area around them as if he were on some secret mission, "I have to ask you something."

Louise had never seen the mayor so flustered. She noticed a slight flush on his cheeks. "Are you all right?" she asked with a touch of concern.

"I'm fine. Listen, Ethel, she . . . well, um, she's been so generous helping me out at the office lately, I wanted to do something extra nice for her. You know, buy her a special gift." He whispered the last words, Louise figured, so that the two patrons and the postal worker would not be privy to their conversation.

Louise calmed down. So that was it. Amusement replaced her fears.

"Anyway, I don't have a clue what to get her for a gift. Since I want something special, and since you and your sisters know her best, I thought maybe you could give me some ideas."

"I see. Well, I will need to give the matter some thought, Lloyd, but I can get back to you in the next couple of days."

He looked around again, giving Louise that feeling of being caught up in an espionage thriller. "Okay, that will be fine. I appreciate it," he called over his shoulder as he left the building. Louise purchased some stamps and then headed for home.

"Hi, Louise. What's new?" Jane asked as Louise entered the inn.

Louise explained the problem that Lloyd was having to Jane, and when Alice stepped into the foyer, Louise explained it again.

"Well, there's a hat Aunt Ethel's taken a fancy to in Potterston," Alice said.

"I know she's been wanting a bread-baking machine. Said she's finished with making bread the old-fashioned way," Jane said with a twinkle in her eye. "She's really gone high tech."

"Indeed." Louise tapped her finger against her lips. "No, I do not think those will work. He is looking for something really special." Louise put the stamps in the top drawer of the front desk. "How about we think on it and get together to talk about it in a little while?"

Jane and Alice agreed.

Later, Ethel breezed in through the back door. "Hello all," she announced as she made her way to the living room.

"Hello, Auntie," Jane said, lifting her gaze from the pages of her magazine.

Alice and Louise chimed in with their greetings. Alice sat reading a mystery. Ethel, taking a seat nearby, clucked her tongue. "I don't know how you can read that stuff, Alice. Doesn't it give you nightmares?"

Alice glanced up. "Not at all. It's like a puzzle, and I like trying to figure out the missing pieces before the author tells me."

Ethel waved her hand. "Well, I think I'll stick to my homemaker magazines and farm news." Ethel turned her attention to Louise. "You still working on that afghan, Louise? Land's sake, I'd never have the patience for it. I would go to the General Store, buy an afghan and be done with it," she said to anyone who would listen.

"Oh, but Auntie, those afghans aren't nearly as beautiful as the ones Louise makes," Jane said, her tone a trifle defensive.

"That's true enough," Ethel agreed.

"Besides that, I enjoy making them. It gives me something to do with my hands," Louise interjected.

"That's good, I suppose. You know what the Bible says, 'Idle hands are the devil's workshop.'"

"Auntie, that's not in the Bible," Jane corrected.

Ethel looked positively aghast. Louise had seen Ethel wear that expression before, when she had found out the sisters were turning their home into a bed and breakfast.

"You don't mean it?" Ethel held her hand against her chest from the sheer distress of the revelation.

"I'm afraid so," Alice said.

"Land's sake, I've been quoting that for years, all the while thinking it was in the Good Book."

The sisters shook their heads.

After the moment of shock wore off, Ethel finally shrugged. "Well, it's a good one. It ought to be in there."

"There is a verse close to that, Aunt Ethel," Louise said, treading lightly. "In I Timothy 5:13, it says, 'Besides, they get into the habit of being idle and going about from house to house. And not only do they become idlers, but also gossips and busybodies, saying things they ought not to.' I guess the lesson is either way, it is best to stay busy and keep out of trouble."

"Well said, Louise," Ethel stated matter-of-factly.

The sisters shared a knowing glance and hid their

amusement. It seemed that Ethel was the only one who did not see herself in that verse. Louise supposed most folks had trouble recognizing themselves in a negative light.

"And speaking of idle hands, where is that laptop?" Ethel wanted to know.

"It's over here," Jane said, hauling it over to Ethel. "I wanted to keep things picked up, so I tucked it away."

Ethel's eyes lit up with the sight of her electronic friend. She opened the laptop and punched the power button. Drumming her fingers on her leg, she waited for everything to boot up.

Jane and Alice went back to their reading, and Louise went to work on her afghan while Ethel worked her way to the over-seventies chat room.

Someone stepped through the front door of the inn.

"I wonder who that could be," Louise commented.

"Hello, ladies. I wonder if any of you have seen Ethel?" Lloyd asked when he entered the room.

"Well, I'm right here, Lloyd, are you blind?" Ethel said with a chuckle.

"Oh, I didn't see you there, Ethel." He slipped onto the seat beside her. "What are you doing?"

Alice and Louise looked at each other, then over to Ethel. Louise wondered if she was already in the chat room and what Lloyd would think of it.

"Oh, I was just visiting in a chat room," she said clicking it off. "Nothing important."

"What on earth were you doing in a chat room, Ethel?" Lloyd asked incredulously.

"I told you I've been learning about the computer," she said a bit defensively.

"Well, I know, but a chat room?"

"After all, I rather enjoy conversing with those people. I've exchanged recipes with one lady, and a gentleman told me where I could get discount coupons for walking shoes. No harm in that." She straightened herself and lifted her head a bit piously.

Lloyd scratched his head. "No, I guess not. Just surprised me, that's all."

Ethel changed the subject. "What are you doing here, Lloyd?"

"I was looking for you."

"I know that," she said with a touch of impatience. "Why were you looking for me?"

"Thought I'd see if you wanted to go to Potterston for Italian food."

Ethel considered a moment. "Well, I would need to go home and change clothes first. This skirt is a mite uncomfortable." Ethel tugged at her waistband.

"That will be fine. I'll just wait here—if that will be okay with these ladies."

"Of course it is," Jane answered.

Ethel heaved herself up from the sofa. "All right. You be good to my nieces, you hear me," she said.

"I'll do my best, Ethel," Lloyd promised.

Lloyd walked her to the back door. Louise heard the door close, and then Lloyd returned to the living room.

"What is on your mind, Lloyd?" Louise asked as she watched him pace.

He turned around. "I guess you heard Ethel talk about visiting that chat room?"

Louise hoped he was not going to ask them to stop her. She did not feel it was their place to interfere with Ethel's personal life.

"We were aware of it, all right," Alice said, her voice heavy with disapproval.

Lloyd turned to Alice. "Did Louise tell you ladies that I wanted to get a special gift for Ethel for all she's been doing to help me out at the office lately?"

Jane and Alice smiled. "Yes, she told us."

"Well, I'm thinking if I could find out which chat room she was visiting, maybe I could sneak in there myself and talk to her, get an idea of what she might like for a present."

Louise was not at all sure if she liked the idea: It sounded rather devious. "Well, I don't know, Lloyd."

He held up his hand. "Now, I know what you're thinking,

Louise. You think it's a little underhanded, but I'm only doing it to find out a way to make her happy."

Jane piped up. "I think it's a great idea," she said, her eyes sparkling. "The hard part will be in getting her to tell a perfect stranger the truth about what she likes."

Lloyd made a face. "Hadn't thought about that. You're probably right. Maybe she wouldn't tell me." His eyes lit up like he had an idea. "Hey, if I pose as a woman, she might be more willing to talk."

Alice laughed and put her book down. "Well, there's no harm in trying. If she's going to be hanging out in the chat room, she may as well be talking to you."

"You feeling like a mother hen, Alice?" Lloyd asked.

She shrugged. "Just want to be careful, that's all."

Right then Wendell came over and curled up in Alice's lap. Jane laughed.

"That Wendell does as he pleases, and it's as though we have no choice in the matter whatsoever," Alice said.

Lloyd grinned. "Cats do seem to have a mind of their own." He made his way back into the kitchen.

Alice stroked Wendell until he settled into a rhythmic purr.

"Here she comes," Lloyd said as though he were at a surprise birthday party. "So will you ladies find out what chat room Ethel frequents, and I will visit her there."

"I already know the chat room," Jane said, putting aside her magazine.

"What is it?" he asked eagerly.

"An 'Over-Seventies Chat Room.'"

"Really?"

"That's the one. I'll write down its Internet address." Jane crossed her heart and held up her hand.

"Great. I'll plan on it then. You all have been a great help. Thanks."

He quickly sat back in his chair just as Ethel came through the back door. She made her way into the living room. "I'm ready to go," she announced.

Louise glanced over at the computer, thinking how the world had changed during the last twenty years. Technology had opened a whole new world. She hoped it was a good thing for Ethel and Lloyd.

Margaret stepped into the inn and pulled off her jacket.

Alice turned to see her. "Well, hello. I was just on my way to the kitchen to make some tea. Want to join me?"

"Sounds heavenly."

"How was your day?" Alice asked, lifting the teakettle and filling it at the tap.

"I had a nice time with Wilma. I took her out to eat,

and we visited awhile at her place. Physical therapy is really helping her make progress. I'll be out of here before you know it."

Once the kettle was filled, Alice placed it on the stove and turned on the flame. "We are certainly in no hurry to have you leave us, Margaret. You have been a joy," Alice said.

"You all are very kind, Alice. I will never forget you for that." She shrugged, "Besides, I live in Philadelphia, that's not so far away that I can't come back to visit."

Alice sat down at the kitchen table with Margaret. "That will suit us fine. By the way, we would love to have Wilma come back and visit longer when she is feeling better."

Margaret seemed surprised. "Really?"

Alice chuckled. "Does that seem odd to you?"

"Well, let's face it, Wilma is not the easiest person in the world to get along with." She laughed.

"Aw, she's fine. Remember, we have Aunt Ethel."

Margaret's hand quickly smothered her giggle.

Alice thought a moment, wondering how to approach the subject of Margaret's son. "How have you been, I mean, since that confrontation with your son?"

Margaret let out a sigh. "It's just so hard. I know he means well, Alice, and I love him dearly, but I'm not ready to throw away my chance for happiness with Michael simply because my son wants me to, you know?"

Alice nodded. "Have you told Michael?"

"Yes. I decided we should be honest and forthright with each other." Margaret crossed her arms over her chest. "We're both frustrated with the whole matter. His daughter, my son." She shrugged. "I love him, but I want our children's blessings too."

"And if they won't give them to you?" Alice asked.

Margaret shook her head. "I don't know. I just don't know."

The teakettle called out from the stove, causing Alice to jump into action, retrieving cups and saucers, brewing tea, gathering sugar and cream. Once the brewing had finished, she poured them each a cup, and they added sugar and cream according to their own tastes.

"If only I could see what the future held for us." Margaret stared into the cup cradled in her hands.

"I think that's best left to the Lord," Alice said thoughtfully, musing on her own life. "All we can do is pray and leave it there."

"Of course, you're right." Margaret took a drink from her cup, then added thoughtfully, "I just pray that my future includes Michael Lawton."

Chapter Twenty-Three

*O*nce Louise had finished putting her room in order, she went down to the kitchen for something to eat. Not knowing Jane's plans for lunch, Louise decided to satisfy her hunger with a light snack.

Rummaging through the refrigerator, Louise pulled out a wedge of cheese and some grapes and placed them on a sheet of wax paper on the counter. After cutting a couple of slices of cheese, she arranged them on a plate. She washed off a cluster of grapes at the sink, added them to her plate, then got the milk out of the refrigerator. She walked over to the cupboard and reached in for a glass, and a picture fell onto the counter.

How odd that a picture would be in the kitchen cupboard. She glanced down to look at it. There stood Jane in front of her old place of employment, the restaurant in San Francisco. She was wearing a large, white chef's hat; a long, white apron; and a wide smile. Louise could not help wondering if Jane missed her work there. While they would miss her terribly if she decided to go back to California, Louise would not want to keep her in Acorn Hill if her heart was not there. She knew Alice would feel the same way.

She thought that perhaps she should talk it over with Alice. All the secrecy surrounding Jane of late could have something to do with this picture. Possibly she and Alice could come up with some way that would make Jane's decision easier, if indeed there was a decision to make.

Louise wondered if she could be overreacting. *After all, Jane says that she is happy here. But what about all the mystery? She definitely has something up her sleeve.*

Though it went quite against her nature to spy on anyone, she thought just maybe a little snooping here and there might bring things to light so that they could encourage Jane to follow her dreams, wherever they might lead her.

There was a noise near the back door. Louise peeked out and saw that Jane was coming. Quickly, Louise placed the picture back in the cupboard behind the glasses where it had been previously. There was no need to confront Jane now. Louise would talk to Alice the first chance she got. Though she resisted the idea that she and Alice might become the snoop sisters, Louise would do whatever she could to help Jane.

"*Yoo-hoo*," Ethel called from the back door. "Anybody home?"

Jane blew a lock of hair from her face. "Hi, Auntie," she said with slightly less enthusiasm than usual. Her aunt did not always pick the best times to show up. Jane was working on a lemon meringue pie for dinner and the meringue was not cooperating. While baking, she had been preoccupied with her trips to Potterston and her secret. She hoped to tell her sisters soon. Another glance at her meringue and she groaned.

"Oh my," Ethel said, shaking her head. "What happened to that?"

Jane's dark mood grew a bit darker. She bit her tongue. No use taking things out on her aunt. "I've just had too much on my mind today. I think I left out the cream of tartar."

"Land's sake, Jane, how can you do a thing like that?" Ethel pulled off her coat and placed it on the back of a kitchen chair. She rolled up her sleeves as if she meant business. "Meringue has always been one of my specialties."

If there was one thing Jane did not want at the moment, it was Ethel's help in the kitchen. She needed to divert her aunt's attention and fast.

Ethel walked over and washed her hands.

"So, Auntie, how are you enjoying your chat room?" Jane asked, while disposing of the limp meringue so that Ethel could not mourn over it. She prayed that Ethel's mind would switch gears and that she would head for the computer.

Ethel wiped her hands on a paper towel. "Well, that's why I came over, to see what's going on today," she said with a sheepish grin.

"Help yourself. Michael's laptop is in the living room, as always."

"I suppose I'll have to give this up soon enough. He won't be around forever," Ethel called over her shoulder, apparently her contribution to the meringue already forgotten.

Jane breathed a sigh of relief and set to work on a new meringue. This time, she did not allow her thoughts to stray until the meringue had been whipped across the pie in big puffy heaps and baked to a light golden brown.

Remembering her picture, Jane quickly went over to the cupboard to get it. She looked around to make sure no one was near the kitchen. When Alice had walked into the kitchen days earlier, Jane did not have time to think, so she stashed the photograph in the cupboard so that her sister would not see it. With it hidden, she forgot about it for a time. Could one of the sisters have seen it? She thought a moment. No, she would certainly have asked her what it was doing in the kitchen cupboard. Jane shook the worry from her mind. No one could have seen it. At least, she hoped not.

She straightened the rest of the kitchen and placed the lemon meringue pie in the refrigerator. After wiping her hands on a kitchen towel, she decided to see what Ethel was up to.

Ethel did not bother looking up when Jane entered the room. Her gaze was fixed on the computer screen. Jane flopped down beside her. "What's going on today?" She wondered if Mayor Tynan had checked into the chat room yet.

"Oh, not too much. I've been talking to this new lady who showed up a couple of days ago. Calls herself Lola." Ethel said, studying the screen.

Jane felt sure that had to be Lloyd. "That's a pretty name. What does she talk about?"

"Oh, mostly she's been talking about how she has a birthday coming up, and her husband wants to know what to give her, and she is trying to think of what she would really like," Ethel said with a casual tone.

She appeared completely unaware of the woman's true identity. Maybe Alice was right. It was kind of scary how people could pass themselves off as someone else.

"So what do you think?" Ethel was asking.

"I'm sorry, Auntie. I missed what you said."

"What kind of gift ideas should I give her?"

"Tell her something you would want if it were you."

Ethel's eyes looked toward the ceiling. Jane could almost hear Ethel's mental wheels turning as she cranked out images of possible gift ideas.

"Oh goodness, I don't know. I suppose I would want a day at the beauty shop to get my hair and nails done, then go out to dinner." Ethel shrugged. "What could be better than that?"

Jane shook her head. "You've got me there."

"I think I'll tell her that. See what she says." Ethel tapped the letters on the keyboard, then clicked "enter" to send the message.

Lola wrote back that that was a good suggestion. Maybe she would tell her husband about it. Ethel sat up an inch, as if proud for helping Lola think of a present.

Another message flashed from Lola. Ethel read it out loud. "I'm glad I have you to talk to. My daughter worries about me being in a chat room. I wouldn't talk to the men, though, just the women. I'm very careful about such things. How about you?"

Jane smiled to herself. Lloyd wanted to make sure Ethel took care of herself on the Web. She wondered just how Ethel would feel once she found out that Lola was actually Lloyd.

Louise checked in her closet once more, but still could not find her missing pictures. She sat on the edge of her bed and tried to remember. Had she lent any pictures to

Cynthia? It didn't seem likely. She felt sure she would have remembered something like that, especially with her most treasured pictures. Still, if they were not in her photograph album, she had to have put them somewhere.

But where?

She decided to set the matter aside. No sense in letting it spoil her day. The pictures would turn up. They had to. She slowly flipped through the album, reliving days of yesteryear with Eliot and Cynthia in their home. With her finger, she traced Eliot's image on a picture. She smiled. If she had it to do over again, she would not fuss at Eliot for leaving his socks on the floor or complain when he left the top off the tooth-paste. Well, not as much as she had, anyway. Funny how things that were once so important pale when . . .

Her gaze fell upon the little girl in the picture. Cynthia. She lovingly touched the little girl on the photo. Where did the time go, child? She glanced at her watch. Just after dinner she would call Cynthia and remind her how much she loved her.

With a grateful heart, she carefully tucked her photo album back in the closet to be enjoyed at another time.

It was evening at Grace Chapel Inn. The quiet town of Acorn Hill had rolled up its sidewalks and closed its shop doors for the night when the Howard sisters, Margaret and

Michael, and the Stanfords gathered in the parlor for a time of fellowship and refreshments. A sweet camaraderie reigned over the little group who had found comfort in the presence of one another.

After serving chocolate cake that Michael had purchased in Potterston, along with coffee and tea from the inn's kitchen, Jane placed a couple of CDs in the player, allowing classical music to fill the room like the soft background in a painting.

Wendell sauntered into the parlor. Alice watched as he looked around a moment, lifted his nose haughtily, then turned on his paws and padded from the room. Obviously it was not the social affair he wished to attend.

Michael and Ralph swapped fishing tales while the women slipped into comfortable conversation.

"I just love the wallpaper in this room," Margaret said, looking around with pleasure. "It gives me the feeling of spring."

Alice glanced at the familiar wall covering of green ivy and lavender violets. "You know, I feel the same way. I think that's why I like to come in here when days are dreary. It reminds me of spring."

Margaret nodded.

"So how is your sister coming along, Margaret?" Louise asked.

"She's feeling great. As I've told you before, when she gets her sass back, I know she's better." She stirred cream into her second cup of coffee and tapped the spoon gently on the rim of the cup. "Well, trust me, she has it back."

They laughed.

"In fact, I told her you wanted her to visit when she's well, Alice. She was delighted and says she now has another incentive to get through therapy."

"Great. We'll look forward to her coming. Let's hope she has a complete recovery."

"Sounds good."

"Who is this you're talking about?" Bernadine wanted to know.

Margaret explained about her sister's ill health and how Alice had taken care of her.

"So, Bernadine, are you and Ralph having a good time here at Acorn Hill?" Alice asked.

Bernadine's face lit up. "We couldn't have picked a better place, with kinder folks," she said with a wide grin. "Now, mind you, I don't mean we don't have that back home, but it's nice to have a change of scenery."

"We're happy you're enjoying your stay," Alice said.

The women grew silent, making it obvious that the men were now talking in whispers.

Bernadine looked over at them. "Now don't you two

be talking about us," she warned, flashing a wink at Margaret.

Ralph looked up. "Just telling him my fishing secrets," he said in all innocence.

"What, you're afraid we'll hear and rush out to the nearest creek to show you up?" Bernadine teased.

"A man can't be too careful, you know," Ralph shot back.

The group enjoyed their time together as the clock inched forward. When the evening was finally spent, the guests retreated to their rooms and Michael put on his jacket. The sisters cleared the dishes, and as they stepped into the foyer to take their things to the kitchen, Michael stopped them.

"I've made a decision tonight." His face looked quite serious as he spoke in a whisper, and Alice felt a touch of anxiety. "I'm going to ask Margaret to marry me."

Relief for Alice turned to pure joy as the meaning of his words had their impact. The sisters surrounded him, congratulating him.

"Have you decided how you want to do it?" Jane asked.

Michael shook his head. "No, I just decided after talking with Ralph."

"So that's what you two were whispering about," Louise said with a grin.

Alice noticed a flush starting at Michael's neck and working its way up.

"Why don't you ask her right here," Jane suggested. "You could do it tomorrow night. We could plan a romantic dinner with candlelight. Louise could play dinner music," she looked to Louise, who nodded her approval, "and then you can propose." Always the romantic, Jane smiled dreamily, waiting for his response.

"I couldn't let you go to that trouble without paying for it. If you'll agree to allow me to pay you as I would at a nice restaurant, I will happily agree."

"Done," Jane said with a snap of her head. "Plan on tomorrow night, say, seven o'clock for dinner?"

"I'll be here. You ladies are the greatest," he said.

"We'll see you then," Jane said.

With a spring in his step, Michael turned and walked out the door.

Chapter Twenty-Four

$\mathcal{B}$y six thirty the next evening, Grace Chapel Inn was abuzz as Alice, Jane and Louise scurried excitedly around the kitchen and dining room getting things in place for Michael and Margaret's special night. The Stanfords had gone out for the evening, and Margaret was in her room getting ready. Alice smiled as she thought of Margaret's assumption that Michael was taking her out for the evening.

Alice stood beside Jane and admired the table. Jane had arranged ivy in a large seashell on the table and set candles on each side among the leaves, which tied in beautifully with the green walls. The dishes were arranged for an elegant formal dinner. When the doorbell sounded, the sisters flew into action. Jane reached over and lit the candles, then nodded toward Louise and Alice. They quickly took their places. Louise went into the parlor, left the door open, and began playing romantic melodies, which made their way softly to the dining room. Alice went to the front door to usher Michael into the foyer. He stood there with a dozen red roses in hand, gazing up at Margaret as she descended the stairs.

With one look at the flowers, Margaret gasped. "Michael, more roses? They're beautiful, but you are spoiling me," she said upon joining him.

"Not as beautiful as you, and I want to spoil you. You're worth it," he returned.

Alice felt a flush of embarrassment for intruding at such a moment. "If you'll allow me," she said, taking the roses and escorting them into the dining room.

"What's going on?" Margaret asked.

"You'll see," Michael said.

Margaret looked with astonishment from the dining room table back to Michael. "Michael?" she asked, clearly perplexed.

He just smiled.

"If you like, I can put these in a vase for you," Alice said, admiring the roses. As though in a daze, Margaret nodded her assent. Alice sighed as she observed the look on Margaret's face.

Jane clapped her hands when she saw Alice enter the kitchen with the roses. "Oh my." She walked over and dipped her face into the bouquet, breathing deeply of their scent. "*Mmm*." She lifted her head, her face displaying obvious pleasure. "I've got just the thing," Jane whispered with a snap of her fingers. She stepped over to a cupboard and pulled out a crystal vase from the back.

Alice let out a slight gasp. "Jane, this is beautiful. Wherever did you get it?"

"One of my wedding gifts," she answered with a shrug. "Might as well let someone else enjoy it."

Alice patted her sister's shoulder. She wondered if this whole thing was hard on Jane, but her fears were quickly forgotten as Jane perked up.

"You take those out, and I'll get the first course ready to serve."

The dinner for the lovers passed like a dream. It started with tomato-ice appetizer and cheese pastry fingers, then worked its way to the main course of lobster thermidor with pilaf, buttered French green beans, skillet cherry tomatoes, and a seeded savory long loaf. Finally, the feast ended with dishes of snow pudding.

After dinner, Alice ushered the happy couple into the living room in front of a blazing fire, then discreetly left them alone. Michael and Margaret sat on the sofa and sipped café espresso. They walked down memory lane together, reminiscing about their high school days, old friends, and finally their love for each other. Their espresso had run out by the time they finished talking.

Michael took Margaret's cup from her hand and placed

it on a nearby stand. His eyes met hers as he made his way back to her. He knelt in front of her. She looked at him in surprise, her eyes wide, the flames from the hearth shining from them. Michael reached for her hand and took it into his own.

"Margaret, you were once a wonderful memory that carried me through many lonely nights in my youth. I was devastated when I lost you so long ago." He paused a moment and looked into the fireplace, as if remembering, then turned back to her. "I don't want to lose you ever again. You are a part of my past, you are a part of my present, and I want to make you a part of my future." He reached into his pocket and removed a tiny jewelry box. He opened the lid and turned the box toward her. "I love you with all my heart, Margaret Ballard. Will you marry me?"

Margaret threw her arms around him, and held him tight. "Oh yes! I will marry you, Michael." Her cheek, wet with tears, pressed against the side of his face. "The very words I longed to say forty-six years ago, I finally can release to you with all my heart." She choked back a sob. "I love you, Michael Lawton" she whispered into his ear. "I love you."

Michael's hand caressed the back of her head as he pulled her to him and kissed her tenderly.

Soon afterward the inn was a place of commotion. Ralph and Bernadine had returned. They, together with the sisters, beamed as the couple shared the news of their engagement, showed off Margaret's diamond, and talked excitedly about the entire evening. Michael paid the sisters handsomely for their efforts despite their protests, and it was close to midnight by the time he departed and the inn quieted down as everyone went off to bed.

As Alice snuggled into her thick covers, she knew this was a night the sisters would not soon forget—a night when love had once again touched the heart of Grace Chapel Inn.

"So they're getting married, huh?" Ethel asked as she sat on the sofa in the living room, staring at the computer screen.

"Yes, they are indeed," Louise answered, knitting needles in motion, hoping that Ethel would not pump her with "twenty questions," but all the while knowing she could expect no less from her dear aunt.

"Well, I hope they haven't rushed into this," Ethel said, her lips pulled into a firm line of disapproval.

"It is not as though they just met. They knew each other years before."

"Yes, but people change, mind you. I don't know what they're in an all-fired hurry about anyway."

Louise shrugged, wishing for once Ethel could keep her

opinions at bay. "Ralph told Michael that at their age they cannot afford to wait."

"Oh pish-posh," Ethel said with a wave of her hand. "Sounds just like an insurance salesman, always scaring people into buying something. I've never seen the likes," she grumbled.

"Well, it is what they wanted, after all, so I am happy for them."

"What do their kids think about it?" Ethel looked up from her screen as if she could not afford to miss what Louise was about to say.

Oh dear, here come the twenty questions. "I don't know. It only just happened, and I doubt if they asked permission ahead of time. After all, they are adults."

"I'll bet the kids will have something to say about it all right." Ethel whistled.

Louise motioned with her hands for Ethel to be silent. "Don't whistle. Jane might walk in and hear you. I would prefer she not get started up again."

Ethel leaned in and whispered, "She still practicing her whistling?"

With a grimace, Louise nodded.

Ethel chuckled. "Well, you got to give that girl credit for trying. Once she sets her mind to something, she doesn't give up easily."

"You have that right." Louise groaned, thinking back on Jane's vocal and piano attempts. She could only hope that Jane's longing to whistle would soon abate.

"Well, anyway, I say Margaret and Michael will have their hands full once their kids get wind of the engagement."

Louise could not help feeling a bit of dread over the matter herself. Time would tell.

Jane entered the inn through the front door.

"Hi," she said, kicking off her shoes as she entered the living room. "These things are killing me." She edged her shoes away from the entrance.

"Didn't you just buy those?" Ethel asked.

Jane headed for the kitchen with her package in hand. "Uh-huh. I haven't broken them in yet."

"Where you been?" Ethel wanted to know.

Jane had already reached the dining room. "Oh, I went over to Wild Things to get some flowers and talked awhile to Craig," she said, referring to the owner.

Louise heard Jane scrambling around the kitchen before she returned with a vase filled with a small bouquet of flowers.

"Those are pretty, Jane," Louise said.

"For Father's study," Jane said proudly, adjusting a flower here and there. "I'll be right back," she called over her shoulder as she headed for the study.

"You girls are good to keep flowers in Daniel's study. He would have liked that."

Louise could see that Ethel highly approved of their ritual. "Kind of makes us feel as though he is still around," Louise said. "Just one way to remember."

Ethel grew pensive. "I sure do miss him."

"I know. We do too."

Jane stepped back into the room. "So, Auntie, are you in your chat room?" she asked, sitting down beside her on the sofa.

Her question seemed to shake Ethel from her thoughts. "Oh dear, I'd forgotten what I was doing." She looked at her screen, and it had gone dark. "Oh no, what did I do?"

"It's just gone to sleep," Jane said. "Here." Jane pressed the space bar and everything lit up again.

Ethel shook her head. "I'll never remember all this stuff."

"You're doing fine, Auntie. I'm proud of you for learning the computer. It's not an easy thing to do, especially when you're older."

Louise worked a couple of stubborn stitches, thinking that she had all that she could do to finish her knitting.

"Well, I'm not all *that* old," Ethel said as if a bit put out by the comment.

Jane and Louise shared a slight grin. "Oh, I'm sorry, I just meant, you know, not in your twenties or whatever."

"*Humph*," Ethel said, turning her attention to the computer screen.

"Have you heard any more from Lola?" Jane asked.

"Who is Lola?" Louise asked with apparent innocence.

"She's Auntie's new cyberfriend."

Ethel looked up with utmost pride at this announcement. "I met her a few days ago in—" she turned to Jane. "What did you call it?"

"Cyberspace."

"Right. I met her a few days ago in cyberspace."

Louise watched her aunt's eyes twinkle with her new-found vocabulary.

"Lola is about to have a birthday. Her husband wanted to know what she wanted for a present, and she couldn't think of anything. She asked me what she should ask for, so I gave her some ideas," Ethel said, looking rather smug.

"Well, how nice that you could help her. Do you think she will use your suggestions?" Louise asked, exchanging a knowing glance with Jane.

Lines creased Ethel's forehead. "I haven't heard from Lola in a couple of days. I don't know. I hope she's not going to stop coming into the chat room." She turned to Jane. "Do you think she'll show up again?"

"She might later. People sometimes get busy and have to save the computer for another time."

"I expect that's so," Ethel said. She closed out of her windows on the computer and proceeded to turn it off. "Well, I've killed enough time here. I'd better hightail it back home and get some work done."

Once she had left, Louise whispered, "So what is going on with that? You think Lola is actually Lloyd?"

"Oh, I'm sure of it. Especially since she . . . or he . . . asked about the birthday gift."

"Do you know what she told him?"

"She said a day at the beauty shop, followed by dinner. You know how Auntie likes to be pampered."

"Oh, do I ever."

Just then Alice came in the front door, carrying a bundle of mail. "Hi, all," she said, pulling off her jacket and setting the mail on the sofa beside her.

"How was your day?" Louise asked, picking up her knitting once again.

"Not bad. More student training today. There were so many nurses on hand that they let me off early." Alice turned her attention to the mail. She began to sort through the envelopes. Then her fingers stopped. Louise watched her, noting the puzzlement on her face.

"Is everything all right, Alice?"

"*Hmm?*" She looked up, "Oh yes, everything is fine. Jane, this is for you." She handed a large envelope to Jane, then gave Louise a glance that told her it was another mysterious package.

Jane read the envelope, then started to get up.

"Anything exciting, Jane?" Louise wanted to know.

"What? Oh no, I don't think so." She started to leave the room.

"Jane," Louise said.

She turned around.

"I know it is none of my business, but well, I have been wondering about things lately. I mean, what is all the mystery? You go to Potterston twice a week without telling us why, and now you are getting these packages. I have been trying to make sense of it. Are you looking for another job?" Louise had not really meant to ask that question, but it was out before she could stop herself.

Practically gaping, Jane looked first at Louise and then at Alice. "Is that what you thought? No, no, a thousand times no! I love this place. Why would I want to leave?"

Obvious relief washed over Louise and Alice. "Well, we didn't know. You have just been acting, well, a little strange lately," Louise said.

Jane smiled. "Everything is fine and I do not plan to leave Grace Chapel Inn. Okay?"

The sisters smiled and said in unison, "Okay."

Jane turned and walked out of the room. Alice smiled at Louise. "Well, I certainly feel better. How about you?"

Louise picked up her knitting. "I am just happy that we do not have to worry about it anymore," she said with a chuckle.

"Louise?"

"Yes?" she answered, working her stitches across the next row of her afghan.

"We let her get away without telling us what it is that she is up to."

Louise continued to knit until the meaning of the words had made an impact. "Oh dear," was all she said.

Chapter Twenty-Five

"What are you doing out here, Alice?" Jane asked as she stepped onto the front porch.

"Oh, it turned out to be such a lovely day, I decided to sweep the porch," she answered, pulling her broom across the floor. She stopped and bent over to pick up a piece of paper, then continued on her way.

"It is nice out today," Jane said, stepping over to the edge of the porch and lifting her face to the sunshine. The sky looked scrubbed clean as far as the eye could see. Not a cloud in sight. "After all the cold and wind we've been having, I'm always surprised when a day like this one pops up."

"I know." Alice stopped sweeping and walked over to her sister to look out across the front lawn. She leaned her chin against the broom handle. "It is a beautiful day for a walk," Alice said with a sigh.

Jane looked at her. "Why haven't you and Vera been walking lately?" Jane asked.

"She's had a bad cold. Doing better now, but still doesn't want to overdo things."

"Well, my dinner plans are all set. You have the afternoon off. Want to go for a walk?"

Alice brightened. "That's a great idea. Just let me finish sweeping up, and then we can go."

"All right, I'll go let Louise know so she won't wonder where we are." Jane went back into the inn and picked up her sweater. Then she walked over to the parlor door. She could hear Louise's student plunking away at the keys. Jane hesitated, not wanting to interrupt. Perhaps she should write a note. Just then the music stopped. Jane tapped on the door.

"Come in," Louise said.

Jane poked her head in. "Just wanted you to know Alice and I are going for a walk. We won't be gone long."

"Thank you, Jane," Louise answered. Wendell slipped out of the parlor through the door just before Jane closed it. Evidently he had listened to all the music that he could take. As the door latched into place, Jane could hear Louise already back to teaching.

No question about it, her sister was a natural teacher. She worked well with youngsters, and she knew her music. Jane thought of Alice's work with the ANGELs. She did a fine job working with children too. Although Jane loved children and got along with them, her calling always seemed to place her in the kitchen handling food or around a table feeding young and old alike. She smiled thinking how blessed she was to work at something she loved to do.

"You ready to go?" Alice asked as she met Jane in the foyer.

"Ready." Jane pulled the ribbon free from her hair and looped the band tighter around her ponytail. Wendell came along and stroked himself thoroughly as he moved around her legs, purring all the while. She stooped down. "What's the matter, ol' boy, you feel lonely?" The ribbon trailed from her fingers, and Wendell immediately pounced on it, bringing the ribbon to life as he tossed it about between his paws.

Alice watched and laughed.

"All right, you," Jane said, getting her ribbon and tying it back around her ponytail. She gave Wendell another stroke or two, then she stood to go.

Together Alice and Jane stepped into the sunshine. Jane's skin tingled with the touch of the crisp afternoon air. Heading toward Hill Street, they took in the vivid display of golds and russets from distant oaks and maples.

"It truly is a great day for a walk, Jane. Thank you for mentioning it."

"I'm glad we could do this together. We don't have the chance very often."

"I enjoy walking through Acorn Hill, especially in the fall. Look at that berry bush," Alice said, pointing.

"Beautiful. You know, I've seen birds get a little, um, tipsy on those berries," Jane said with a laugh.

Alice chuckled. "Well, that's what they get for over-indulging." She paused to gaze upon the tree. "I do enjoy their mature color this time of year."

Content in their thoughts, the two lapsed into comfortable silence.

"Land's sake, you never know who you're going to bump into on the streets of Acorn Hill," Ethel called out behind them as she and Lloyd exited the Coffee Shop.

Alice and Jane swiveled around and waved at the couple. A red truck came slowly down the street. "There's Fred," Alice said, her arm waving widely about in a friendly greeting. He beeped his horn and waved his arm out the window.

It was just that kind of a day.

"That's one thing I like about a small town," Jane said. "Everybody knows everybody."

"True. Of course, everybody knows everybody's business, too, especially if Aunt Ethel has anything to say about it."

Jane giggled. "That's for sure."

"A person can hardly sneeze without someone running to get you a tissue." Alice laughed. "But I wouldn't have it any other way." Alice lifted her face to the breeze. "I know you enjoyed San Francisco, but I could never be happy in a big city. I guess I'm just a small-town girl."

"Big cities can be fun. They offer a lot of amusements from which to choose, but a small town certainly has its charms. Especially Acorn Hill."

"*Mmm*, do you smell that?" Alice asked. "I think Clarissa is making hot cinnamon rolls at the bakery today."

The mere thought of them made Jane's mouth water. "Hey, want to go in?" she asked.

"You don't have to ask me twice," Alice said, already making her way toward the Good Apple Bakery.

"Hello, ladies." A tall woman in her seventies, wearing a blue-and-white dress that hung loosely over her small frame, stood behind the counter."

"How's the arthritis today, Clarissa?" Alice asked.

The woman shrugged. "Oh, I have my good days and bad days just like most folks. I guess I could use a little oil in the joints every now and then," she joked as she tucked a stray hair back under her hair net. "What can I get for you two?"

"We couldn't help smelling those wonderful cinnamon rolls, Clarissa. Any chance we could get them hot out of the oven?" Alice wanted to know.

Clarissa chuckled. "You sure like those cinnamon rolls, don't you, Alice?"

"That makes two of us," Jane joined in, already imagining the taste.

Alice blushed a little and nodded. "Wish I could eat them and stay as thin as you. I don't know how you do it, working in a bakery."

Clarissa shrugged. "It gets old after a while. Doesn't tempt me so much now as it did in my younger days. I'm not as much of a sweets eater as I used to be."

Alice shook her head. "I like food, period."

"That makes two of us again," Jane said with a laugh, thinking of how her days were filled with food and baking. All the more reason for her to continue jogging, which, she scolded herself, she had not been doing faithfully lately.

"Well, little wonder, having a cook like that at your house," Clarissa said, pointing to Jane.

"What can I say? Guilty as charged," Jane said, enjoying the compliment.

"Okay, two cinnamon rolls coming up. You have time to stay? I'll bring you some coffee and tea."

"That would be great," Alice said. She followed Jane to a small table, and they settled into their places.

"Did you notice that wedding cake in the corner of the shop?" Jane asked, after she spotted the cake display.

Alice thought a moment, then brightened when she turned to it. "Oh yes, it's just beautiful."

Jane leaned in with a conspiratorial manner. "You know, I was thinking—"

Alice held up her hand. "Oh no, you'd better stop right there. When you start thinking with a look like that on your face, it usually gets me into trouble."

"You make me sound like Lucy Ricardo. I'm not quite that bad," Jane said with a grin. It tickled Jane to no end that her sisters thought her too adventurous. "Besides, this won't get you into trouble. I promise." She made the scouts honor sign.

"Okay, what were you thinking?"

Jane licked her lips. "What if we threw a small engagement tea for Michael and Margaret? We could even invite their kids so they can see how happy their parents are now."

With some hesitation, Alice answered, "I don't know, Jane. Their kids haven't been too thrilled up to now, and we don't know how they feel about the engagement at this point."

Jane considered this. "You know, we could invite them over on the spur of the moment, say, tomorrow evening for dessert, and just get a feel for things. I remember Margaret saying Greg would be in Potterston today and tomorrow to visit Wilma. I could call him tonight. I might even ask Ralph to talk some sense into these kids."

"Hey, you might be onto something there."

Jane giggled. "Why not try? Then if all goes well with tomorrow's get-together, we could then start plans for the engagement tea. Have the bakery prepare the cake. I'll get a few flowers from Craig, that kind of thing. Nothing major, just a nice little celebration with the couple, their kids, and the inn guests. Michael gave us far too much money for the dinner the other night. I could use what was left after expenses and put it toward this little celebration. What do you think?"

"We'd have to do it soon. I don't know how much longer Margaret will be at the inn."

Jane frowned while considering this. She came up with an idea, not a perfect solution, but a possible one. "Hey, I've got it. We could do it Sunday afternoon. Everyone would be off work so they would most likely be able to come."

"Sunday? Is that too soon? How can you get everything ready by then?"

Though Jane was not completely sure about the timing, she did not want to let on to Alice. "Sure. Well, that is, if their kids don't already have plans. I'll just call them rather than sending out invitations. If they can't come, we'll try another time. Besides, you said yourself you don't know how much longer Margaret will be with us." Jane thought some more. "Let's see, cake, flowers—I'm not really doing all that much." Jane clapped her hands. "Oh, it will be blast!"

Alice hesitated and then finally sighed. "Well, I suppose

we could try it. Besides, I learned long ago that once you get an idea in your head, I'm wasting my breath to try to talk you out of it."

"That bad, huh?"

Alice nodded. "Let's just hope the kids are happy about it when the time comes."

"Well, we might find out tomorrow." Jane looked at Alice's worried expression and laughed. "You worry too much." She went over the preparations in her thoughts and practically had the inn decorated before they ever left the bakery.

When they arrived back at the inn, Alice and Jane saw Ethel sitting on the sofa happily typing away on the laptop.

"Hi," Ethel said without lifting her eyes.

Jane walked over and sat down on the sofa beside Ethel. "How's it going, Auntie?" Jane stretched her neck to get a look at the screen.

"Fine. I was just talking with Lola about her birthday gift. She's getting excited now." Ethel clicked out of the windows and turned off the computer.

"You don't have to stop on our account," Jane protested, feeling put out that she did not get to read Ethel's chat with her friend.

"No, it was time to get off. I've been on it too long anyway."

"What's the matter, you don't seem yourself today," Jane said, eyeing her aunt carefully.

"Oh, it's nothing."

Jane knew better. "Come on, it's something. You might as well tell us. I'm not giving you any tea until you do."

Ethel's eyes sparkled. "That's a good tactic. Maybe I'll try that the next time I'm trying to fish out some juicy tidbit."

Alice shook her head and Jane laughed.

"Well, all this talk with Lola about her birthday just makes me think how nice it is to be remembered. Lloyd is not one for remembering things."

"Well, the gift of time and affection means much more than trinkets, Auntie. Lloyd gives you that." After all, Jane thought the poor man deserved some credit.

Ethel considered this a moment, then a smile lit her face. "Come to think of it, you're right. He is a good man, just forgetful."

Jane grinned. "That's right."

"Okay, I told you what was the matter. Now, how about some tea," Ethel said in her snap-to-it voice.

Chapter Twenty-Six

"Oh my, how lovely," Margaret said the next evening when she and Michael stepped into the dining room after their return from a light dinner. "Your table looks elegant as always."

Jane felt especially pleased. "Well, I thought we would have some guests over for dessert tonight."

Margaret smiled. "How nice."

"You're invited, you know." Jane beamed.

"Thank you."

"And your kids," Jane continued.

Alice looked at Louise, who cocked an eyebrow, and together they watched the whole scene play out.

"We'll have such a lovely time—" Margaret stopped herself. "Who?"

Jane put down a plate and turned to her.

Uh-oh, here it comes. Alice braced herself.

"Your kids." She looked first at Michael. "I've invited Sherri. Actually, I invited her whole family, but her husband was taking Abby to ballet. I guess it's their weekly ritual for him to take her to ballet lessons and then out for a special treat."

Michael nodded but stood mute.

Then Jane turned to Margaret. "And Greg was in Potterston, so he happily agreed to come over for dessert."

"Happily?" Margaret asked in disbelief.

Jane fudged a little. "Well, he agreed anyway." She resumed her perky attitude. "It will be great fun." Then as if oblivious to any possible tension around her, she went back to her food preparations.

Michael cleared his throat. "*Um*, I think you need to know something," he said.

Jane and Alice looked at him. Alice did not like the cloud over his face.

"They don't know we're engaged yet."

"We figured as much, that's why we called this gathering together," Jane said without skipping a beat. She pulled silverware from the drawer. "Oh, did we mention that we want to have an engagement tea for you Sunday afternoon? Well, we couldn't have the engagement tea if we didn't have your children's blessings, so we thought we'd better get that ironed out before Sunday." She smiled and began to set the silverware on a tray.

Michael and Margaret looked stunned. Alice mentally ran through her CPR training.

Jane stopped and looked at them. "You don't mind, do you? The engagement tea, I mean?"

Margaret just stared.

"Of course not—providing everything works out with the kids. And, uh, thank you," Michael managed through shallow breaths.

"You're welcome." Jane smiled pleasantly. "We won't talk about the engagement, unless you do." She smiled again. "Now, relax. We're going to have a great time."

Michael and Margaret stood motionless. At least they had not keeled over. Alice thought that had to be a good sign.

Alice could not believe the calm with which Jane handled everything. Louise, too, watched their sister with wonder.

"Are Lloyd and Aunt Ethel coming?" Alice finally asked.

Jane shook her head. "Lloyd asked her to attend a meeting with him tonight in Potterston."

A moment later Sherri stepped through the front door with Greg right behind her.

"Hi, Sherri," Jane said, extending her hand. "Greg." She shook his hand. Ralph and Bernadine soon joined them, completing the party. After the formalities, everyone gathered in the dining room for dessert and coffee.

Once seated, Greg asked, "So, what's the occasion?"

Michael cleared his throat and locked eyes with Jane. Alice looked at Margaret who sat mute and pale.

"Oh, just thought it would be nice to have a get-together." Jane said.

Michael visibly relaxed in his seat.

Alice sat speechless, watching Jane at her best, flitting around in her hospitality mode, again oblivious to tension as she did what she loved most.

Alice and Louise shared a glance. Louise shrugged, helping Alice to relax a little. *Might as well make the most of it*, she decided.

Louise offered the blessing for their repast, and in no time the room was filled with happy chatter as all enjoyed the rich aroma of coffee while savoring slices of spicy mince and pumpkin pie. Alice was delighted to see Sherri and Greg not only talking, but also laughing with the others. Ralph kept everyone in stitches as he shared stories from his and Bernadine's Southern hometown.

After dessert, the group retired to the living room, where they played a round of charades and talked together over another round of tea and coffee.

Finally, Louise and Jane settled in their chairs to watch Margaret and Michael square off in a game of checkers. In another corner, Ralph and Bernadine shared their story with Sherri and Greg. Alice eased into a nearby chair. She was not trying to eavesdrop exactly, but what did it hurt if she happened to overhear a little of their discussion?

"First off, I applaud you, Sherri and Greg, for coming here tonight. I know you're struggling with your parents' relationship."

Sherri stared aimlessly into her coffee mug. Greg studied his fingers.

"Our children felt the same way about us," Ralph said, reaching over to hold Bernadine's free hand.

Sherri and Greg looked at them.

"You see, they felt we were replacing our spouses who had died. They couldn't see that we weren't replacing our spouses, just trying to make a new life for ourselves." He paused. "In other words, picking up the pieces." He said the words like a man who had experienced great pain.

Alice glanced over. Ralph had Sherri's and Greg's complete attention. Alice offered a silent prayer.

"We always wanted what was best for our kids. Valued their happiness above all things. So when they reacted unkindly toward our union, I couldn't understand it. I figured they'd want us happy after living in grief for so long." He shook his head. "But they couldn't see past their own sadness." He took a drink from his cup. "After some time, though, they saw how happy we were together. My daughter told me she hadn't seen me that happy since before her mother had taken ill. She said she realized how selfish she had been, putting her own feelings above what was best for me and for Bernadine."

"She wasn't being selfish, she was being loyal," Sherri said, raising her eyebrows.

"That's what she thought too—at first. Until I asked her, 'Would your mom want you to react this way, or would she want you to support me and my happiness?'" His face lit up. "Well, I've got to tell you my wife always put others first. We both knew she would want my happiness and for us to make the most of our time left here on this earth." He looked straight at Sherri. "It doesn't mean I loved her any less. It simply means I've had to let her go."

Tears spilled from Sherri's eyes and made wet tracks down her cheeks. She wiped them with a napkin. When Alice looked at Greg, his head was down. He seemed to be mulling over the matter in his mind.

"We only want what's best for them," Greg said, almost in a whisper.

"And who could know what's best for them better than they?" Ralph asked.

Greg considered this but said nothing.

They talked a little longer, but the words were lost to Alice until Ralph's voice broke through once more.

"Well, I've given you much to think on. You're good

people. Things will work out all right. You'll see." He squeezed Bernadine's hand. "Now, I'm a might tired, Bernie," he said with a chuckle. "If you younguns will excuse us, I think we'll head for bed."

Sherri walked over to Michael. "Daddy, can we talk?" Michael looked up with surprise. "Sure, kiddo." He excused himself and followed her into the foyer.

Greg walked over to Margaret. "Um, Mom, would you come with me for a minute?" he asked, motioning her to follow. She glanced at the sisters, then walked toward Greg.

The sisters retreated to the kitchen and began to clean up. Once the kitchen sparkled, they heard calls of "Goodbye, ladies" and "Thank you," coming from the living room. They walked out to see everyone but Margaret leaving.

"We had a wonderful time," Sherri said to the sisters.

Greg shook the sisters' hands. "Thank you for a great evening." He looked as though he really meant it. He glanced at Margaret. "See you tomorrow, Mom."

She nodded.

"Tomorrow, Dad?" Sherri asked.

"I'll be there, sweetheart," Michael answered. He leaned over and kissed Margaret's cheek, then said to her, "I'll pick you up tomorrow morning at eight thirty."

"I'll be ready," Margaret said.

Alice closed the door behind them, then turned to a smiling Margaret.

"All four of us are meeting for breakfast in the morning. Pray."

Jane squealed, the sisters clapped their hands. Alice thought there just might be a wedding yet.

Peace settled over Alice when she slipped beneath her covers that night. Though she did not know what the future held for her special friends, she knew the One who did. . . .

The next morning Ethel arrived just as Louise and Jane finished cleaning the kitchen after breakfast. Alice had already gone to work. They slipped into places at the table.

"After Lloyd and I went to that meeting last night, he took me out to dinner. It almost killed me."

"Why is that, Auntie? Did you have something bad to eat?" Jane asked with concern.

"Did you get food poisoning?" Louise joined in.

"Land's sake, no. I wanted to know what happened with Michael and Margaret, and I had to wait until this morning to find out."

Ethel's no-nonsense ways never ceased to tickle and surprise Jane. To hide her amusement, she decided that she better get up from the table. "Let me get us some tea," she said, rising to put the pot on the stove.

"Well, what happened?" Ethel asked Louise.

"We don't know yet."

"What do you mean, you don't know? You were right here last night. Did anything happen with the kids?" Ethel blew out an exasperated sigh. "I tell you, I don't know how you girls can miss so much with things going on right under your noses."

Jane wanted to suggest that perhaps Ethel might start a class called Snooping 101, but thought better of it.

"Everything went smoothly. The kids were meeting them for breakfast this morning," Louise offered without elaboration.

Ethel's eyes widened. "Do tell." She scooted her chair closer to the table, looking as though she had not had this much fun in ages. "Oh, I hope things work out for them."

"I thought you felt they were rushing," Louise said with a cocked eyebrow.

"I did, but knowing they wanted to go ahead with their plans, I feel bad the kids are trying to talk them out of it." She placed her arms on the table and leaned in on her elbows. "You think they'll settle things this morning?" she asked in a secretive manner, as if they might be overheard.

"I hope so," Jane said.

Ethel frowned. "It's a dirty, rotten shame. Those kids are trying to run their lives, I tell you. A dirty, rotten shame." Ethel turned her head and *tsk*-ed profusely.

One look at Ethel's face told Jane her aunt really did feel bad about the whole matter. She hoped that Ethel would not decide to take matters into her own hands and try to work things out. The sisters had enough to worry about without adding that to the mix.

"Well, we have prayed about the matter, and it is in the Lord's hands now. We will see how He leads," Louise said.

"Of course, that's right. That's always the best thing to do. Pray, I mean. That precious couple." Ethel *tsk*-ed some more.

"So how are things going for you and Lola in the chat room, Auntie?" Jane asked in an attempt to keep Ethel's mind from concocting any scheme on the engaged couple's behalf. She poured everyone a cup of tea.

Ethel picked up her cup and sipped a little. "Oh, fine. I think she finally told her husband what she wanted for her birthday."

"Did she decide on what you suggested, the day of pampering?" Jane asked with interest.

"Yes, I believe she did," Ethel answered with a shred of pride, no doubt for having been the one responsible for the idea. "I told her she was lucky to have a husband who remembered birthdays and such. Lots of men don't do that." She took another drink. "I know Lloyd would never remember." As if reading Jane's mind, Ethel answered Jane's unspoken question. "I told Lola all about that too. Oh, Lloyd's a good man and all. I just think he's a little, well, absent-minded now and then."

"You told Lola about Lloyd and that he wouldn't remember birthdays and such?" Jane asked, trying desperately not to laugh.

"I sure did. I probably shouldn't tell her so much about my personal life, but we get along well, and it's easy to share with her. Plus, I'll most likely never meet her here on this earth, so what does it matter?" Ethel took another drink.

The sisters shared a glance. Jane walked over to the stove and busied herself pouring the remaining water from the pot and rinsing it out.

"Well, I hope you were not too harsh about Lloyd with her. I mean, you would not want to give her the wrong impression about the dear man," Louise wisely suggested.

"Oh no, I wouldn't say anything bad about him, just that he's a little forgetful. But then most men are," Ethel said, chuckling at her own comment.

"Would you be terribly disappointed if Lloyd didn't remember a special day, Auntie?" Jane asked, putting the pot back on the stove and walking over to the table to sit down.

Ethel considered this. "Well, I would be disappointed, but it wouldn't be the end of the world. I'd just remind him, and then he would feel bad and take me out to some nice restaurant, so it would all work out in the end."

They all laughed together.

Jane chuckled to herself. Little did Ethel know that she was playing right into Lloyd's hands.

Chapter Twenty-Seven

*T*he sisters still had no word from Michael and Margaret by the time Alice returned home from work. Rather than sitting at the inn and twiddling her thumbs, Alice met up with Vera and they went for a walk. Fresh air and exercise always made Alice feel better, especially when she could visit with Vera.

"I've missed our walks, Vera. I'm glad your health is on the mend."

"Me too. It feels good to be out of the house. I'm just thankful we've had these beautiful fall days interspersed with the chilly ones." Vera kicked a pebble from her path.

"I know. It makes me sad to see the autumn season leaving us. I hate to see it go. Though I confess I enjoy all the other seasons as well when they first arrive."

"Well, the good thing about winter for me is I get to enjoy Christmas break."

Alice chuckled. "Things should slow down for us at the inn too."

"Seems to me I remember your thinking about that in

the past, and you always end up getting unexpected guests or something happens to keep you hopping," Vera reminded her.

Alice laughed, remembering just such incidents in days gone by. "I suppose you're right. I shouldn't complain. Hey, do you want to stop in at the Coffee Shop? I'm a little chilly. Something warm to drink sounds good right about now, and I can fill you in on last night's get-together."

"I think that's a great idea."

Alice and Vera stepped into the shop and slid into one of the booths.

"Hi, ladies, what can I get you?" Hope Collins, the Coffee Shop waitress, stood before them, looking neat in her pink uniform and wearing a big smile. Her naturally dark hair had blond highlights in it.

"I like your hair, Hope," Alice said cheerfully, thinking how Hope always looked attractive.

The waitress absently touched her highlights. "Thanks. I just got it done last night," she said with a smidgen of pride in her voice.

"Well, it's a nice color for you," Vera added.

"I think I'll have some tea, Hope."

"Don't you want a slice of blackberry pie?" she asked with a wink.

Alice smiled, knowing that Hope had served Alice's

father blackberry pie almost every day when he had visited the Coffee Shop.

Vera's eyes lit up. "Oh boy, that does sound good."

"Okay, I'll make that tea and a serving of blackberry pie."

"Make that one tea, one coffee, and two pieces of black-berry pie," Vera said with a laugh. "And could I get some cream with that?"

Despite the nearness to dinnertime, Alice did not object.

"No problem. I'll be back in a jif."

"Alice, how are things going with the ANGELs? Didn't you say you got that little problem ironed out between the girls?"

"Yes, thanks to Annie Burton." Alice thought of the child and smiled.

"She is a special girl, isn't she?

"That she is." Alice waited while Hope set their cups and saucers on the table. A teabag string and tag hung over the side of Alice's cup, which Hope filled with hot water. She poured coffee into Vera's cup.

Vera stirred the cream in her coffee. "So what ended up being the problem?"

"Oh, some jealousy thing. You know how girls that age can be." Alice pumped her teabag in the water a couple of times, then lifted the bag and placed it by the edge of her saucer.

Vera nodded. "I remember well when my own girls were that age. They were always in a tiff about something or another."

Alice and Vera each took a sip from their cups. Placing her cup back on the saucer, Vera looked up at Alice. "So, how did your gathering go with Michael, Margaret and the kids last night?"

Alice told Vera about the previous night's gathering, and that Michael and Margaret had gone to breakfast with the kids in the morning and not yet returned.

"Well, that sounds promising," Vera encouraged.

Alice smiled. "It does, doesn't it?" Then her smile faded.

"What is it?"

"Oh, I'm just wondering why they're not back yet. They know we are anxiously waiting to hear how things are going. I hope everything is all right."

Vera shrugged. "Could be any number of things. It might mean they are having a good day together."

"True. I think Wilma had a therapy session today, so perhaps they just went ahead and took her to it."

"You and your sisters have grown very fond of that couple, haven't you?"

"We really have. I mean, we enjoy most of the guests who come to the inn, but Michael and Margaret are something very special."

"Well, I hope things work out for them. You'll have to let me know what happens. I'll be praying for them and for you."

Vera and Alice finished their drinks and pie, paid their bill, then headed out the door to finish their walk.

After her walk, Alice settled in the living room, finally getting a chance to read her book. Louise sat on the sofa, working on her afghan. Jane walked in from the kitchen and plopped down to read a magazine. Alice looked up.

"I wish they would hurry and get here," Jane said with a grin.

"I know. It's hard for me to concentrate on my book."

"I can't tell you how many stitches I have dropped," Louise said with a chuckle.

Jane laughed. "We're a mess."

Before they could return to what they had been doing, the front door opened and closed.

For a moment the sisters remained silent.

"Well, I guess we better see who is at the door," Alice said with a laugh, pulling herself up from the chair.

Jane and Louise followed practically on her heels. Once in the foyer, they stopped short when they faced Margaret, Michael, Greg and Sherri. No one was smiling.

An awkward silence filled the room. Alice felt her heart

beat and decided that she was too old to deal with such things. Unfortunately, sometimes being a friend called for facing difficult situations, such as the one in which she currently found herself. What was a friend to do?

Just as she was about to utter a greeting, Michael's expression changed into a huge grin. "Sherri and Greg want to know what time they should be here for the engagement tea."

Alice let out the breath she had not realized she was holding. In a matter of seconds, everyone fell into a heap of hugs, congratulations and laughter.

Sherri and Greg explained how Ralph had helped them to see their own selfishness. They had thought that they had their parents' best interests at heart, but Ralph showed Sherri and Greg their true motives.

The group celebrated over tea and coffee and a flurry of conversation about the upcoming engagement tea. After a little while, their guests left and the sisters prepared for dinner.

After dinner Louise decided to practice the piano. When she entered the parlor and sat down at the bench, she noticed a card propped up on the piano. The writing on the envelope simply read, "Mrs. Smith."

Louise carefully opened the envelope and pulled out a card from one of her students.

Dear Mrs. Smith,

Sometimes I worry that you don't know how happy it makes me to have you for my teacher.

When I play something beautiful I feel that God is close to me. And I know that you are very pashient and kind.

Thank you for all that you do for me. I will never forget you.

Love,

Janet Springer

Tears blurred her vision as she reread the card. The words of encouragement and affirmation warmed her heart and told her that God was using her in a special way. It always amazed Louise when He took the time to remind her of His nearness. Nothing could move her more. She had no doubt He cared about every aspect of her life.

She put the card back inside the envelope and pulled it tight against her chest.

Alice stepped into the parlor. "Oh, I'm sorry, Louise, I didn't know you were in here."

"That's fine, Alice. I'm finished."

"Isn't it wonderful how everything turned out for Michael and Margaret? I still can't get over it."

Louise nodded. "You know, it is funny. We pray about things, and then when God answers, we are surprised."

Alice chuckled. "You're right."

"Sometimes I am amazed when He shows me time and again how actively involved He is in my life. How can we question it? After all, He knows the very number of hairs on our heads."

Alice nodded. "And that changes every time we comb through our hair."

Louise laughed. "Just the same, it shows how intimately involved He is with every detail of our lives."

Alice studied Louise for a moment. "I know you really believe that."

"Oh, I do. I have never been more sure of anything in my life."

After lunch the next day, Alice came down the stairs with her mystery book in her hands. She hoped to spend some time catching up on her reading. With all the interruptions in her life lately, she began to wonder if she would ever reach the ending of this mystery. She hoped that things would settle down a little and that she could relax.

Though she enjoyed her work at the hospital, she treasured such moments of rest at the inn. The start of her work week came all too soon. A contented sigh escaped her, and she shivered slightly. She loved to read. She had stopped in her book at a very crucial part and could hardly wait to dig in and see what was happening with the characters.

She could not imagine anything more wonderful than occasional solitude, except, perhaps, a piece of blackberry pie or a walk with Vera on a crisp fall afternoon. She smiled at the thought. No doubt about it, she had much for which to be thankful. She descended the last step just as the front door opened.

Lloyd Tynan entered, flushed and quite out of breath with excitement.

"Lloyd, are you all right?" she asked.

"I'm doing fine, Alice. I had to sneak in here while Ethel was in town so she wouldn't see me. I wondered if you could go with me to pick out her special gift?"

Alice thought he looked as eager as a puppy finding a new home. "Well, I thought you already knew what you were going to get her."

"Yes, I have an idea, but I was hoping for a woman's input. And who but you and your sisters know Ethel so well? If you can't go, perhaps Jane or Louise could accompany me," Lloyd suggested.

Alice thought a second. She knew that Jane had gone to Potterston, and that Louise had another headache and was resting in her room. "Well, I think they are busy right now."

His face showed his disappointment, as if he expected her

to turn him down. Alice turned over her book in her hands and glanced once more at the title. *Without a Trace*. She groaned inwardly, sensing that her would-be restful afternoon was fading with not a trace left behind. Oh well, she told herself, *friends are more important than restful times alone*. At least she was struggling to convince herself of that. Thoughts of Annie's lesson with the ANGELs came to her mind. "We have this moment today to do something good for someone else, to reach out to a neighbor and lend a helping hand," Annie had reminded them. With a gentle sigh, Alice walked over and placed her book on the desk. "Just let me get my jacket."

Lloyd straightened and adjusted his bow tie, which he did whenever he was excited.

Alice pulled her blue jacket from the closet, then stopped at the front desk and scribbled a note to Jane and Louise, letting them know where she had gone. She placed the note in a prominent place on the desk. Grabbing her purse, she made her way to the door with Lloyd smiling like a Cheshire cat beside her. This gift obviously meant a lot to him, and he wanted it to be perfect when he gave it to Ethel. Though her plans had been disrupted, Alice decided she had made the right choice to go along. There would be time enough to rest when she was too old to do anything else. Now was the time for her to reach out and help a friend. And so she would.

Chapter Twenty-Eight

*L*ouise felt refreshed and well rested when she woke up from her nap, her headache gone. The card from her student still brightened her thoughts. Rising from her bed, she walked over to the dresser and combed her hair into place. She picked up her glasses, then walked to the closet and retrieved her photograph album, realizing she had been doing that a lot of late. She could not imagine what was making her so sentimental. Feelings of life passing her by had plagued her the last time she browsed through the pages, but her heart felt much lighter now.

Louise straightened the covering on her bed and carefully sat down with the album firmly on her lap. Once again she traveled through the memories, but this time with a sense of purpose. Each picture represented a scene in her life, a moment in time when life had been good and meaningful. She remembered and cherished every one.

There was the time that four-year-old Cynthia had decided to make her mother a snack and walked over to the refrigerator to take out the milk. The gallon had proved too heavy for her, and she had spilled the carton on the floor, splattering milk in every direction. When Louise had walked in, she had seen the fear on Cynthia's face.

"I'm sorry, Mommy. I wanted to make you a snack," Cynthia had said, referring to their afternoon snack time routine.

"It's all right, dear. Step over to the side and Mommy will clean it up." Louise had grabbed the mop, but before she started cleaning, she had bent down to give Cynthia a reassuring hug.

Cynthia had told her countless times through the years how much that hug had meant to her when she had failed in her own eyes. That same memory had pulled her through times in her adult life when she believed that she had done less than her best.

Louise thought it interesting how little things could mean so much. A hug at the right time. A phone call. She hoped that she would always know when the time was right to do a particular task, and she hoped that she would be obedient when the tug came to her heart.

She continued through the pages. Scenes of Cynthia as a toddler, Eliot with Cynthia, family shots—she treasured them all. Coming to the pages with missing photos, she stopped. That matter still puzzled her. She could not imagine how they would have fallen from her album. And if they had fallen out, where were they now?

She tried to think it through, but the answer eluded her. After thinking awhile, she reluctantly closed her album. She had far too much to do to spend time worrying about the pictures. After all, they would surely turn up one day. At least she hoped they would.

After dinner, Jane went up to her room. Sitting on her couch, she set some of the decorative pillows aside and settled in to put the finishing touches on her project. She could not help feeling a little proud when she thought of all the work that had gone into it. She hoped that her sisters would be just as excited once they learned the truth.

Before she knew it, an hour had passed and her project was completed. She traced the edges with her fingers, feeling a wonderful sense of accomplishment.

Glancing at her watch, Jane frowned. Her guest should have arrived already. Still, with all her excitement, she refused to allow worry to clutter her mind. Presumably, that guest would arrive shortly, and then together they could approach her sisters.

Standing, she put the pillows back in place and straightened them. She left her project behind, walked over to her mirror, brushed through her ponytail, and tucked her blouse neatly back into place beneath her belt. Satisfied, she left her room.

Once she arrived in the living room, she found Louise working on her afghan. "Is Alice still with Lloyd?"

Louise stopped knitting and looked up. "Yes. She will certainly be tired before this evening is through," Louise said with a hint of worry in her voice.

"She will be tired, but you know Alice. She likes helping people. I'm sure she is enjoying herself." Jane settled on a chair. "It's probably a good thing she's going along. Men so often manage to mess things up when it comes to gift-giving." She laughed.

Louise returned to her knitting, and Jane relaxed, letting her mind wander.

"What are you thinking about?" Louise asked after a while.

"Oh, I don't know, just thinking about Mother."

Louise displayed a tender smile.

"Do you think I'm silly, Louise?"

"What do you mean?"

"How I go on about Mother from time to time. I mean, I can't help wondering what she was like, how she would react in a certain situation, how she would feel if I did this or that."

"I don't think that is silly in the least, Jane. We all have an innate love for our parents. You are no exception to that rule. Since you never physically got to know Mother, it seems only natural that you would long for a glimpse of her through photographs or whatever means available."

"Thanks for understanding."

"Remember, one day we shall all be together again."

"I really believe that," Jane said with excitement, thankful for her strengthened faith and a heritage that put God and family first.

"Any chance I could sit down and kick off my shoes," Alice said with a sigh when she shuffled into the living room.

Jane and Louise laughed together. "That bad?" Jane asked.

"Let's just say I have never before seen a man worry over his purchases like that man does." Alice dropped onto the sofa with a thunk and peeled off her shoes.

"Would you like something to drink, Alice?" Jane asked.

"No, thank you, Jane. I'm too tired to swallow."

"I thought that Lloyd already knew what to get Ethel after Lola talked with Ethel in the chat room." Louise said while working the stitches on her afghan.

"Well, that's what I thought, too. Ultimately, he ended up arranging for what she had suggested. But of course, that was after he went through countless stores ruling out other gifts that caught his fancy." Alice sighed. "I must admit I had fun being a part of it, though."

Jane looked at Louise. "What did I tell you?"

Louise smiled and nodded.

"I'm looking forward to hearing all about it once Ethel receives her present."

"Oh, I'm sure she will be over here in two seconds flat once she gets back from her big evening," Jane said with a laugh.

"No question about that," Louise added.

Wendell sauntered into the room and jumped up on Alice's lap. Trying to get comfortable, he pawed her legs a few times, then eased in for a nice nap.

"Why is it I feel that the only reason you like me is so I can be your bed?" Alice asked with a laugh, gently stroking the tabby's fur.

Jane giggled as she watched Wendell get comfortable. "Hey, did Lloyd tell you where he was taking Auntie for dinner?"

"Some nice place in Philadelphia."

"Philadelphia!" Jane whistled. Her whistle was not the weak little gust of air kind that hardly makes any noise, mind you, but an honest-to-goodness, Bing Crosby type of whistle.

Alice's eyes widened.

Louise dropped her knitting and her head jerked up. "Jane, did you do that?" she asked.

Jane lifted her chin ever so slightly, and she nodded. She did not let them know that she had surprised herself.

Alice and Louise both clapped and congratulated her on her musical abilities. They pumped her so full of compliments that Jane felt as though she might be nominated for Female Vocalist of the Year.

"Just goes to show that with a little practice, you can do anything, maybe even sing." She heard a moan and looked over at Louise. Her head drooped suspiciously over the afghan upon which her fingers worked feverishly. Jane's eyes narrowed. She felt sure Louise was attempting to ignore her comment. *Oh well.* It did not matter in the least. She had proved to them she could whistle and that was that. She decided to change the subject.

"Well, Lloyd sure is going all out for Auntie. There will be no living with her after all that." Jane kicked off her shoes and tucked her feet beneath her.

"That is the truth of it," Louise said, stopping long enough to count her stitches, then clicking the needles once again.

"I think he's taking her there for the afternoon." Alice scratched Wendell behind the ears. "Your afghan is coming right along, Louise," Alice said.

"It is, isn't it?" Louise smiled as she looked over her project. "Alice, I have been meaning to ask you something. Would the hospital be interested in crocheted hats for the infants in their birthing ward?" She stopped to pick up a dropped stitch before adding, "I would donate them, of course."

"Oh, what a lovely idea, Louise." Alice seemed to consider the matter. "Are you sure you have the time for such a project?"

"Well, I would not be able to do it full-time, but I thought perhaps once in a while I could donate a box of caps. Your hospital doesn't have so many babies being born that I could not keep up. At least, they don't seem to have that many, do they?"

Alice laughed. "No, I would say Potterston's baby ward is fairly manageable."

"Good. As soon as I finish this afghan, I'll get started on some colorful little caps. That settles the matter of what project I will work on next. Makes me feel better too, to know I am doing some good."

Jane shook her head. "You are a marvel, Louise."

Louise looked up with surprise.

"Well, you and Alice both are always thinking of others," Jane said.

"And you don't?" Alice piped up.

"Well—"

"Well," Louise interrupted "you just feed anybody and everybody who walks through that front door. Not to mention all the banquets that you manage for the church."

"I would say we have a mutual admiration society going on here," Alice said with a chuckle.

Jane and Louise smiled. Jane glanced at her watch.

"Jane, why do you keep looking at your watch? Are you going somewhere tonight?" Alice asked.

"No, nowhere."

"You have a television program you wanted to see?" Alice prompted further.

"No, no program."

Alice frowned. Jane had to hide her smile behind her hand. She knew she was driving her sisters crazy with all her secrecy. She wondered how she could keep evading their questions, but she did not have to worry because just then someone entered the inn. She could only hope it was the guest for whom she had been waiting.

"I'll go see who it is," Jane said before Alice or Louise could get up. But before Jane could leave her seat, her guest arrived at the living room entrance.

"Hello, Mother," the woman said.

Louise dropped her knitting needles. "Cynthia!"

Cynthia went over to her mother, who was already meeting her halfway.

"What a blessed surprise! How were you able to come by tonight? Are you staying overnight or did you stop only to say hello and have to be on your way? Are you hungry? Do you want something to eat or drink?" The questions tumbled over one another as Louise seemed overcome with excitement at the sight of her daughter.

Cynthia laughed. "*Hmm*, let's see, which question should I answer first?"

Laughing, Jane and Alice made their way toward Cynthia to give her a round of hugs. Once the commotion finally died down, everyone found a seat.

"If you'll excuse me, I think I'll go into the kitchen and make us something to drink," Jane said, nodding toward Cynthia.

"Could you use some help, Jane?" Cynthia asked.

"That would be great," Jane responded.

"While you girls are getting the drinks, I'll light the fire in the hearth, and we'll prepare for a cozy visit," Alice said. "Louise, you can just relax until you're over the shock."

"Well, hurry back, Cynthia. I want to hear all your news."

"And you can think up some more questions, Mother," Cynthia called over her shoulder as she followed Jane into the kitchen. They pushed through the swinging door and Cynthia whispered, "Did you get it finished?"

"It's all done and it's beautiful, if I do say so myself," Jane said excitedly.

"I can't wait to see it. Do you think they suspect anything?" Cynthia asked as she pulled cups and saucers from the cabinet while Jane put a pot of water on the stove and clicked on the burner.

Jane shook her head. "They know something is up because I keep going to Potterston. I think that is driving Alice crazy." Jane laughed. "But they haven't pressed too hard for the answers. I don't think I could have stalled much longer though. Alice kept probing for answers tonight."

"That's too funny. So how are we going to do this?"

"Well, I thought I could let you serve the drinks, and while you're doing that, I'll go upstairs and get it from my room, then bring it down and present it to them." Jane felt like a little girl with a big secret. "How long do you get to stay?"

Cynthia frowned. "Just until after breakfast. My business meeting is in Maryland, so I'll have to get going after that."

Jane thought a moment. "Oh, that's right. Well, at least we get you for tonight," Jane said brightly. "We're going to have such fun. Though I know we can't keep you up too late since you have a trip ahead of you."

Cynthia laughed. "I don't care. I'll be fine. Since I don't get to come here very often, I would rather pack in as much fun tonight as we can."

Jane nodded. "Did you see how your mother lit up when she saw you?"

"Yes, I did. It's so good to see her. I miss her." A look of regret shadowed her face.

Jane took her hand. "Now don't be sad. This is a happy time. Louise knows you make every effort to come and see her when you can, and you call her faithfully. You've been a wonderful daughter to her. That's the important thing. Besides that, you've made her very happy tonight." Jane squeezed Cynthia's hand and smiled. The kettle whistled its readiness, and the two went to work gathering the tea fixings on a tray.

"Okay, I'll slip upstairs while you keep them occupied with the tea," Jane whispered.

"Sounds good. I can't wait."

Full of excitement, Jane and Cynthia stepped back into the living room.

Chapter Twenty-Nine

O h, I love this peach tea," Alice said, placing her cup back on the saucer.

"It is good," Louise agreed. "Jane has a gift for finding the best flavors."

"So, Cynthia, tell me what brings you here tonight. I've never been so surprised in all my life," Louise said before taking a sip of her drink.

Yellow and bluish flames danced in the hearth. Jane could hear the wood crackling and popping as she stood to the side of the living-room entrance, just out of sight. She held her treasure in her arms, waiting for the right moment to enter.

"I'm on my way to Maryland for a business trip. I had hoped to get here sooner today, but I had trouble getting away from the office," Cynthia said with a tinge of sadness in her voice.

"Well, dear, you must not give that another thought. You are here now and that is all that matters to me," Louise said with a smile.

"Thanks, Mother."

A pause followed, giving Jane just the opportunity she needed to make her entrance. When she walked into the room, everyone looked up.

"Why, Jane, what is that you have there?" Alice wanted to know.

"Oh, you'll see. Go over to the sofa, and I'll sit in between you and Louise," Jane said to Alice.

Alice picked up her tea and walked over to the sofa and sat down. She looked at Cynthia. "Do you want to come around behind the sofa to see this, Cynthia, or would you rather look at it later?" Jane asked, thinking Cynthia might like to watch her mother's expression.

"I'll wait, thank you, Aunt Jane."

Jane smiled. Once she had her sisters' full attention, she stood before them and held up what was in her hands. "As you know, I've been spending a lot of time in Potterston lately."

Louise and Alice nodded.

"I told you I was meeting with some friends, which was true, but it wasn't the whole truth."

Louise and Alice exchanged an uncertain glance.

"You see, I got to thinking I wanted to throw myself into something worthwhile—"

Alice started to say something but Jane held up her hand to stop her. "I know you think I do worthwhile things in the kitchen, but I wanted something else. You know what I mean?"

Louise nodded as if she understood completely.

"Well, anyway, when Ruth Kincade and I went shopping in Potterston, I came upon a scrapbooking store."

Alice and Louise both made a face as though they had no idea what she was talking about.

"I know. I had never heard of it either. Anyway, it's a store where they sell items to help people move their priceless photos from shoeboxes into scrapbooks that are sure to become family treasures. These aren't just pages thrown together, but rather they are quite elaborate books that tell a history of a chosen memorable event. In my case, I have created a history of our family, showing snapshots of our lives when we were younger, and then each of our lives as we have grown up." Jane studied her sisters' expressions to see if they had an inkling of where she was going with this introduction. They looked puzzled.

"Maybe you've noticed some missing photos in your own picture albums?"

Louise's eyes widened. "Oh my, so you have them!"

Jane laughed and nodded. "I'm sorry. I had to sneak in and get some of your photographs and send them to Cynthia. She then took them to a photography store, where she had them copied. Then she sent them all back to me. So your originals are still intact, and I have copies in this scrapbook."

"The envelopes with no return address," Alice said.

"Right." Jane smiled.

Louise looked at Cynthia. "You were in on this?" she asked incredulously.

Cynthia nodded with pride. "We're quite devious, I must confess," she said, wiggling her eyebrows.

"I should say so," Louise said, laughing with Alice.

Jane continued. "The acid-free paper these scrapbooking stores sell is made to last for many years, and it comes in all sorts of different colors. They also sell paper trimmers, safe adhesive, black markers for journaling, die cuts, large stickers and drawings. You name it, they sell it. They have colored pencils and markers, letter stickers for titles, fast-drying pens and soft-graphite pencils for labeling the backs of photos, everything you can imagine to help one make the most memorable scrapbook."

"My, that does sound rather involved," Louise said.

"It is. Also, it requires a lot of time. It took me forever just to figure out what supplies to buy and then to organize the photos in chronological order. That's why I've been so busy even when I wasn't in Potterston." Jane paused to take a breath. "I have created a scrapbook for our family, and this is what I want to show you." Jane scrunched in between her two sisters on the sofa. She opened her album and watched with sheer pleasure the surprise on her sisters' faces.

"Oh my, Jane, the pictures are even matted on the page. How nice," Alice exclaimed.

"Well, now that I've seen Mother's and Aunt Alice's initial reactions, I think I'll join you," Cynthia said, walking behind the sofa to look over Jane's shoulder.

One by one, Jane turned the pages while everyone oohed and aahed with every display. She felt a true sense of accomplishment in completing the scrapbook for their family.

"This is exquisite, Jane," Louise said with emotion.

"Oh, Louise, do you remember when Mother and Father bought us that bicycle?" Alice asked, pointing to a photo of Louise sitting on a two-wheel bicycle with Alice on the handlebar.

"Oh my, I sure do," Louise said. "Why, we thought they had given us the world when they rolled that bicycle into the living room at Christmastime."

The pages showed moments from their childhood, their graduations, Louise's and Jane's weddings, Cynthia's babyhood, and Jane's stay in California.

"Ah, the envelope from San Francisco," Alice said.

The final pictures were of the sisters in front of Grace Chapel Inn. By the time they had finished reading through all the writings and looking at the pictures, Alice and Louise both had to wipe away tears. Their reactions were everything for which Jane could have hoped.

"I can only imagine how much time and effort went into this, Jane. A gift of time and love is truly the loveliest gift any of us can give to another. Thank you so much," Louise said, pulling Jane into a warm embrace.

"This is a beautiful gift, Jane. One we will treasure always."

"Well, I couldn't have done it without my cohort in crime," Jane said, looking back at Cynthia.

"I did very little. You did all the work. Besides, it gave me a chance to see pictures I had never seen before, and to relive snatches of my childhood that I hadn't visited in quite some time." Cynthia walked around and knelt down beside her mother. "Thank you for giving me a wonderful childhood, Mother. I've always been thankful for my heritage, and I count myself very blessed to be your daughter."

Fresh tears fell from Louise's eyes. "Now look what you have done. I'm weeping like a schoolgirl," Louise said, laughing.

Jane rose from the sofa to get some tissues for her sisters. She could not have been more pleased with their response to her efforts. It had been worth every struggle. Plucking the tissues from the holder, she made her way back to her sisters while her father's words echoed through her mind, "*Making a memory is saving a treasure for tomorrow.*" Jane heartily agreed.

~

After a leisurely breakfast, the sisters sat around visiting with Cynthia until she announced she had to leave. Though Alice knew Louise was sorry to see Cynthia go, Louise handled herself very well. Mother and daughter hugged fiercely at the door with promises to call and write each other. Alice's heart constricted with the thought of how Louise must feel saying good-bye to Cynthia, not knowing when she would get to hug her again. But Louise had told her sisters many times that she had learned to enjoy the moments that she and Cynthia did have rather than sulk over the moments they did not have.

When lunchtime rolled around, the sisters worked together in the kitchen.

"I can't tell you how much I appreciated all your efforts in making that scrapbook, Jane. And to have Cynthia stop by so unexpectedly, well, that just made my whole year," Louise said, lifting out plates from the cabinet.

"I'm so glad you like the scrapbook. We knew you would be happy to see Cynthia. She couldn't wait to get here. She really misses you."

Louise nodded. "I miss her too. But these little snatches of time together surely help."

"That they do," Jane said with a nod of her head. She turned to Alice. "So what are Margaret's plans today?"

"She was going to spend the afternoon with Wilma, I believe."

Shortly after lunch, the Stanfords came down the stairs with their luggage.

"Well, I guess it's time to hightail it back home," Ralph said in his southern drawl.

Alice looked up from the foyer. "Oh dear, is it that time already?"

"It won't be our last time here, though, we can tell you that," Bernadine said.

"I'm so glad you enjoyed your stay, and I thank you for all you did to help Margaret and Michael," Alice said.

"It was our pleasure. We hope they'll be as happy as we are," Ralph said.

While Alice settled up their paperwork, Jane and Louise came into the foyer to say good-bye to their guests.

"I can't remember when we've gotten so attached to our guests as we have in the last few weeks," Jane said as the Stanfords walked to their car.

Louise and Alice nodded in agreement.

"You know, I think I could get into this bed-and-breakfast thing," Jane said with a chuckle.

"Well, it's a good thing, because I think we're stuck," Alice said lightheartedly. "Let's pour our drinks and take them into the parlor."

"Great idea."

Once the sisters were settled in the parlor, Margaret appeared at the door. "I thought I might find you in here."

"Oh, Margaret, would you like some tea or coffee? Some pastry?" Jane asked.

"No, thank you." Margaret patted her stomach, "I've had more than enough to eat. Wilma is feeling better, and we've been eating out far too much. If I stayed around here any longer, I'd jump to the next dress size."

Everyone laughed and then they talked awhile about Wilma's progress and how the Lord continued to strengthen her. They also talked more in depth about the breakfast with Sherri and Greg and what a wonderful time they had had together.

Just when Alice thought the day could not get any better, Ethel breezed through the front door with all the excitement of a teenager. She stopped at the parlor door, hesitated only a second, then plunged ahead, telling all about her day with Lloyd: their sumptuous dinner and his surprise of a day of pampering, complete with breakfast at the Good Apple bakery, a trip to Potterston to a day spa to have a facial, and finally, a trip to the beauty shop to have her hair and nails done.

"If I had known he would go to all this trouble, I would have helped him in his office a long time ago," Ethel said with a chuckle.

"So however did Lloyd manage to come up with the perfect gift?" Jane teased.

"Oh, I know all about that," Ethel said with a wave of her hand. "That rascal got into the chat room and weaseled it out of me. Lola, indeed!"

Everyone laughed.

Alice smiled as she watched her aunt excitedly tell of her wonderful date. Glancing around the room filled with friends and family, Alice offered a prayer of thanks for this special time that she would tuck away in her memory and retrieve time and again for years to come.

Chapter Thirty

A ruffle of wind rattled the windowpane, causing Alice to stir. She glanced at the clock on her stand. She had a little time before church to see if Jane needed help to get ready for the afternoon engagement tea, though it would not take much preparation. She stretched and yawned, then noticed the ray of sunlight that fell across her quilt. Good. The weather would hold out for Margaret and Michael.

The couple had been through quite a lot already. Alice knew that they were in love or else they never would have withstood the storms that had come their way. She thought it a lovely story, really—meeting all those years ago, then separated by miles and years. Wrinkles and gray hairs later, they met and resumed where they had left off. Alice plumped her pillow a moment and lingered in the morning calm. *Margaret and Michael still see each other as the youngsters of years before. Funny how we do that*, she thought.

Mark Graves came to mind. He had not changed much. He was still handsome with charcoal-colored hair. Well, so he had a little gray at his temples and around the edges of his beard. Nevertheless, he looked much the same as when they had dated years before.

Even now, Alice could see his long strides as he walked across the campus lawn, meeting her after classes with a huge grin on his face. Hard to believe so many years had passed between them. Life had kept them busy, Mark with his veterinarian career and Alice with nursing responsibilities at the hospital. A shadow fell over her. The heart attack had been a wake-up call to which Mark seemed to pay attention. His interests now leaned toward God and knowing Him better. She felt thankful for that.

Alice sighed and wondered what the future held for them. If their relationship never grew into anything more than friendship, she felt certain they would always have a special bond.

Well, I'll never get anything done at this rate. She threw off her covers and dangled her feet from the bed. She ran her fingers through the tangles in her hair, attempting to lessen the shock of her first morning look in the mirror.

It didn't work.

"Mirror, mirror on the wall, I wish you'd lie to me just once," she grumbled. Alice collected the things that she needed for the shower and passed her mirror again. She stopped and turned around. Shaking her finger at the offensive piece of furniture she whispered, "One of these days, I'm going to get rid of you."

After dressing for church, Alice left her bedroom to head for the kitchen. Thoughts of breakfast lifted her disposition considerably. She noticed Margaret's door open and started to pass by when Margaret called to her.

"Do you have a minute?"

"Sure." Alice stepped inside the room. A look of apprehension covered Margaret's face. "Are you all right?"

Margaret smiled and nodded. "Just a little, oh, I don't know, maybe afraid." She sat on the bed and Alice eased down beside her.

"Afraid? But why?"

"I feel like I've stepped into a dream, Alice. I mean how strange after all this time, we're together again."

Alice smiled. "I was thinking that earlier. How wonderful for the both of you."

"You're right. But then again, that's the thing that's bothering me. It's almost too wonderful. I'm afraid something will come along and burst our bubble."

Alice took Margaret's hand and looked her straight in the eyes. "God has blessed your relationship with Michael. Don't question it. Enjoy it. You've been given a second chance together. This season of life is meant for the two of you. Take pleasure in the journey. Grow old together."

"Too late for that," Margaret said with a giggle.

Alice shrugged. "Old is a relative term, you know. Besides, I don't feel old, do you?"

Margaret shook her head. "I haven't felt this young in years."

Alice squeezed Margaret's hand. "So there you are. Don't worry about things, Margaret. The kids are trying to work with both of you, you love each other, and most important of all, you both love the Lord. He will guide you in your new life together."

Margaret blew out a breath of relief. "You're right, as always."

"By the way," Alice said, rising from the bed, "have you decided on when you're getting married?"

Margaret considered this. "We're still talking about all that. Michael keeps reminding me what Ralph said about not waiting too long at our age."

They both laughed.

"We'll probably get married in a couple of months, if Michael has his way."

"Will you be moving to Florida then?"

"No, I believe Michael will keep his home down there so that we will have a place to visit, but he'll move to Pennsylvania with me. We're talking about moving to Potterston to be closer to Wilma, since she has no one to help her really. She's too sassy for anyone else to put up with her." Margaret shrugged.

"I understand. How does Greg feel about that?"

"I haven't told him yet, but he won't mind. As you know, Greg travels a lot to Potterston with his sales job, so I would most likely see him as much as I do now."

Alice nodded. "Sounds like you've figured out a good plan. Will you miss Philadelphia?"

Margaret studied her fingers. "I will miss my friends there. I have a good church, and it will be hard to leave it behind." She looked up at Alice and brightened. "Still, we're not so far away that we can't visit."

"I'm glad." Alice waited a moment. "Well, I'd better get downstairs and help Jane with breakfast so we can go to church and get back to prepare for your tea."

Margaret giggled. "I have to pinch myself. I can't believe all this is really happening."

"Well, it's happening, so you'd better get ready," Alice said with a chuckle before she turned and walked out the door.

Jane, Louise and Alice joined together to get things ready for the engagement tea. They really did not have much to do. Margaret had insisted that they keep things simple. She did not want a big "to-do," as she called it. So, according to her requests, the guests would have refreshments of cake, punch, coffee and tea, some mints and nuts, and that was it.

Fred and Vera Humbert came by early to help set up some extra chairs in the parlor. Jane had a lovely white linen tablecloth spread across the dining-room table, where flower petals circled a beautiful heart-shaped topiary. Dessert plates, napkins, polished silverware, carafes for coffee and tea, bowls of butter mints and raw cashew nuts, and especially the cake all gave the table a festive look.

"Oh, Jane, everything is lovely," Vera said.

"Thank you. We didn't do all that much, but simple is nice."

"I agree," Louise added when she walked into the room.

"Ditto," Alice said, slipping in from the kitchen.

Jane put her hands on her hips and scrutinized the place. "Looks like we're ready," she stated with a grin.

"It's a good thing, too," Ethel said as she and Lloyd stepped in from the kitchen.

"Auntie, I didn't hear you come in," Jane said, reaching over to give Ethel a hug. Jane stepped back and looked at her aunt. "My, don't you look lovely today." Jane eyed the cream-colored dress sprinkled with leaves of brown, gold and rust.

Ethel looked down as if she could not remember what she had put on in the morning. "Oh, this old thing?"

Jane nodded with a smile. This was a ritual to which Jane had been accustomed for years.

Ethel waved her hand. "It's old, but the material wears well. And I thank you for the compliment."

"How are you, Lloyd?" Jane asked.

"I'm doing mighty fine, Jane. Yes, mighty fine," he answered, rocking on his heels. "I suppose Ethel told you about our special day and her present?" His eyes sparkled.

"Yes, indeed, she did," Louise offered.

A soft blush touched Ethel's cheeks. Jane expected Lloyd to tuck his thumbs under his arms any minute and puff his chest out in pride. Instead, he straightened, giving himself the appearance of having grown an inch.

"You did a good job, Lloyd," Alice said. "What a thoughtful gift idea."

He stared at the floor. "Well, I guess I can't take all the credit. Lola helped me out."

Everyone laughed.

"So, Auntie, have you been in the chat room lately?" Jane straightened a misplaced fork on the table.

"Whatever for? The only person I wanted to talk to was Lola, and she doesn't get on anymore." Ethel looked at Lloyd and chuckled. "Of course, if I find out she's back on the computer, I just might check it out."

"Oh no," Lloyd said. "I can't have the rumor get out that I'm known as Lola in a chat room."

"Oh, Lloyd," Ethel said with a hearty chuckle before tapping him playfully on the arm, "you're such a kidder."

"Hey, we thought the party was in the parlor," Vera and Fred said, entering the dining room.

"The parlor is for later. We are waiting here for the happy couple." Louise turned to Jane. "Is Sherri bringing her family?"

"As far as I know."

"How about Greg, is he coming?" Vera wanted to know. Jane nodded.

"I thought this wasn't supposed to be a big shindig," Ethel said, pulling a piece of lint from the sleeve of her dress.

"It's not a big shindig. Just having the people closest to them." Jane put her finger to her mouth. "Did you hear the front door?"

Everyone turned toward the dining room entrance just as Sherri, with her husband Jeremy and their daughter Abby, entered. Greg Ballard was not too far behind.

The room soon filled with chatter amongst the guests, and in no time Margaret and Michael walked into the room. Congratulations and good wishes abounded. Jane scooped pieces of cake onto dessert plates, and the guests helped themselves to mints and nuts. Alice and Louise served cups of coffee, tea and punch, and with dessert finished, Jane suggested that all proceed with their drinks to the parlor.

Alice and Jane lingered, making sure that everything was in order, while Louise slid onto the piano bench in the parlor and began to play soothing music.

"Alice, would you mind making a toast to Margaret and Michael when we get in there?" Jane asked.

"A toast?"

"Well, we can lift our coffee cups or whatever, but just say something nice about their future together. Maybe some others will want to join in. Then perhaps you could close everything with prayer?"

"That sounds like a wonderful idea, Jane. I would be happy to do that."

"Great."

The sisters entered the parlor, noting that the guests were engrossed in conversation while Louise's beautiful music wafted through the air. Jane nodded toward Alice, who stayed standing near the piano. Alice bent over and whispered something to Louise, who finished playing her piece.

The room fell into a comfortable quiet. Everyone looked toward Alice, who stood before the group. "I want to thank you all for coming to join us in the celebration of this happy event," she said, "the engagement of Michael Lawton and Margaret Ballard."

Applause broke out among the small group.

"Though we didn't know them forty-six years ago, it has been our pleasure to know them for, what, the last month?"

Margaret and Michael nodded together.

"It seems a short time, and yet you have already captured our hearts. We feel as though you are family."

Jane and Louise smiled their agreement.

"We wanted to take just a moment to let you know we are thankful the Lord has brought you our way, and we pray God's richest blessings on your lives together."

Alice raised her cup. "To the happy couple."

Everyone raised their cups. "To the happy couple."

Fred Humbert cleared his throat. "I've appreciated getting to know you, Michael. You know you have to come back and visit because I've heard you brag about being a checkers champion, but you haven't played me yet."

Vera poked Fred's side as laughter filled the room.

One by one, they took turns around the room, each guest telling the couple what a difference knowing them had made. Finally, once the last toast had been given, laughter turned to expressions of thankfulness as Alice offered a beautiful prayer of blessing.

After prayer, Louise played soft, happy music once more and the guests stayed awhile, sharing and talking together.

"Margaret?" Sherri said.

Jane looked up to see Sherri, Jeremy and Abby all standing near Michael and Margaret. "I just want to say thank you for making Dad so happy. I'll look forward to having you in the family." Sherri reached over and gave Margaret a hug while Jane held back a tear.

"Um, Michael?" Greg stood before them now. He looked down at his feet. "I've been a jerk, and I—"

"Say no more."

Greg looked up with surprise.

Michael held up a hand. "You were protecting your mother, and I respect you for that."

Greg released a smile. "Thanks," he said, holding out his hand. The two shook hands heartily. Greg turned to his mother and gave her a hug. "I wish you both years of happiness together." He hugged Margaret once more before leaving.

Jane released a deep breath. Things had turned out all right after all.

The afternoon soon blended into evening, and Jane, Louise and Alice watched as the last guest left the inn, leaving the sisters alone once again. Alice prepared to close the front door, then glanced at the plaque hanging there.

"A place where one can be refreshed and encouraged. A place of hope and healing. A place where God is at home." She turned to Jane and Louise. "Somehow, I think Father would be pleased."

Louise nodded. "Who could have known the ministry that we would have here at Grace Chapel Inn?"

In the soft glow of the foyer light, Jane looked to her sisters and whispered, "God knew."

Contented, the sisters stepped toward the living room. "I hope Margaret and Michael have a long, wonderful life together," Jane said.

"If we all could learn to take one day at a time, it would make such a difference in our lives. What is it they say, 'Live like you're dying tomorrow and pray like you're living forever'?"

Jane studied Louise a moment. "That's so true, Louise."

"Well, I mean, we have *this* moment, here, right now, to make a difference," Louise said. "Whether we have lots of time or a little, it is up to us to make the most of the time we are given."

"Well said, sister. And on a lighter note, I say right now we use our time to go back into the kitchen and eat some more of that cake before Aunt Ethel comes by in the morning," Alice said.

"Oh, you," Louise said with a laugh as they all headed for the kitchen.

Wrapped in the sheer pleasure of their kinship and love for one another, Jane felt a deep gratitude that she had this moment to share with her sisters.

Tales from Grace Chapel Inn®

The Price of Fame
by Carolyne Aarsen

Ready to Wed
by Melody Carlson

Hidden History
by Melody Carlson

Back Home Again
by Melody Carlson

Recipes & Wooden Spoons
by Judy Baer

Once you visit the charming village of Acorn Hill, you'll never want to leave. Here, the three Howard sisters reunite after their father's death and turn the family home into a bed-and-breakfast. They rekindle old memories, rediscover the bonds of sisterhood, revel in the blessings of friendship and meet many fascinating guests along the way.

Diann Hunt writes fiction with a hefty dose of romance and humor. She will do just about anything (within reason) for chocolate. She has published three novellas and twelve novels, including Hot Tropics and Cold Feet, Hot Flashes and Cold Cream *and* Be Sweet. *Diann lives in Indiana, has been happily married forever, loves her family, chocolate, her friends, chocolate, her dog and, well, chocolate.*